Sea Lord

(Book 2 of the Owerd Chronicles)

A sequel to "Owerd the Briton"

By

James Gault

Copyright © James Gault 2023

All rights reserved

This is a work of fiction. Some of the characters in this story were real people who lived at the time. Their characterization, words and actions are fictitious.

"Of all the animals on earth we least know what is good for us. My opinion is, that what is best for us is our admiration of good."

— Homer, <u>The Iliad</u>

The land of the Englisc, despite wealth in terms of gold and silver, was in a state of depressive frustration. Drought, hunger and Normans stalked their land in 1070 and there seemed little the resident Saxons and Britons could do about it. The aim had become survival. Much the same could be said for Owerd: a Briton, a knight and a convalescent recovering at his manor of Birdlip after a severe thrashing received whilst helping defeat an invasion of the south-west by Earl Harold Godwinson's sons. What made matters worse was his agonizing over the circumstances that had led him to fight for the Norman occupiers against the family of the very man who had knighted him in the first place. His shock and dismay when he had first realized the extent of his torn allegiance had almost caused his death and still lingered as he slowly recovered from his physical wounds.

Outwardly, Owerd looked to be the same man; tall, well-muscled and still impressively handsome in appearance despite the multitude of fresh scars scattered almost randomly over his body. He had attended, albeit listlessly, to both the business of the manor and the business of regaining his strength throughout the months since his return from four weeks of post-battle recovery in Cornwall. That recovery, aided by the ministrations of Wenna, his brief lover whilst there, had at least made him functional once more. To those that knew him, though, it was evident that his heart wasn't in it. Hilda, his wife and long-term love, determined to snap him out of it, whatever "it" might be. The opportunity for a gentle probe into his state of mind arose after one evening meal when he still sat staring disinterestedly at an untouched bowl of now-cold pottage well after the servants had retired for the night.

'You have been behaving like a lost puppy since your return from Launceston, my love, so tell me exactly what ails you so we might come to find some cure'.

Owerd paused for quite some time in silence to seek some answer for his wife that might make sense. Eventually he gave a deep sigh and began.

'From my earliest days I have been told that God put us on this earth for a reason. I just cannot find what that reason might be. I chose to follow the way of a warrior and was bound to the earls Harold and Edwin. Life and my role had direction: I trained, worked and fought for them as they required of me. I was content. Now Earl Harold is dead and Earl Edwin has shown himself to be a weak leader who repeatedly gets his followers killed for no good outcome. These Norman invaders have shown themselves to be arrogant and ruthless yet William is now king and if we are to have any order in our lives his rule must be respected, though that sits ill with me. I hear stories of a man called Hereward who stokes rebellion over in the east and Edwin flirts with rebellion when it is convenient to him but I feel both are doomed. So, what is my role to be? I feel like a warrior without a cause. Does that explain my dilemma?'

Hilda, though now lady of the manor, was once a slave. She well knew the challenge involved in constantly being told what do regardless of right or wrong.

'You are now a knight, my love, you have choices. Your cause is perhaps whatever is right. It matters not the task or who orders the task, but the task itself. If it is the right thing to do, the Christian thing if you will, then your conscience will let you know. I have faith that you will always choose right over wrong, my dear, but for now your role is to get ready for whatever may come and that means getting stronger in body and soul. For now, though, I believe a good night's sleep to be in order'.

She had a quiet word with Osric, the sergeant of their eight housecarls, the next morning before they all filed in to the common-room to break their fast.

'Perhaps a light workout at the pells this morning my lord, followed by a bout or two. What say you?'

'That will suit me fine, thank you Osric'. This was said contentedly but without notable enthusiasm.

After fifteen minutes at the pells a warm glow was evident on Owerd's features but he could hardly be described as dripping in sweat.

'Time for a bout, my lord', called Osric, who then passed his lord and master his mail shirt and a blunted sword. Dressed and armed, Owerd looked curiously at Osric who had not armed himself.

'A touch hard to fight myself, Osric, are you not thinking of joining me?'

'Not me today, sir, your opponent is just behind you'.

Owerd spun around to see Hilda armed, in mail and looking deadly serious as she strode toward him. There were no preliminaries. Hilda launched a vicious series of strikes at Owerd's torso, most of which landed heavily and would cause bruising. He was late in properly defending himself and slow in its execution but there was no let-up in the assault. Hilda had an excellent grasp of swordcraft and was using every trick in the book to land a blow, occasionally dropping to the ground and gaining yet another success on his legs. Belatedly Owerd tried a few tentative attacking strokes of his own but his sword was flicked aside with disdain and Hilda pressed home a forceful counter-attack on each occasion. It took nearly twenty minutes and a world of pain before Owerd finally found his temper developing from annoyance to anger and he attacked vigorously. He went to end the fight with a feint to the left followed immediately by a strike at Hilda's chest, only to find his sword knocked from his hand.

'You are getting your strength back Owerd, but you need to work harder on your speed'.

Having said that, Hilda simply walked away to get changed. Owerd was left in a degree of shock that would doubtless take some time to settle. He was smart enough to know, though, that he had just received a necessary wake-up call, though he had not expected it to come from his lady. He resolved to recover his originally high level of fighting ability without further delay.

The weeks that followed were blessedly free of interruptions from beyond the manor and that allowed Owerd and his housecarls to focus on their warrior skills.

Morale was soaring. A minor distraction involved reports of drunkenness and brawling by one of the tenants that became too significant to ignore.

'It is Oxenblod, my lord', reported Edward the steward, 'he is belligerent at the best of times but lately he is ever demanding ale, threatening violence to any that approach him and declares himself unable to pay his rent. His wife Sibbe, on the few occasions she is seen about, is covered in bruises and I hear he savagely beat her only yesterday'.

'I cannot be seen to interfere between man and wife, Edward', replied Owerd, 'but mayhap I could pay them a visit and see what might be resolved'.

'Take care, my lord, he can be a brute and without respect for any when in his cups'.

The two senior housecarls Osric and Cuthbert, joined Owerd as they rode out to the Oxenblods' farm the next day. He was uncertain about how he might approach this situation as, despite a personal loathing of wife-beating, or indeed any attack upon women, people generally frowned on any form of external interference between man and wife. He decided to withhold judgement until he could see for himself how matters lay. Initial impressions were not promising. The sound of their horses had drawn Oxenblod out from his hovel and his state of disarray was a match for the home itself which looked to be on the verge of collapse. The man himself was unkempt and with a surly expression that oozed belligerence.

'Hail Master Oxenblod', called Owerd, 'how goes it with yourself and Mistress Oxenblod?'

'Well enough!'

Owerd could almost feel Osric behind him bristling at the lack of respect his lord was being shown, but decided to ignore it and slipped from the saddle.

'Did the corn-seed I provided prosper; are the chickens laying well?'

'Well enough', came the repeated, though obviously reluctant, response.

'So why is it Master Oxenblod that you claim to be unable to pay the last Quarter's rent?'

'The wife has been poorly and my time has been taken up attending to her. We don't all have servants to look to our needs'.

Regardless of the insulting comment, this was the opening Owerd needed and he walked directly for the hovel's doorway. Oxenblod remained where he was, barring the way.

'If she is poorly, she needs be tended. I will see to your wife myself, stand aside'.

The man could not help but notice that Owerd's hand had gone to the hilt of his sword and grudgingly stood aside. Bending low and entering the hovel, the smell of mead, stale food and body odour was unavoidable. In the dim light, movement in one corner caught his eye and he sighted the one he took to be Sibbe Oxenblod prostrate on the dirt floor. She was evidently in a bad way and pain showed in her face and voice. It was hard to see any detail but a large dark patch around her jaw indicated a substantial bruise. He was about to kneel and examine her further when there was a commotion outside and he instead left to see to that. Cuthbert had a cursing Oxenblod grasped from behind in a bear-hug while Osric sought to rip an axe handle from the man's hand.

'He thought to bludgeon us', said Osric.

'Bind him', directed Owerd. 'Once he is secure, we need to get word to Wyld the birthing woman, who is the closest thing we have here to a physic. Oxenblod can be brought back to the manor-house and I will have Edward bring a cart back here for the woman: she can't be left here alone'.

With their snarling prisoner bound at the end of a long rope they all made their way back to the manor-house and once in sight, Osric peeled off the locate Wyld.

'Put him in the barn until I decide what to do with him', Owerd ordered Cuthbert.

By lunchtime Sibbe was back on a spare cot in the newly-build accommodation building being tended to by Wyld with a concerned Hilda hovering nearby. She was in a worse state than any had imagined: bruising to much of her body, malnourished and with at least a fractured jaw. Owerd consulted Edward and all of his housecarls about what to do with Oxenblod, for whom none had any sympathy. Worse punishments were mooted by some, but it was eventually decided that banishment would be

7

suitable. Accordingly, he was taken by cart to the edge of the manor the next morning and sent on his way with a warning that, should he be seen again in Birdlip, he would be flogged and lose an eye. Owerd was pleased that he had consulted his team, as were they, and grateful that no blood had needed to be shed.

II

The business of the manor continued unabated, with the most pressing business, at least according to Dobson the horse-master, being oats. More to the point was their seemingly never-ending need for those oats.

'Including the foals, my lord, we now have over forty horses: with the land as it is, their consumption of oats is enormous. With famine ever present we will need those oats for our people: what the horses need is more grassy land. We are already beginning to overgraze: we need to sell some horses or obtain some more grazing land'.

'I accept what you say, Dobson', muttered Owerd with a frown, 'but acquiring more land will not be easy. I know we suffered last time we offered some of the stock for sale through Edlif at Cirencester but perhaps we can try that again, just a few of those less-attractive for breeding. Meanwhile I will investigate the purchase of some more land nearby'.

Dobson left the manor-house mollified, then a window into the outside world opened up with the arrival of a monk.

'By all the saints above, it's Brother Cerdic come to visit', called Owerd as he warmly greeted the monk that he had spent time and hardships with when a fellow novice. 'Welcome Cerdic', he added as he was joined by Hilda in ushering him into their common-room. 'Are you still a king's messenger and in your usual rush, or can you spend some time with us?'

'I am back at Evesham Abbey, Owerd, but on my way with a message for the king from my lord abbott. I can stay a little while, but just a little refreshment will happily see me back on my way'.

Seated over a plate each of cold meats and cups of light beer, the three friends began to share news and memories.

'Stigand has been deposed as Archbishop of Canterbury and replaced by a Norman abbott named Lanfranc. He is a Benedictine which augured well at first but he seems to be doing little to constrain the plundering of monasteries that we hear is happening everywhere. My lord abbott is unsure how high this pillaging is being authorized or sanctioned but I am on my way with a humble, though probably fruitless, request for the king to stamp it out. He has other worries: the Danes are back at it. King Sweyn's sons brought a large fleet across and had a go at landing in the south-east, including Dover by all accounts, but failed. Next it was York's turn and that place was savaged in company with rebellious northerners before the Danes retired to sit on the Humber River for a while. Eventually King Sweyn joined them himself and they had another go down south, meeting up with that Hereward fellow at Ely but there were no major landings and they took what booty they could and left. Suspicions are rife that William paid them off yet again. That brings you up to date on what I know, except to add that our gracious King had a fierce anger upon him when he learned that the northerners had sided with the Danes and had burned his nice new castles in York. He took his general fitzOsbern with him and began destroying everything up there in sight'.

Hilda intervened with a question. 'So, Sir William fitzOsbern is well and able to fight still?'

'Yes, for now, my lady. He had some unknown illness or injury a while back and had to return to Normandy for some months to recuperate'. That caused a satisfied smile to appear on Hilda's face, knowing as she did who had most likely caused his injury – herself in avoiding an imminent rape. Cerdic continued 'but he is now back in the fray with a vengeance, wreaking havoc in the north of the country, although the king has reportedly returned to Winchester. Misery is becoming the staple diet up north; it is certainly the case that there is little left to eat; even less for the poor of course'.

That gave Owerd cause to pause, thinking of the heavy consumption of oats by his horses. He would need to bolster the manor's food stocks, he thought. Then he burst into a bout of ironical laughter – Sigria the maid had just brought in more light beer and a platter of oatcakes. He smiled at the others but made no comment.

The sun had just begun its gentle descent as Brother Cerdic rode off to continue his journey to the king. No sooner had he disappeared along the track than the clatter of hooves signified more visitors, this time a knight and what were presumably his two bodyguards. The knight, a smartly attired young Norman dismounted and introduced himself as Sieur Raymond of Foxcote. He offered a shake of the hand to Owerd.

'I take you to be Sir Owerd', he began, 'it is my great pleasure to meet a knight so widely well-spoken of as yourself, sir. I have a message for you from our sheriff', he added as he passed over a thin parchment.

Owerd inwardly groaned. No missive from Sheriff Roger of Gloucester was ever likely to be good news. What the brief note contained was a politely worded request to act in the sheriff's stead in chairing the forthcoming Hundred Court at Cheltenham. 'You had best come in and explain this for me Sieur Raymond: it makes little sense to me at present'.

Seated at table with Hilda, refreshments served and the visitor's men being looked after by the steward, Raymond began to clarify the sheriff's request, although it was apparent to all that "request" was a euphemism for a directive.

'A local farmer along the track between here and Gloucester has reported finding three bodies on his land. I was tasked to check and one of my men has since confirmed the find. The Hundred Court has been ordered to convene in Cheltenham for Sext next Monday to investigate the matter'.

'So, why involve me? Why does the sheriff not handle the matter with his own men?'

'It happens, Sir Owerd, that as you hold your land directly from the king, you are the only tenant-in-chief within the Hundred who resides here. All others, including myself, hold their land in a secondary manner through some lord such as Bishop Odo. I might also mention, though

12

it hasn't been acknowledged aloud, that having someone other than a Norman lord handle proceedings in this particular case would be politically prudent'.

'What significance does that have?'

Sieur Raymond leaned forward with a conspiratorial look. 'I am informed that our sheriff intends to invoke the law of Murdrum. If it cannot be shown that the bodies are not Norman, then the Hundred will be liable for a fine. Unless some remission is offered, which is doubtful as the sheriff stands to take one-third for himself, that fine would be four hundred Marks, conceivably triple that as there are three bodies. Most manors in the Hundred, mine own included, would be impoverished by such an amount'.

Hilda had gone a little pale whilst listening to this discussion and excused herself to attend to some household duties. Those "household duties" entailed hurriedly finding and briefing Osric who disappeared into the storage area and could then have been seen leading his horse on to the road to Gloucester. Feeling better, she rejoined the others in the common-room just as Owerd was asking Raymond about his manor and family.

'So, what exactly is your role in this Raymond?'

'The Hundred Court requires the attendance of two knights, sir. I am to be your colleague at the court'.

'Is Foxcote far from here?' The question came from Hilda who pointedly looked out to the sinking sun. 'I am sure my husband would welcome some fresh company for the night, Sieur Raymond, 'as would I. Will you stay?'

This was agreed, much to the relief of Hilda who needed plenty of time for Osric to complete the task he had been given. They further agreed that Owerd and Raymond would inspect the site next day where the bodies still lay. The remainder of the afternoon and evening was spent in sharing news of happenings around the country and observations on aspects of manor management. Raymond turned out to be a pleasant and unassuming young man who was a refreshing change from many of the Normans they had met. He was originally a lowly and landless knight of Bayeux in Normandy to whom Bishop Odo had offered tenancy of the manor in Foxcote, one of very many he now owned from the king. The bishop enjoyed their rents, but took neither part nor interest in their care or management.

'Our good bishop serves God, but serves himself in equal measure', Raymond commented in one unguarded moment after several cups of wine.

Summer sunshine prevailed the next day as the two knights each with a pair of housecarls, rode out toward Gloucester. One of Raymond's men was tasked to ride ahead to identify the location concerned and they all dismounted when he halted and pointed off the track. It was only fifty paces from the track where the heavily decomposed bodies lay in a shallow stream-bed but the smell assaulted them well before they were close. Owerd retired to his horse trying not to breathe and recovered a spare undershirt from his saddle which he tied around his mouth and nostrils before returning to the bodies. Raymond followed suit. The bodies themselves were little more than skeletons and no cause of death was obvious.

'What is that around the neck on that one?' Owerd pointed and one of Raymond's men drew his knife and cut a cord around the neck, lifting a small iron charm in the shape of a hammer. 'There be another one on his fellow', he said as he grimaced and pulled a second charm free.

'Look here my lords', called Osric as he lifted a rusty iron sword clear of some undergrowth. 'There are silver pennies here in the grass, too'.

The cloying stench discouraged any further inspection and the group retired to the main track to examine their finds.

'What say you, Raymond? These look like Norse or Viking charms to me. Are those two from around the necks not Thor's Hammer symbols?'

'Mjolnir my lords', interposed one of Raymond's men, 'the Norse name for Thor's Hammer. I have encountered a few Vikings in my time and that sword, such as it is, is typical Viking'.

'I bow to your better knowledge', Raymond told his man. 'I believe, Owerd, that we can now confidently assert that these bodies are not of Norman origin.'

'I agree. As my manor is closer than yours, I will have a work party bury these remains and we can attend the Hundred on Monday with some confidence'.

The two parties separated for their homeward journeys.

That evening as Owerd and his lady settled down for the night in their chamber, Hilda confessed.

'Owerd, I told you of William fitzOsbern's attack. What I did not mention is that he had previously sent an officer and two soldiers to take me to him in Oxford by force. I had sounded the alarm and the tenants and I dealt with them. Those bodies you examined today are almost certainly of those three Normans. Osric has confirmed it. Whilst we were at supper last evening, I had him ride to the spot they had been disposed of and place some typical Viking items around the site. I could not tell you earlier or you might have shown knowledge of events'.

'My Lord and all the saints, Hilda, this is a pretty pickle. We will just have to continue as we are and hope the sheriff accepts the tale we tell, although he will be reluctant to give up his share of a hefty fine'.

'Could we pay him off: we have plenty of silver from the cartload of Hereford geld money that I took?'

'O Lord!' That was the closest Owerd was going to come to a curse. 'I forgot about that. Where is it stashed?'

'It is untouched: in the stable block behind the hay'.

'That must be near a hundred pounds of silver: we must get rid of it. Who knows of it?'

'All of our soldiers. Sorry, my love, I was determined to strike a blow at Sir William for his attack and failed to think through the consequences'.

'There is naught to be done about it tonight, my love, let me sleep upon it and maybe some solution might offer itself in the morning'.

Owerd drifted off to a restless sleep dreaming of himself, Hilda and the housecarls hanging from makeshift gallows in front of the manor-house. He awoke with a start at daybreak, relieved to detect no change to normality, and with a rough plan of action in mind. A hastily arranged breakfast meeting with Hilda and the housecarls provided a salutary lesson for Owerd in the meaning of loyalty. There was not the slightest murmur of dissension from his plan until he suggested that, having been exposed to much risk, each of the men should be permitted to take a share of coins from the collected loot. That generated instant uproar, which in the confines of the common-room, sounded more like a town riot. The soldiers were unanimous and vocal in their dismissal of any thought of being "paid" for their efforts above their usual daily allowance.

Unusually, it was Cuthbert who expressed their collective opinion. 'My lord, we were employed by yourself and Lady Hilda at a fair rate to look after your security, that of the manor and all your other interests. Short of cold-blooded murder, we are your men for whatever task you or your lady ask of us. We have each pledged our loyalty: that has no boundaries calling for extra reward'. That was the longest speech anyone had ever heard from Cuthbert but there were knowing smiles and nods of affirmation all around. Owerd felt a little chastised and was humbled by their expression of loyalty, although what proportion was awarded to himself rather than to Hilda remained obscure.

Their meeting ended in a flurry of activity as they all went about their various tasks such that by the end of the week Osric was able to report that all was in readiness.

III

Monthly meetings of the Hundred rarely attracted much attention and attendance was usually so poor that the sheriff could collect a reasonable amount in fines for those failing to turn up. That was not going to be the case today. As Owerd rode with four housecarls up to the church where the Hundred routinely met he was faced with a crowd of two or three hundred men, women and even children all gathered in front. Dismounting he had his men remain with the horses while he strode to the front of the church where two stools had been placed. Sieur Raymond stood beside one of them looking a touch nervous but the crowd became silent as Owerd approached and he detected no threat. Maybe it was simply the warm sunshine that had brought everyone out, he thought, though he immediately dismissed that option, knowing that word would inevitably have spread like wildfire of something serious afoot.

He was met by a tall, well-muscled man of middle years who looked just like what he turned out to be: a rustic farmer who had done well. He was also the chief tithingman of the Hundred, responsible for its general lawfulness and tax collection. Owerd smiled politely to each as he was introduced to the eleven other freeholders who made up the rest of the Court, although it turned out that some were also tenant tithingmen. They all formed up on either side of himself and Raymond who were both invited to sit. The rest of the Court and observers were expected to remain standing and with such a large crowd Owerd thought it best to do likewise but stood on the stool instead. He noticed a monk walk alongside as he did so but took little notice.

'This Court of the Hundred of Dudstone and Kings Barton is convened by his lordship the sheriff of Gloucestershire and hereby brought to order. I am a knight of Birdlip and my colleague is a knight of Foxcote, both in this shire. Together with the twelve good men you see beside us, we fully and legally constitute this court which is required most importantly to address a serious crime recently brought to our attention'. There was whisper through the crowd as he said that but he clearly had their undivided attention.

'The bodies of three unfortunate souls have been found in suspicious circumstances within the Hundred. That a crime has been committed is without doubt. Should the bodies be found to be of Norman stock then the crime becomes that much more serious, being an affront to the king. Heavy fines could be imposed on the people of this Hundred. I require any man who knows anything of this matter to speak now'. He had almost said "or woman" but the evidence of women was rarely taken seriously and had no weight in law. He was met by disturbed muttering but no-one spoke aloud.

'I can inform the Hundred that my colleague and I investigated the site of the crime and discovered certain items'. Here he waved Osric forward who handed him the evidence collected. 'Two of the dead wore Norse tokens of their false god Thor. Another had an old sword of Norse origin'. He held each item aloft for the crowd to view. 'Some scattered coins were also found. It is our view that this crime is a case of a gang of thieves falling out over stolen silver with fatal consequences. That they were not God-fearing Christian Normans is without doubt'. Owerd turned to the Court's twelve freeholders and the general crowd inviting agreement or any dissent. There was certainly none of the latter and the universal sense of relief was palpable. 'Then that is the decision of this Court. If there are other business matters members of the Hundred wish to raise, they can be addressed with the Tithingmen separately. Court closed'.

There was much muttering in the crowd and a broad movement away, except for the monk who had stood beside him.

'The sheriff is not going to like this Sir Owerd', he whispered. 'He sent me to monitor proceedings and I can only report back that everything was done properly in a well-ordered meeting. I have no doubt, though, that he was looking forward to a hefty fine and perhaps thereby coming to the notice of the king. Take care how you present the decision of the Court my lord'. A lone voice could then be heard from the back of the crowd. 'Someone should buy that knight an ale'. A good thought, Owerd agreed, and invited the chief tithingman to lead him in the direction of an ale-seller. Raymond and his own men joined them and they had only a few minutes' walk before being sat on stools each enjoying a cup of ale, for which Owerd ended up paying.

'I cannot disagree with anything you said Owerd', began Raymond being cautious in his choice of words, 'but I am at a loss as to how you came to the conclusion that they were thieves. Apart from those few coins we saw no evidence of plunder'.

'Not here Raymond. I will let you know the rest of the tale on our way to the sheriff'.

Their arrival at Gloucester was expected, but not the appearance of Gloucester itself which, to Owerd, looked like a massive building site. Workers, most looking decidedly unhappy about it, struggled with timber and earthworks, clearly the ingredients of a new motte and bailey castle. An amazing amount of work had been accomplished since Owerd last visited Gloucester but there was much left to do before the place looked seriously like a castle. Sheriff Roger still lived in his original and virtually untouched dwelling, which seemed much like the peaceful eye of a storm as work progressed all around it. Peaceful would not describe the sheriff's demeanour, though, when Owerd and Raymond were shown into his office. The monk had made it here beforehand and had obviously briefed him on the outcome of the Hundred Court. He stood near the sheriff as the two knights entered.

Sheriff Roger sat red-faced and glowering behind his desk. 'I thought better of you Sir Owerd; not having previously taken you as a man given to surrendering to pressure from a bunch of self-serving thegns and serfs eager to escape a fine. I had already written to the king informing him of these murders and assuring him that I had tasked a fearless knight, you by name, to resolve the matter. How wrong I was! I see I shall need look elsewhere in future when I seek integrity and honour'.

'My lord!' Even the monk was startled by this venomous comment. Owerd noticed that Raymond's hand had automatically gone to the hilt of his sword. His own eyes narrowed and he took half a pace forward as he assumed an icy calmness.

'Caution, my lord sheriff', he warned 'I have oft heard of questions of honour and integrity being resolved at the point of a sword'.

'You threaten me?' The sheriff was noticeably shaken and seemed on the verge of calling for his guards.

'I threaten no-one, Roger'. He deliberately omitted any honorifics and smiled. 'Why should such a thing be called for when I come here to present such good news?'

That completely threw the sheriff. 'What good news?'

'I am given to understand that whilst I was absent on the king's business in Cornwall with Sir Brian of Brittany a shipment of Geld from Sir William fitzOsbern was stolen on its way to the king. With the help of Sieur Raymond here I have found it. It appears relatively untouched and comprises what I believe to be a very large amount of silver. I am sure Sir William and the king will both be grateful to you for its recovery'.

There was silence in the room for a full minute.

'Where is this silver now, Sir Owerd?' It was only in his imagination but Owerd was picturing the sheriff inwardly salivating at this revelation.

'It rests safely under guard by my men, sheriff'.

'We must recover it to the castle here as soon as possible', the sheriff declared as he summoned his guards.

Within the hour a cart and escort of twelve guards, all that could be spared from any other duty, were mustered at the castle gateway and, with Owerd, Raymond and Sheriff Roger leading, rode out toward the road to Cirencester. The monk who had monitored Court proceedings attached himself to the group. They all arrived at the site of the crime within another hour, having left the cart to make its own way behind. They were met by two of Owerd's housecarls who took them past three shallow graves and toward a copse of trees. There, watched over by two other housecarls and nestled in long grass, lay a score of sealed timber casks. One cask, a little smaller than the others, was open and the silver it contained shone brightly in the fading sun.

'Open two more of the larger casks', ordered the sheriff. His men obliged and stood aside for Roger to dip his hand inside to check the casks' contents.

'You will note, sheriff, that this stash of plunder lies only forty paces from where the remains were found of what I believe to have been the thieves. There was also a scattering of pennies discovered with the bodies which I suspect came from the open cask and perchance caused their feuding and demise. If you are content to now assume custody of this money, I have had a long day and would retire to my manor'.

'Yes, I will take charge of this find; you may go'. There was no hint of apology or commendation from the sheriff, neither of which Owerd expected, so he gathered his men to ride back to Birdlip. He was just getting comfortable in the saddle when the monk, also mounted, leaned over and whispered 'I would never wish to gamble with you Sir Owerd. I now find I need to be on my way back to Winchester where my own lord awaits my report. Fare thee well'. There was an audible "clink" as the monk settled his robe about him. It caught Owerd's attention just as the man was adjusting something at his waist. Realization hit him like a hammer: the man was an armed warrior monk.

Back at the manor-house a nervous Hilda came out to meet the returning men. Owerd leapt from his horse and swept her into his arms to a few light-hearted cat-calls from his men.

'It went perfectly, my love; I expect we can now rest easy for a while. Time to celebrate, I think'.

With the horses seen to, Dobson the horse-master and all the housecarls joined Owerd and Hilda in the common-room and toasted each other and a successful venture. Owerd congratulated his men on their performance and looked upon them with pride and no small measure of relief. They were all a trifle tipsy by the time they went their various ways to retire for the night.

The morning brought renewed joy to the manor in the form of a bright clear day with warm sunshine and no threat of rain. The tenant farmers were contentedly in their fields, the birds chirping happily in the sky and tranquility prevailed over all. Dobson was seen riding up on his borrowed mule whilst from the other direction a rider much in a hurry pulled in at the water trough and dismounted. The two greeted each other in friendly fashion and after a brief rest the unknown rider remounted and proceeded on his way.

'Who was that fellow in a hurry?' Owerd's enquiry was mere curiosity; he was mentally preparing himself for the inevitable requests from Dobson for more land, hay and oats. He received exactly what he expected.

'He claimed to be one of the sheriff's men, though lightly dressed as a messenger. He said he was on his way to Winchester with some report or other for the king. For my part, my lord, I seek some silver and use of the cart to fetch more hay and oats from Cirencester'.

'I can guess what the messenger's report is all about. As far as the feed for the horses is concerned, that will be fine. In fact, I think I might come with you. It would be an opportunity to assess what land on the way could be suitable for grazing.'

Hilda had overheard that last remark. 'Take the men with you', she said, 'they will just get bored hanging round here'.

'Less talk of hanging my dear, we may be Christian but you never know when the ancient gods are listening. Good idea, though, I'll take the men'.

It took no more than thirty minutes for the cart to be readied, the housecarls mounted and the relaxed Birdlip group to be trotting leisurely toward Cirencester. The grasses at this time of the year were slightly browned off and failed to excite Owerd much as he sought good pasture. What did increase his level of excitement, though in a surprisingly humorous way if the reaction of his men was anything to go by, was the sight ahead of them of a lone figure walking slowly towards them. What brought wide smiles to their faces was the fact that the man was stark naked.

'What ho, young fellow, mayhap you could tell us your story'. Owerd's smile vanished as he also noticed bruising about the man face and body.

'Sheriff's man', the figure gasped, 'set upon by ruffians not half a league along the track from here'. He was evidently in poor humour from his encounter. Owerd reached into his saddle-bag, withdrew a spare linen undershirt and tossed it to the man just as the cart drew up alongside them.

'It is the messenger I met at the manor gateway, my lord, although he looked better dressed at the time'. Dobson could not resist adding his own humorous touch.

Owerd's warrior instincts kicked in and he soon gathered the whole tale of woe. The soldier had been dressed and armed lightly, just a seax, to aid a rapid journey to Winchester. He had encountered a flock of sheep blocking the track. The shepherd, if that is what he was, made no attempt to move them off the track so the soldier had slowed his horse to a walk and attempted to force his way through the flock. No sooner was he in the middle and obstructed all around, than four others ran from the hedgerow and pulled him to the ground. He was then beaten, stripped and sent on his way.

'I need a sacrificial lamb, men, who is it to be?' Groans all around resulted as the men all guessed what Owerd had in mind.

'I suppose it may as well be me', declared Cuthbert as he stripped off his sword and gave it to the soldier who was now resting in the cart.

'Two scouts either side in the fields, the rest with me. We will stay just out of sight of you Cuthbert but hopefully within hearing. You scouts will need to keep up with Cuthbert as far as you are able whilst remaining unseen. I want none to escape but as we are without mail, I want caution all around. I doubt they are well armed but they are not worth injuries to ourselves or the horses'.

As Cuthbert rode off at little more than a walk, the others checked their swords were free and waited until he was just out of sight before following.

Hearing a loud cry from ahead less than ten minutes later, Owerd urged his horse to the gallop and drew his sword as the others did likewise. Around a tight turn in the track, they came upon the expected flock of sheep with five men in their midst surrounding Cuthbert who was trying valiantly to hold his seat. He was fighting a losing battle and was slowly but roughly pulled to the ground. He sensibly gave up the fight and lay still, which was especially wise as two arrows flew from the hedgerow over his head. Two very surprised ambushers took arrows to their bodies as the others stood in shock at being ambushed themselves. Their paralysis did not last long and all three of those still able rushed to flee down the track. They were overtaken by all four of Owerd's scouts and thrown to the ground either by sword strike or by being run down beneath flying hooves.

The tidying up process was straightforward. Two of the miscreants were dead, two wounded, of which one unlikely to survive, and one loudly proclaiming his innocence. Regardless, those living were bound and placed on the cart. Only a few spear-throws off the track, they found the messenger's horse and a sack full of clothes and minor valuables. The messenger extracted his own gear and the rest was thrown on the cart with the prisoners.

'I fear the horse-feed will need to wait Dobson; these characters will need to be taken to the sheriff in Gloucester. Osric, you go with them to explain the situation'. To the soldier, who gave his name as Cerdic, he asked him whether he would return to Gloucester or, if well enough, continue his journey.

'I am most thankful to you and your men sir', he said, 'and would prefer not to risk the ire of the sheriff by delaying his message any further. My feet are not much up to walking but I can ride, so will continue on my way'.

The sheep were something more of a challenge. Cirencester was the closest settlement, so it was decided that two of Owerd's men would herd them along in that direction with one other, Rhys, riding ahead into farmsteads to see if he could locate their owner. That left three men with Owerd, who shrugged his shoulders and decided that they would return to Birdlip.

-IV-

Despite the sun lingering in the sky, as it did at this time of year, it was almost dark by the time Rhys and his temporary shepherds returned to the manor. It was definitely dark before Osric and Dobson returned. Hilda had kept lamps burning and food warming until they all arrived back so it was a weary but comfortable gathering as they sat to share their stories.

'We were lucky I went ahead of the others', said Rhys. 'It was only a couple of leagues down the track when I came upon a very irate farmer and a whole bunch of his tenants – all armed and fit to murder anyone found with a flock of sheep. It helped not to begin with that I was stinking of sheep shit!'

'And still do', said one of the other Waelisc men, easing the taunt with a hearty chuckle.

'Anyway', Rhys continued, 'the man was very grateful to have his flock returned and indicated that he might call on you to thank thee in person'.

The mood was made somewhat more sombre when Osric and Dobson arrived.

Owerd met them at the door. 'How did the sheriff react to the tale?'

'He was unhappy from the moment of our arrival at having his meal disturbed', said Osric. 'He listened to our description of events, took a look at the prisoners and had them all hanged on the spot: live, wounded or dead already. It was not a pretty sight'.

That effectively put a damper on the evening's conversation and it was a thoughtful group that gradually disbursed and retired for the night.

A brighter and cloudless day welcomed them all next morning with the manor settling back into a more relaxed existence. Owerd looked around at men and women beavering away at various tasks, seemingly without a worry in the world. He began to wonder why he was not feeling quite the same. He had a beautiful, loving and capable wife; a manor that was now flourishing, besides two other manors that he had left much to their own devices; and silver aplenty. He should, he thought, be one of the most contented men in the land. But he was not, and he could not quite identify what might be missing. Wandering into the common-room he joined Hilda who was seated with a small cloak that she was making for their daughter.

'I am feeling restless, my love, and know not why. We should be as contented as cows in clover just now but I seem to have an itch I cannot scratch'.

'Is your conscience troubling you over those men that were killed?'

'No, I feel sad that men are brought so low as to do as they did, but their fate was sealed when they chose that course. Perhaps we should visit my other manors and make an adventure of it'.

'It sounds to me', said Hilda looking at him piercingly, 'that you are simply bored. Go entertain our daughter, she would welcome your company and you seem to need the diversion'.

Owerd did just as Hilda suggested and enjoyed playing for a while with their two-year-old Breanna. He was evidently not as much fun to play with as Sigria the maid though, so he was soon ignored and left to tend to manor business. Most of that business was readily sorted, including the departure of Dobson to fetch more hay and oats, though this time Owerd sent an escort of four housecarls with him. Routine then settled again on the manor and continued that way for almost four days. The burst of summer weather had passed and rain clouds loomed across a grey sky as a monk rode up to the gate and dismounted.

'Good day to you brother', greeted Hilda. 'How may we assist you?'

'I seek Sir Owerd, lady'.

'You had best come in and take some refreshment, my husband is out the back pretending to know something about making ale. You may leave your sword on the table in the hall'.

The monk was shocked. 'How did you know that I was carrying a sword?'

'I was brought up in a community of warrior monks near Evesham. I spent many a time cutting and stitching access pockets such as that you have in your habit'.

Having been summoned by the steward, Owerd arrived shortly, rubbing his hands to free them of malt. He recognized the monk. 'Ho, Brother, you are the mysterious warrior monk who monitored the Hundred Court for our beloved sheriff'.

'No more mysterious than any other monk, Sir Owerd. My name is John and I act for a number of men, not all of them beloved. On this occasion, I act for the king. You are summoned to Winchester'. With that he handed a thin scroll across the table. The crown seal was readily visible.

Owerd took the scroll leaned back on his stool and looked hard at Brother John. 'You are an Intelligencer, I think', he said. 'Do you know perchance what this summons is about?'

'I know only what I am told, Sir Owerd'. He said no more and seemed to be simply waiting for Owerd to open the message. Instead, he turned to Hilda. 'My lady, when you mentioned being with monks near Evesham, did you by any chance mean at Bredon?'

Hilda looked startled, as did Owerd who was now paying even more attention to the monk.

'I did mean Bredon, yes'.

'In which case you would have met my brother Radwulf perhaps?'

Hilda stared at the man. Owerd was so startled he stood and knocked over his stool before asking 'when you say "brother" did you mean kin?'

What followed was enlightening for all three present and discussion and reminiscences continued into the night when they dined together privately.

'I avenged his death', declared Owerd somewhat later as they prepared to retire.

'As a man of God, I should frown on any act of vengeance, Owerd, but as a simple man I thank you. I will keep you in my prayers'.

As they broke their fast the next morning Owerd introduced Brother John to the housecarls as a friend. As the monk saddled up to leave, he took Owerd aside, thanking him for his hospitality.

'Do you recall the two main precepts of Saint Benedict, Sir Owerd?'

'Humility and Obedience', replied Owerd confidently, 'how could I ever forget?'

'The reason I ask, Owerd, is that if what I believe the king has in mind for you comes to pass, you could become quite a powerful man. It would be wise to bear those precepts in mind, for our king has a tendency to destroy those he thinks at all lacking in those qualities, especially powerful men. If you or your lady ever seek my assistance, you can always reach me through the Abbot of the Benedictine Monastery in Westminster. Fare thee well'.

Much of that day was spent equipping himself and four housecarls for a stay of unknown length in Winchester. The summons from the king had been brief and vague: simply to present himself at Winchester at the earliest practical date. He decided to leave Osric in charge at Birdlip and take Cuthbert, Rhys, Ralph and the Cornishman Osbald. They were all keen to go, if for no other reason than as a break from the routine of the manor. Hilda made sure that they were well clothed and provisioned and gave Owerd a suitably memorable night before he left the next morning.

A steady pace and overnight roadside camping had them in Winchester by the afternoon of the third day. Owerd made himself known to the Chamberlain and was allotted accommodation for himself and his men. There was no indication as to when the king might see him, so he busied himself making sure both men and horses were suitably cared for, then wandered back to his allotted room to wash and change into more suitable clothing. He dined with many others in the Great Hall that evening, sitting well down the table and nervous in case Sir William fitzOsbern was about. He chatted amicably with a young knight who sat next to him, but in the main was ignored.

It was not until after Terce the next day that a Page found him to tell him that he was invited to dine with his majesty around Sext and should wait upon him in the Great Hall. Going there well before the sun reached its zenith, he found the hall as crowded as usual but with Bishop Odo presiding at the top table and no sign of the king. Worrying that there had been some misunderstanding, he discreetly beckoned a passing Page to enquire of the king.

'He is dining privately today, my lord. If you have urgent business with him you should speak with the Chamberlain. He is just over there', and pointed.

'What are you doing in here, Sir Owerd? The king is expecting you in his chambers. Follow me!'

Entering a sumptuous and well-guarded room after being announced, Owerd was surprised to see a table laid for three, with the king and one other already seated.

'Join us Sir Owerd', said the king, 'better late than never'.

Owerd flushed, apologized profusely for mistaking the dining location and took the third seat.

'Eat!' With that simple royal command, the threesome began to politely devour a range of small pastries and the like in quantities and varieties that Owerd had never previously seen. Only when they each had finished eating and small beer was presented at table did any conversation occur.

'This is Sieur Charles, the head of our exchequer', said the king. 'He is here simply for awareness of your tasking and to follow through with meeting all financial requirements that arise. This business is between ourselves. What do you know of Scipfryd?'

'The way we go about providing ships of war, Your Grace. I only know it is an obligation on certain places to provide a ship or ships depending upon the size of their land'.

'Yes: and what do we get for that? We shall tell you. We get a ragged bunch of mixed ships with a ragged bunch of mariners - what you call in Englisc "butsecarls" – who may or may not be trained. Your King Harold had lots of such ships and where were they when needed? We shall tell you that too; they were abandoned, no supplies, no mariners. That system is no good. Now we find that pirates can attack our trading ships at will and raiders can sit in the Humber or Thames and threaten our lands yet seem unassailable. This cannot go on'. King William was clearly working himself up into a rage.

'You, Sir Owerd, are going to change this situation. We want warships that can put the fear of God into pirates and sweep them from the sea. We want any who think of attacking this island to think again. We want a proper navy. Do you understand us?'

'I understand, Your Grace. I am, though, but a simple warrior. How can I help?'

'Do not assume a false mantle of humility with us Sir Owerd. You may be a warrior; we have adequate testament to that. But you are not simple; we have received adequate testament to that also. We need someone that we can trust who has shown both honesty and a capacity to lead from the front. Importantly, we have been advised that most mariners are Danes, Britons or Englisc. They do not respond well to Norman supervision. As a Briton we expect you to solve that problem, and it helps that you can write in Latin. Do not think that we expect you to single-handedly produce a navy. What we need is a small force – like a cavalry squadron if you will – that can make pirates or invaders think again before threatening us. They must be made to see that they stand to pay a heavy price for any upset to our peace and order. You will be provided with a house and funds. You have until Spring'.

King William stood, which was the clear sign that their discussion was over, so Owerd bowed and left the room, followed by Sieur Charles. To say that his head was spinning was a significant understatement: more a state of utter confusion mixed with fear of what the king may do when he realized that Owerd had no idea about how to go about this task. Fortunately, Sieur Charles took him by the elbow and led him to a minor office next to the Royal Exchequer.

'You must understand', began Sieur Charles as they sat together at a small table, 'the king's pride has been sorely tested of late. The return to Englisc shores of King Sweyn and his sons demonstrated the vulnerability of the king's land forces, which could not attack their ships even though in plain sight. How you go about restoring that pride is up to you, but I can assure you that there will be as much in the way of silver as you need. You will raise orders on the exchequer each month for the amount needed or for one-off payments which, if large, may be paid by grant of land. All correspondence is to be with me alone and in Latin, which is to include a report on progress for the king each month. You are also provided with a house to use as a base and I will have a page escort you there shortly. There is also this'. He handed over a large purse of silver and a parchment with the king's seal which read –

This identifies Sir Owerd of Birdlip who acts as His Majesty King William's Master of Mariners. He is authorized in the king's name to buy, rent or seize ships, men, horses or other goods as he may choose and direct. He is to be afforded every courtesy and cooperation.

The letter was signed with an elaborate vertical cross and the letters "W. Rex". Owerd stared blankly at the letter for some time, not quite comprehending the enormous change in his status that had occurred over the course of a single meal and the daunting task that accompanied it.

'If I may suggest', added Sieur Charles after a little while, 'you may find it helpful to call on Master Stephen fitzAirard who captains the king's flagship, the "Mora". He has a house not far away in Southampton'.

-V-

Led to a modest manor-house just outside the palace enclosure, Owerd was startled to see that this was the home of the late Queen Edith which he had visited once or twice previously. There were servants in residence who were expecting him and he was offered refreshments as soon as he entered. The steward was a lively but very slim older man, past his prime but still full of energy.

'I am Aelfric, sir, welcome. I have been left to tend this residence ever since our beloved king Edward passed on. I do recall you visiting our great lady Edith, God bless her. The place has been vacant for some months. Bishop Odo kept ladies here for a while but those relationships did not last and he has since found a more suitable arrangement. There is a cook, a workman and one maidservant'.

'I will need accommodation for four housecarls, can the house fit them in somewhere?'

'No doubt at all, my lord, there is an extra accommodation building at the rear with rooms, though they be small, for up to a dozen men. Stables too'.

Owerd walked through the house, examining the luxurious furnishings, then took Aelfric with him to the stables and spare accommodation, both rather austere by comparison. It was all well-kept and he pronounced himself satisfied.

'We will need plenty of ale, small beer and a little wine, Aelfric. Please let the cook know that there will be five for the evening meal. Meanwhile, I shall fetch my men and our horses'.

A brisk walk back to the palace had him reunited with his beloved horse and then, with the aid of a palace guardsman, his housecarls. Back at the manor-house he sat them down in what would be used as a common-room and explained the new situation. The simplest way of doing so would be to read out the king's letter, which he then did. When he had finished there were wide eyes, dropped jaws and utter silence.

'I see that has you all wonderfully excited', he commented with amusement. 'I have until next Spring to put this sea force together. I am still feeling my way and doing so mainly in the dark, but your own roles remain unchanged, at least for now. I am thinking that with four of the men here at any one time and four at Birdlip, we could rotate one man every few weeks to share out the joy. Any thoughts?'

Cuthbert was the first to find his voice. 'I still have no understanding of what all this means, my lord, but it does seem to me that you must stand very high in the king's favour. If I had a cup of ale at hand, I could offer my congratulations and toast your good fortune'.

'Subtle as ever, Cuthbert'. Owerd sent for ale and they all toasted the new Master of Mariners, though none knew what that position entailed. 'My first duty is to call on

King William's leading shipmaster. We ride for Southampton in the morning'.

The ride to the bustling port was a pleasant trot of around three leagues in warming sunshine and with rolling green fields to either side. Southampton was entirely new to all of them but the extensive earthworks happening provided a reminder of Gloucester as yet another of William's ubiquitous castles was being constructed. Directions to Master fitzAirard's house was readily obtained and it was obvious why on arrival as the place had been built on a grand scale. Having been announced, Owerd walked into a luxurious side room where his host was seated on a quilted couch with a large cup of wine in one hand and a heavily bandaged foot resting on a footstool.

'Welcome, sir, please excuse me not standing, my feet ail me something wicked these days. My physik urges me to drink no more wine but purgatory must need wait. Please join me in a cup'.

Seated comfortably with his wine, which to Owerd's taste seemed exceptionally good, he examined the renowned ship's captain with undisguised interest. Of around forty years of age, bearded and neatly groomed, he was muscular but showing the effects of much self-indulgence. He decided to explain the reason for his visit by passing across the king's edict. Master Stephen examined it closely and chuckled.

'Not an edict that I would welcome, Sir Owerd. You have quite a task ahead of you'.

'All the more so, sir, as I am a landsman, not a sailor, which is why I come to seek your advice. The king seems concerned that the Englisc system of Scipfryd failed King Harold and he is left with no defence against marauding raiders and pirates'.

'Well, I can testify to the truth of that Owerd. My vessel "Mora" is one of the better warships, a good-sized Drakkar. Sailing to Hastings, though, we were loaded with horses and knights and would have been hard pressed to fight any sea battle. The other vessels King William used for his troops were even worse prepared, basically just transports. We were fortunate indeed that Harold's forces were not even at sea. The problem with Scipfryd is that one needs to know when and where and for how long the threat will arise and know in sufficient time to prepare and sustain the ships. I suspect you will need a different approach to satisfy our king, who is no fool'.

'As for the ships themselves, Owerd, you will need other advice, I fear. It is many a year since we Normans went a-Viking. We have fought many a land battle since, but designing warships is, to us, something of a lost art. I can tell you what types may be around, but that is not much. The Norman fleet was largely dismantled on arrival and the Englisc ships, at least the better ones, were stolen away to Ireland by Harold's sons. What vessels remain in the country, or the condition of those, I have not maintained a knowledge, but I fear we have ceded the seas to others. My advice is to think afresh'.

'Can you offer any thoughts on what I should be looking for in any new vessels?'

Stephen sat back and called for more wine as he contemplated that question. 'The design of ships, like the art of sailing itself, is not something that can simply be told of, nor even read of, it must be done. That takes years of practice. I can pass on to you some understanding of ships and how they might be made and managed, but that would be sufficient only to give you enough knowledge to hold a conversation with someone experienced or explain what you wanted. Do you perchance have a few days at leisure so you could attend me here for that? I would welcome the company'.

What resulted was Owerd being housed each night for a few days with Sir fitzAirard while his men were given silver and the freedom to roam the port. He was introduced to charts, keels, ballast, sails and the other instruments of the sea together with many of his host's nostalgic yarns about the vagaries of winds, currents and storms. After three days of having his head filled with nautical detail, enough at least to hold a sensible conversation with a sailor, he gathered his men and returned to Winchester to plot his next steps.

'What I need to find is an experienced and reliable ship-master', he told the men. 'One who is not Norman'.

'Plenty around where we just came from', said Osbald the Cornish, 'there were boats aplenty moored along the Test River'.

'The trick will be to find one that is not making lots of silver trading over the sea', added Cuthbert.

'We can spend a day in the port on the morrow, asking about', said Owerd doubtfully. 'We also need to find what warships may be about and what builders of ships there may be. I fear we may be searching as in the fog for a while. Let us eat and sleep upon it'.

The trip back to Southampton was taken next day with all in a mood that matched the weather: gloomy. It looked like one of those summer storms would shortly be upon them and they hurried along the well-worn track expecting a deluge at any minute. The storm hit them as they entered the town's main street which led down to the port and they sought urgent shelter. It was Cuthbert, never one to miss an opportunity for a cup of liquor, that spotted the ale-house and they drew up outside the inauspiciously named "Sinking Ship". Shaking rainwater from their cloaks, they secured the horses outside and ducked below a low doorway into the gloom of the near-empty ale-house.

A burly man of middle years who looked like he enjoyed his own products overmuch offered them small beer or ale then, taking a second look at Owerd, added wine to his offerings. Ale was the drink of choice and Owerd asked also what food might be had. Whatever else he may have been, the owner knew his business and they were soon treated to jugs of ale with finely made cups at hand together with well-made hot pottage. As Owerd's eyes became more steadily accustomed to the gloom he became conscious of a figure in the far corner slumped at a table by himself and nursing a cup and half-empty jug of drink. He looked for all the world like a man who had the weight of the world on his shoulders. He also looked oddly familiar and Owerd stared hard through the gloom.

Owerd shot to his feet when recognition struck him. 'Hakon, you Danish sinner, how goes it?'

The man looked up at the sound of his name but showed no hint of recognition himself. 'Who disturbs my solitude?'

'It is Owerd, my friend, come join us and tell us your news. How goes the "Merry Widow"?'

Without much enthusiasm, Hakon rose slowly to his feet and stared at Owerd for many a heartbeat. Realization finally came to him and he walked unsteadily forward and gripped Owerd around the shoulders. Owerd had to stop himself from grimacing at the stench of alcohol Hakon breathed over him, but led him to their own table and sat him down.

'This is Master Hakon, master of the vessel "Merry Widow", with whom I have shared a little adventure for our late Queen'. Having introduced him, Owerd pursued the cause of the man's obvious present unhappiness.

'The Gods have turned against me, Sir Owerd, they set Loki upon me'. Hakon was a fervent believer in the Norse Gods and their mysterious ways. 'After the Queen died and left me the ship in her will, my first voyage was a success. I filled her with wool for Flanders and returned with a hold full of French wine. The profit was good and I sought to repeat the venture. I took on another shipload of mixed goods but before clearing the waters off Dover I was set upon by pirates and they cleaned me out. I was lucky to keep my ship and my life but on return to port here the owners of the cargo put a lien on the vessel until I paid the value of their lost cargo. I have not the silver to pay so the ship sits idle and I ease my pain with a little ale'.

'Would you like to seek revenge?'

Owerd's question surprised him, but his eyes became sharper and his head more erect. 'How so?'

'It happens that our new lord and master has tasked me with assembling fighting ships capable of taking on pirates and raiders. I need someone with knowledge of the sea to aid me. I am hopeful that you may be such a man'.

'I have debts but no silver and expect to be digging dirt for the new castle any day now to feed myself. If there is another option, I am your man'.

'Let us go have a look at this ship of yours Hakon. That is if that storm has passed, could you take a look please Ralph?'

With all being clear of rain, though not gloomy skies, the group walked with the horses downhill to the port and Hakon began to look much improved. The vessel itself was on the near end of a jetty with no gangplank and a large sign forbidding entry. Ignoring that, Owerd had a spare plank drawn up to the ship and they embarked, all but Rhys who, in the absence of any arrangement for tethering the horses, was left to hold them. The ship looked to have been left in good condition, although there was no sign of a sail and some of the usual lines and hawsers seemed to be missing. 'Taken by the pirates' explained Hakon.

Before having the time to go a below an angry-looking man strode along the wharf to them, panting in his exertion.

'Can you not read? You cannot go aboard that vessel, she is in my custody until debts are paid', he yelled at them, 'get off her now!'

'Well, she is now in my custody, so kindly leave us be'. Owerd was in no mood to debate the matter.

'I am the Port Reeve and shall be obeyed. If I have to get the sheriff's men you will all be arrested and punishments here are harsh'.

Owerd ignored the man and continued his inspection as the Reeve dashed off to summon the sheriff's men, who arrived sooner than expected. There were four of them, all brandishing spears. Seeing that they were outnumbered by men who were also armed, they slowed their approach and one ran off, presumably for reinforcements. Those reinforcements arrived just as Owerd was finishing his inspection and in much larger numbers than anticipated. There were around a score of guardsmen on foot, led by an officer of some kind on a horse.

'Come off that vessel now and submit', the officer shouted. 'Resist and it will go ill with you'. He spoke in Norman French and displayed the sort of arrogance certain to raise Owerd's ire.

Owerd waved discreetly to Rhys, hoping he would understand, and walked down the plank and toward the officer.

'Get down off that horse', ordered Owerd firmly.

A look of shock came to the officer's face and his hand went to the hilt of his sword.

'If I see an inch of steel out of that scabbard, my man there', and he pointed to Rhys, 'will put a yard of timber through your throat. Now get down of that damned horse'.

Whether it was the sheer authority in Owerd's voice or having looked around and seen the threat of imminent death, the officer slowly dismounted.

Owerd pulled the king's writ from under his cloak and offered it to the sheriff's man. 'I assume you can read', he said with deliberate insult.

The officer read the letter twice, then looked up. 'You are Sir Owerd of Birdlip?'

'I am. I am also the king's Master of Mariners and I am seizing this ship on his authority. Do you challenge my right to do so?'

'No sir, my apologies, the reeve did not explain the circumstances to me. I shall leave you in peace'. With that he waved his men around and they departed the wharf, leaving a confused and angry Port Reeve in their wake. Owerd felt a touch of sympathy for the reeve, so approached him and offered up the king's writ once more. Having given him sufficient time to read it he added that he was seizing the "Merry Widow" in the king's name and she was to be left untouched unless he directed otherwise. A thoroughly chastened reeve was still staring after them as the group departed to look for a horse to rent for Hakon.

-VI-

Back at house in Winchester, Owerd and Hakon sat together at a beautifully polished table and viewed a map of southern England, the first Owerd had ever seen. They were discussing a strategy for sea defence, which to Owerd felt weird. He had a basic knowledge, though, and was able to bring his thoughts as a warrior to bear on the problem.

'These five ports you say are regarded as the key to sea defence are Romney, Dover, Sandwich, Hastings and Hythe. Is that correct?' To a nod of agreement Owerd continued, 'but these ports are all on the coast opposite to Normandy. We no longer face any threat from Normandy, so I fail to see their purpose'.

'They are good ports, Owerd, so they serve well as bases to head in either direction, north or west'.

'I agree with that, but the west is too far to go for any threat from the Irish or Waelisc and by the time they get there it would be all over. The same applies to Danish raiders, with all due respect to your heritage Hakon, their history of attacks puts them far to the north; too far from places like Dover. Let us also not forget that our trading links go mainly from southern ports, although London is especially important. Trade, like monasteries, attracts pirates like honey to the bee. So where does all that leave us?'

'The challenge is too great, Owerd. What you seem to be aiming at is protecting the east, the west and the south. We have far too few ships and men to accomplish that'.

'So, let us focus on what might be achievable. What if we had three smaller forces, one in each area, strong enough to act against pirates and with enough of a sting to deter raiders or delay them until more forces could be mustered?'

'These pirates and raiders should not be underestimated Owerd. These Vikings have been plying their trade for generations, they can be very efficient killers, even in small numbers. They and those that copy them overwhelm their prey by grappling alongside and pouring well-armed warriors on to the victim. They are ruthless and can also be in large numbers. King Sweyn had two or three hundred ships when he threatened William'.

'Well, whatever we decide to do we are going to need ships and men. Ships take more time. Where do we get them and what sort? Let us start with yours Hakon, will you run the "Merry Widow" as a king's ship?'

'I will readily work with you Owerd, but she is no warship and I would like to see some silver for her use'.

'Good! I have a use for her other than for fighting, though my thinking is a little uncertain at this stage. I will make sure you receive fair compensation. What about fighting ships?'

'Some sort of longship would be best. The Snekkar, the Norsemen call them Snekkja, is most favoured, although I have heard of a larger version called Skeid.

Whichever design you choose, Owerd, it will take time to construct and it will be costly'.

'I have been thinking back to my early lessons in Latin and my tutor's use of Roman battle descriptions. They spoke of rams; a contraption called a Corvus and Greek fire. I am sure we could learn from those features somehow. Anyway, it is late: let us retire and think upon it more on the morrow'.

Owerd awoke with a start before the sun had risen having had vivid dreams of Roman galleys ramming Carthaginian Quadriremes – or perhaps the other way around, he was not quite sure. Whatever it was, it gave him the germ of an idea for his king's ships. If the Norse way of sea fighting was to board and subdue the opposing vessels, the trick would be to avoid being boarded. His ships would need to be faster yet maneuverable to avoid the enemy until they could close, perchance to ram or use longer range weapons. Archers, he thought, and in the next instant, fire arrows. He had a plan, though probably one with lots of holes he had not yet foreseen.

The next few weeks had Owerd and his men scouring the southern coast of England for vessels and boat builders while Hakon gathered his crew and set his ship back into good order. They found a good supply of knarrs and cogs suitable for carrying trade goods but far fewer longships, of any type, that were in reasonable condition. The choice of boatbuilders was very limited and Owerd was repeatedly advised to try Dublin in Ireland but persevered and eventually found a keen boatbuilder in a tiny hamlet called Langstone near Portsmouth. He had started work on a new vessel based upon the design of a Snekkar, now derelict, that had been stranded on the stony beach some time past. When questioned, he was excited by the prospect of building further vessels and had a good supply of labourers who were short of employment. More importantly he was both supportive of Owerd's design modifications and keen to see how they worked in practice. He was contracted to build three new vessels subject to the first being of satisfactory quality and performance.

Owerd decided to take Hakon with him to assess the Snekkars they had located for possible purchase whilst Rhys and Osbald were dispatched to recruit archers who were prepared to serve at sea. At three pennies per day, or four if at sea, they were optimistic that in the prevailing hard times being widely experienced they would have reasonable success. Cuthbert was sent back to Birdlip to pass on news of developments and to have Osric join Owerd in Winchester.

Five days later a dusty and flustered Osric arrived at the house in Winchester and hammered urgently upon the door. He was met by the steward Aelfric who, not recognizing the caller, treated him with the barest of civility.

'Yes?' That was the sum of his greeting, accompanied, what is more, by a disdainful stare.

'I need to speak with Sir Owerd as a matter of urgency'.

'Well, he is not here. Come back in a day or so'.

Aelfric must have detected something in the crestfallen look of the caller because he mellowed somewhat. 'If you would tell me who you are and the nature of your business, I might be able to assist you more'.

'I am Osric, Sir Owerd's serjeant of housecarls and bring worrying news of Lady Hilda'.

'Why did you not say so in the first place. Come in serjeant Osric and settle your mind with a cup of light beer. I am Aelfric, steward of the house. Come'.

Despite that inauspicious start, the pair became friendly and discussed options for having some message passed to Owerd, who was away "examining ships" as Aelfric put it. His actual whereabouts were unknown and though the two canvassed a range of options, none were satisfactory and they finally concluded that they could do little until Owerd returned.

Approaching London, Hilda was also looking forward to seeing Owerd after a long ride from Birdlip. When he had ridden off, she had thought he was heading to meet the king at Winchester. Why the change of plan, or whether the king had taken him with his entourage when relocating to Westminster she had no idea. What the guard captain had simply informed her was that he had been directed to escort her and her daughter to meet Owerd, who was apparently in the king's favour, at Westminster. She had been permitted to bring her maid but housecarls would apparently be both unnecessary and undesirable at Court. The captain's own troop of six cavalrymen would provide quite sufficient security he told her.

Approaching the Palace of Westminster, Hilda was hit with the stench of the river that she had almost forgotten. That and the noise and bustle of so many people caused a momentary regret at having left the tranquility of Birdlip but the imminent reunion with Owerd made up for that, she thought. She was led inside, welcomed by the Chamberlain and escorted to a delightful suite with an adjoining room for Sigria and Breanna. Refreshments were already laid out and she helped herself hungrily while waiting for Owerd to arrive.

It was not Owerd who arrived, but Sir William fitzOsbern. 'Stay seated Lady Hilda. You are quite safe and we have matters to discuss'.

Hilda momentarily froze. Her pulse was racing, although she was unsure whether it was simply the shock of seeing this hated man or a mixture of fear and anger. She settled back in her seat determined to show no emotion.

'You will be aware, lady, that I once sent for you on my way north to suppress some rebellious brigands. The three men I sent went missing. Nothing was heard of them until a fortnight past. Their bodies were found near your manor and cleverly disguised by your husband as non-Norman thieves. I now have an eye-witness account, from an ex-tenant of yours named Oxenblod, who swears he was one of a number, led by yourself, who actually killed them. I have a few courses of action open to me. I should properly have you hanged, but I believe my men would enjoy your body first and they would doubtless take their time about it so that not even a desperate whore-house would take you afterwards. I would also have your husband hanged as he is

57

legally responsible for you and your tenants. I would perhaps have him first watch you hang, though you would be in an unattractive state when my men had finished with you'.

Sir William paused to let this threat sink in.

'There is another way', he continued, 'my wife has returned to Normandy. That leaves me lacking in necessary female company and you, being an entirely desirable woman, would fulfil my needs handsomely. You and your daughter would be safe and well looked after here at the palace and treated like royalty as my concubine. The choice of your daughter's future, privilege or poverty, as well as your own and your husband's, rests with you. You will dine with me in the Great Hall this evening and let me know your decision'.

Hilda's fear was nearly all-consuming, as was her sense of outrage. At first glance she was entirely at this hateful man's mercy. At second glance the sorry picture did not change. She was isolated and friendless in this distant Court and escape seemed to be a remote prospect, even if she would be permitted to get outside the palace gates. Could she bear to have that man make use of her body? Would death really be preferable? If it was, could she in all conscience take that course and have Owerd follow her to the gallows whilst her daughter was put out on the streets? Perhaps the least evil course would be to accede to his demands, closing her mind off from her body whenever he was using her. She had been raped before: could she submit to it again?

Her thoughts were swirling around her head with no sign of any sensible outcome. Her thoughts turned to her time in the monastic enclave at Bredon: how she wished she had Radwulf here to hear her confession and receive whispered solutions to her problems. Her mind seemed to stop in mid thought. Radwulf's brother, what was his name - Brother John? And did he not invite them to contact him for assistance? She sent for Sigria.

'Sigria, go around the palace and find me a Page who would be prepared to take a message to the Abbey?'

As her maid departed, Hilda scribbled a note on a piece of parchment and folded it into a small piece addressed to "Brother John, Abbey of Westminster" and hoped that would suffice.

Sigria returned with a bright-eyed lad of around ten years. Three silver pennies bought his promise to try to find Brother John and perhaps await a return message. There was hope, Hilda thought as she sat back with her mind turning blank. Slim hope, but hope nevertheless.

-VII-

Sir William fitzOsbern was in a buoyant mood as he strolled across the palace courtyard. He encountered Brother John coming toward him, head bowed.

'Well, if it isn't our interfering king's intelligencer', he snarled, 'why are you not under a rock somewhere checking on peasants making rude comments about the Pope?'

'My lord, I come to warn you'.

'Spit it out man, nothing much is going to spoil my mood today'.

'The king is not well pleased with you, my lord. He is making preparations to return to Westminster and has it in mind to arrest you or put you to the enquirers. He has become aware of correspondence between yourself and Countess Richilde of Mons offering your troops to fight for Flanders. Supposedly marriage was discussed. That is additional to his awareness of a large shipment of silver in your care destined for the treasury which went missing, though you failed to inform him of that'.

'I made that loss of silver good from my own purse', William declared angrily, 'and if I make a good marriage with Richilde overseas that has naught to do with the king'.

'I believe, my lord, that he has the view that the restored silver came from the purse of the people of Hereford, stoking anger and near rebellion there. The

60

matter of Countess Richilde he sees as disloyalty and he may want the troops here'.

'This is outrageous!' William's mood was no longer buoyant and he was beginning to think that he really could be at risk.

'My lord, we both know that his majesty's moods are unpredictable. If it helps in any way, I happen to know of six transports resting in the port that could be made ready for sea by the morrow'.

'I shall think upon it', muttered a chastened William as he walked back to the palace. 'If I find myself in your debt, you shall not go unrewarded'. He beckoned a serjeant of his guard to approach him. 'Ride to the port. Come back and inform me of how many ships there are there which would be suitable for troop transport and ready to sail'.

That evening the Great Hall was as brightly illuminated as usual but there seemed less menfolk at table. Sir William and his closest advisers had taken up the top table and were in earnest discussion. To those in the know it was apparent that some great deployment was afoot. When Hilda entered there was a sudden lull in the conversation as she captured universal attention. She looked both dramatic and stunningly attractive in a crimson gown, tight fitting to the waist and showing a wealth of cleavage. Head held high she walked confidently forward as William stood and gestured for her to take the seat next to him.

'You look delectable, my dear. Mayhap it is anticipation of the night to come that brings out the best in you as a woman. I take it your answer is positive?'

Hilda smiled coquettishly and whispered in his ear. 'Yes. If I am to be forced to share my bed with you, then I see no reason why I should not enjoy it. I am looking forward to our physical encounter'.

She could probably have said nothing better to dispel William's sour mood brought on by an earlier than anticipated move to the continent. He was determined to have her but at the same time realized that it would needs be a short interlude. Perhaps he should bang her and hang her all in the same night, he thought. The concept amused him: bang then hang, a whole new philosophy. He ate noisily and with relish.

Not knowing where the next meal might be coming from, Hilda also ate well but more daintily than William by a long way. She was nervous and had to occasionally force her hands hard on to the table to stop them shaking. When replete she asked to be excused and stood to leave. William made no effort at discretion or to keep his intentions hidden. 'I have some matters to attend to my dear; I shall join you in your chamber in less than half of an hour'.

The walk to her chamber seemed excessively long and it was with difficulty that she managed not to break in to a run. Once there, she checked that Sigria and her daughter were suitably prepared and gave Sigria her small cloth bag of valuables. 'Go', she said. Slipping off her fine gown she spread it over the back of a chair such that it looked like it had been hurriedly removed and thrown. Changing into riding clothes and swapping her dainty evening slippers for a pair of light boots, she climbed into bed to wait.

Sir William entered her room confidently and well aroused. His sword belt fell to the floor and he began stripping off his clothing as he stared at this much-desired woman tucked neatly below the blanket, smiling at him with her hair artfully spread across the pillow. The faint smell of rose water could be detected. Naked at last, he reached to strip the covering blanket from his victim and was caught by surprise to see her fully dressed. That realization had no sooner become a conscious thought than Hilda was on him with a long-bladed knife. She struck at his heart in a powerful lunge but he was quick and deflected the blow which tore through his side. For a man nearing sixty years, he remained fit and powerful and beside wincing at the instant pain, he showed no disability. He threw her off the bed, cursing the witch he knew her to be, and prepared to beat her to a pulp.

William was certainly quick and strong, to a degree that shocked Hilda and she gasped as she hit the floor with a thud. Suppressing panic, she rolled rapidly out of reach and was half way to her feet when he came at her, closing the gap rapidly and punching her in the stomach and following up with a resounding smack to the head. She reeled and fell once more, landing painfully on something hard. It was his discarded sword. Groggily raising the knife to ward him off, she rolled, grasped the hilt and pulled hard to free it from its scabbard. William stopped short as she aimed the sword's point close to his groin and gave a menacing growl. He well knew that she was a capable user of swords and paused to await developments, while pondering whether he could kick at her legs and avoid any serious sword strike. He decided not.

Very slowly gaining her feet, Hilda kept the sword rock steady. 'Nothing would give me greater pleasure than to slice off a large part off your manhood', she warned, 'now turn around'.

William did as he was ordered, still confident that he could regain the upper hand. She probably had not realized, he thought, that he had placed a guard outside her door. That confidence slipped a little as she walked him through the adjoining room, entering the corridor further away from the guard, who seemed to be listening at her door.

'Stay where you are or he dies', she yelled. 'Do not even try to follow us'.

Down the stairs they went, both being extra cautious, along more corridors, following the route Brother John had described and eventually coming to a heavy door slightly ajar. The dimly lit hallways gave way to starlight with an open paved area leading to another door in the wall. Unfortunately, there was another guard peering at the locking bar to that door, perhaps wondering why it was lying on the paving stones and not in its locked position. He had not noticed them, but surely would at any moment. That is when a figure detached itself from the shadows and struck the man with a firm blow to the side of the head with a cudgel of some sort.

'Go', the man said, 'I will place the locking bar back'.

Hilda pushed William through the doorway at sword-point and stepped outside on to a muddy river bank that smelled as bad as the river alongside. She looked further along the pathway and could just make out the promised row-boat with the silhouettes of Sigria and Breanna seated inside. Sensing that momentary distraction, William made his move and swept his arm back, striking the sword away from his body and pivoting to face her but shying away from the blade in her other hand. He misjudged the momentum of the swing and the stability of the ground. With a shout of despair, he overbalanced and was in the river, floundering and struggling to regain the bank.

Hilda wasted no time but ran down the river bank, took the steps two at a time and leapt into the row-boat, almost tipping it over. There was nothing smoothly organized about their departure; Hilda slashed at the mooring line with her knife and they were carried away in the current. Whether or not William had regained the shore, none of them bothered to concern themselves. Following instructions, they made for the bank at the start of the first sweeping bend, a process that was even more fraught than their departure, with oars going in all directions. There were no steps in sight and the only way to secure the boat was to grab the undergrowth. Even young Breanna managed to end up with muddy hands and knees by the time that they breasted to top of the bank and faced a series of laneways. Navigating by guesswork, Hilda led them through a series of alleys until they reached a much wider throughfare and turned toward the Abbey that could be seen ahead of them standing proud in the night sky.

Hilda tried to orient herself, oddly challenging in the dark. She was supposed to go to the western entrance and was sure this was it just to her left but there were two stout looking ruffians standing at the gateway. They were carrying what looked like cudgels. She tried not to make eye contact and grabbed Breanna's hand with a view to making a quick escape. Increasing her pace, she looked over her shoulder to see one of the men following them. He had broken into a run. Pulling Breanna and Sigria behind her she drew her knife, regretting that she had thrown William's sword into the river.

'Stop, Lady Hilda'. The cry came from the man running toward her. There was a moment of uncertainty as he continued closing. 'I am Brother John's man, here to see that you remain unmolested. Let us get you into sanctuary. Follow me'.

Her hopes of rescue seemed to be on the verge of fulfilment but it would not be a comfortable nor a longer-term solution to her woes. To take her mind of that problem, she focused on the immediate needs of Sigria and Breanna who were both in a confused and upset state. The side chapel where they rested was tucked away off one of the abbey's transepts but was cold, gloomy and uncomfortable. The mixed smells of burned candle-wax and incense permeated the air around them and the slightest noise echoed through the large and otherwise empty building. She delved into the cloth bag of essentials that Sigria had brought and began cutting up an apple into tiny pieces to ease Breanna's evident hunger. She shared the remaining half of the apple with Sigria and hugged her close, both for comfort and warmth.

Every noise in the church fired up their nerves and as daylight broke through the morning gloom the sounds of a small congregation could be heard as they gathered for Mass. That happened twice more before the welcome sight of Brother John appeared with little noise but the swish of his cassock. He had a small basket of equally welcome food, comprising a half loaf of fresh bread, some cheese and a little sliced chicken; even some blackberries. He also presented them with two cloaks with monkish cowls.

'I suggest you keep yourselves covered with these', he said pleasantly. Hilda's hands went to her head and in horror she realized that she was in church with her hair uncovered. In many quarters that would be regarded as advertising for prostitution.

'You will need to stay here until dark, when I will come for you. There is a small guest room attached to the monks' refectory which should prove a little more comfortable until I can deem it safe. We do have watchers. I don't suppose you have coin with you, my lady?'

Hilda failed to understand the significance of those last comments but reached for her own cloth bag of valuables and produced a handful of four or five pennies.

'That should be enough. Consider it the cost of some removals. My men happily work for a regular day's pay but for extra tasks they do appreciate a little additional silver'.

Hilda, her daughter and maid were relocated to the monks' guest room late that evening and settled comfortably, albeit without any fresh clothes to change into. Brother John made regular visits to the palace over the next few days to check the lie of the land as he put it but was adamant that Hilda should remain out of sight until her situation became clearer. What they did know was that Sir William fitzOsbern had sailed with his troops, reportedly for Flanders. What remained uncertain was any writs or warrants relating to Hilda he may have issued before leaving.

This gloomy atmosphere within the monks' guest room contrasted with the bright sunshine prevailing outdoors and the three females were soon becoming impatient and irritable. This was especially so with Breanna who was becoming difficult to manage even for the ever-patient Sigria. The lack of any positive information from the palace remained especially galling and this remained the case for three days until their routine was broken by an agitated monk who came searching for Brother John.

'You had best come, Brother', the monk urged breathlessly, 'there is a man claiming to be Sir Owerd causing mayhem in the palace, demanding a search be made for Lady Hilda and accusing Sir William of suspected kidnap. Bishop Odo has been sent for but the Chamberlain is at a loss as to what to do'.

-VIII-

'This is a very serious accusation Sir Owerd', the Chamberlain tailed off as Brother John strode up to them, addressing Owerd directly.

'The Lady Hilda has been found safe and well, Sir Owerd, together with your daughter and their maid. It would appear that they managed to escape'.

Owerd's next demand, of which there had been many over the past hour, would have been to be taken to them. The only reason that demand was delayed was because Archbishop Odo was storming into the Great Hall exuding irritability and impatience.

'Ah, it's you', he declared on sighting Owerd with the Chamberlain. 'What is this nonsense about an abduction and why is some rustic knight disturbing the peace of the royal palace with wild accusations?'

'Rustic knight I may be, Your Grace, but I am also a king's officer and my wife and daughter were brought here under false pretenses by Sir William fitzOsbern. Based upon his previous behaviour I suspect an immoral purpose to be at the heart of it. I am now told that the man cannot be located, though it appears that my wife and daughter have managed to escape his clutches'.

'You are impugning the honour of one of His Majesty's senior commanders, Sir, and for cert he would call you out were he here to answer your accusations'. He turned to the Chamberlain. 'Where is Sir William as we speak?'

'He cannot be found, Your Grace. I am informed that his soldiers boarded ships two days past and sailed for unknown ports. Whether he was with them is unknown, but he did not advise me of any plans to be absent'.

'His troops make up the majority of the garrison of London. If they really have gone elsewhere then I should have been informed immediately. Who is in charge of the garrison?'

There were blank looks from the Chamberlain. Owerd and Brother John examined dust on the floor. The archbishop looked fit to burst a blood vessel or two and snorted in disgust as he turned to the nearest soldier and told him to fetch the captain of the palace guard. 'For now, he admonished, the security of the city is more important than the happenings to any mere woman. You, Sir Owerd, will remain until we can get to the bottom of the matter, but you will do so with no more fuss and bother about the place. The Chamberlain will assign you a room. You may go.

Owerd inwardly seethed at the disparaging comment about a "mere woman" but bit his tongue. Led across the main street to the abbey, he met up with a relieved and warmly welcoming Hilda and a newly invigorated Breanna. Sigria smiled timidly. Brother John entered also, but remained discreetly quiet whilst the affectionate reunions were made. Once settled, the various stories were told, relatively unemotionally, and the rescue strategy of Brother John was revealed with much satisfaction all round.

'Not entirely a bluff', said he, 'my business is to know the business of others and I can make an educated guess as to the king's likely reaction to Sir William's devious moves, together with Sir William's own reaction once he knew of the king's awareness of them. I would, though, have been delighted beyond measure to have seen his lordship floundering naked in the river. Which reminds me. If not beforehand, the man is now undoubtably the unwavering enemy of you both. He had watchers on the abbey which my men have removed for now, but they have a purpose as yet unfulfilled. I fear you will need your wits about you for some time to come'.

Sporadic cheering could then be heard from outside in the street and John began making a move toward the door when another monk knocked and came in respectfully.

'The king is arriving from Winchester, Brother', he announced.

John had the prescient look of someone who was confidently expecting this to be happening just now and merely nodded his acknowledgement.

'If I may be so bold, Sir Owerd, you stink of horseflesh, leather and sweat. If you are to return to the palace as directed by my lord archbishop then I heartily recommend a bath and some better clothing'. Hilda was vigorously nodding her agreement to this, though looked slightly abashed as she regarded her own disheveled appearance'.

'We go shopping, my dear Hilda. I have brought no other suitable clothing and I take the good brother's observation as nothing but the truth'.

London town was essentially one large market, probably the largest in the land, so it was not difficult to find suitable apparel for them both and also some for Sigria. Some would need to be delivered later but at least they managed to find sufficient for them to walk around without attracting undue attention. They came across one street with a fiery glow which on closer inspection was caused by a series of blacksmiths' furnaces turning out iron and steel in various forms. That gave Owerd thought.

'Mayhap there is an opportunity here to obtain a decent sword for you, my love, what do you think?'

Hilda had become quite used to taking whichever weapons suited her purpose from the manor's store, but the thought of having one of her very own was tempting. 'If you have the silver, Owerd, I would welcome having my own sword'.

There were one or two specialist bladesmiths amongst the shopfronts and they approached one that looked likely.

'My lady would have a sword', he called over the noise of beating metal to one having a small well-guarded display.

'A dress sword for the lady', the man responded casually, 'take one of those over there that would suit a lady of taste'. He pointed to an array of weapons to the side with beautifully crafted hilts and matching scabbards. He spoke directly to Owerd, ignoring Hilda.

'A fighting sword!' Hilda demanded crossly.

The blacksmith looked unconvinced. 'I may have just the thing for a lady like you', he announced as he pulled a sword from beneath a counter 'feel that, good enough for any lady as wants to fight and only six shillings'.

Hilda took the sword and made a few light swings from side to side, then nodded at Owerd. Nothing needed to be said as Owerd drew his own sword and held it upwards in a forward guard position. Hilda took an energetic sideways sweep then struck his sword in the middle. Her own weapon, if that is what it could really be named, shattered into two pieces with Hilda still holding the hilt and the majority of the blade clattering amongst the dealer's other goods. She threw her broken piece on to the ground in disgust.

'That's six shillings you owe me', protested the blacksmith angrily.

Owerd still had his sword in hand and pointed it casually at the man. 'If you try to sell shoddy goods to anyone, make sure you know who you are dealing with first. You lied to my lady about that piece of rubbish. I should run you through for placing her life in danger, which is exactly what it would have been had she attempted to use that piece in anger. Now, go back to your work and try to do better'.

This altercation had drawn quite a crowd of onlookers, some of whom clapped as Hilda walked on. Watching with interest was the bladesmith two stalls up the street and, when Hilda approached, he returned inside his shop and returned with a blade wrapped in an old piece of cloth.

'Try this my lady. It is not Toledo steel but as close as one might find in this land'. The man evidently knew what he was talking about. Toledo steel from Spain produced probably the finest blades anywhere and was known to experts but rare in England. The man was also being honest, which counted for much.

Hilda took the blade and practised a few strikes and swings before turning to Owerd and his sword, now raised once more. A swift but forceful strike hit his blade half way along and there came a resounding sound of steel-on-steel resonating like a bell. She examined the blade. It was unmarked. She nodded to the bladesmith. 'Good balance, fine steel, how much?'

'Well, let me think. I recognize that blade your escort carries, so I believe I know who you are Lady Hilda. The blade itself is a touch short for most men and a touch heavy for most ladies so it is unlikely to be a quick sale. Bearing all that in mind, shall we say one pound?'

Hilda turned to Owerd who nodded. 'Done', she said, 'is there a scabbard that would suit?'

'There is, my lady. I will happily include that with the sale if I could handle Sir Owerd's blade for a few moments'.

Owerd handed over his sword and the smith handled it reverently and stroked the blade from hilt to tip. 'I made this for a warrior monk named Aethelwig. May I ask how you came by it?'

'Brother Aethelwig has since become Abbot Aethelwig of Evesham, my friend', Owerd replied politely, 'he gifted it to me when I first took the warrior's path'.

'I saw it on you once outside the royal palace when delivering some work for Bishop Odo. You were wielding it with great success against a Norman knight and I asked of your name. I am honoured that a such a noble Briton carries it and now doubly so that his lady carries another of my pieces. May they protect you both well into the future'.

Owerd and Hilda walked on toward the palace well satisfied with their purchase and the conversation that accompanied it. Their mood was buoyant although they still harboured doubts about what awaited them at the palace. If Sir William had pursued his vengeance by leaving writs about the murdered Norman soldiers, then they would be in for a difficult, and possibly fatal, time. Side by side and chatting as they were, Hilda was first to notice a rough and ragged individual keeping pace with them on the very edge of the roadway. Not an especially unusual sight, except that he had one hand tucked beneath his tunic. Feigning a faltering step and a slight slip she took the opportunity for a glance to the opposite side. Sure enough, there was a like fellow on the other side of the roadway, similarly attired and clutching something beneath his cloak. She adjusted the small bag of clothing she carried and grasped the hilt of her new sword in one hand and the scabbard in the other.

'Ware ambush, Owerd', she advised quietly. 'One on each side, probably carrying knives or short swords beneath their tunics and keeping pace with us'.

Owerd nodded and continued to make small talk whilst glancing from side to side just sufficiently to sight the two individuals concerned. The couple continued onwards showing no signs of awareness of any threat, though the reduction in traffic as they closed on the palace and abbey was becoming noticeable. Owerd decided to force the issue. He appeared to stumble and fell to the ground with a cry of distress. Hilda went on a pace or two then turned to face what were now the two running men, eager to take advantage of a disabled prey. Hilda's assailant was closest and she had no hesitation in walking forward as she drew her sword and struck the man full in the chest. He came to a shuddering halt as he tried to avoid the point of her blade. He not only failed, his realization that he was under threat himself came too late and his momentum forced the blade even deeper inside him. With a shriek of pain and eyes widening in fear, he collapsed to the ground.

Owerd's assailant was even more confident of success but managed to stop his charge as his target launched himself back to his feet with astonishing speed. Regardless, the man realized that he was now committed to the attack and attempted to duck beneath Owerd's sword to sweep his own weapon across his opponent's legs as he closed within the possible swing of the sword. The man was evidently an experienced and professional killer. Had Owerd not had the quickness of mind and body to step back on his left foot and swing his right foot across the attacker's arm he would have been sorely wounded. Owerd continued to swivel through a full circle and that enabled him to bring his sword low across the man's body. It had the full force of his swing and almost severed the man's left arm as it continued into his body and struck bone.

With both assailants disabled and any witnesses scurrying for anonymous cover, Owerd looked back at Hilda to see her simply watching her assailant's last gasping breaths. He had little idea as to how she was feeling but she was certainly showing no emotion as she turned away from the prone body and joined Owerd. Seeing that the man at Owerd's feet was still alive she placed the point of her sword, still dripping drops of blood, at his throat and looked to be about to finish him off.

'Stop', called Owerd as he kicked the man's dropped knife away from his body. Hilda seemed dazed but did not complete her threatened thrust. Dropping to one knee, Owerd leant over the man who was still alert but clearly in agonizing pain.

'Who sent you?' Owerd's simple question generated nothing but a contemptuous snort and an attempted spit of phlegm before Hilda shifted the point of her sword and pushed it none too gently into his wound. A cry of pain and a torrent of blasphemous curses followed which left Hilda unmoved. She twisted the sword and pushed it a little deeper such that the man's agony could not have been more evident.

'Answer!'

Excruciating pain must have overcome any qualms the man may have had about protecting the sponsor of his work. 'Lord William', he gasped.

Hilda looked to Owerd who nodded as she shifted the point of her sword to the man's throat and pushed hard. With a final gasp, the assassin's body gave a shudder and his life ended.

-IX-

Having collected Sigria and Breanna along the way, the couple began settling into the same palace suite that had previously been assigned to Hilda. Her clothes and minor personal items that had been abandoned lay about untouched, as did a set of male clothing lying on the floor. Owerd raised his eyebrows at the sight and especially at the crimson gown spread carefully across the back of a gilded chair.

'Would you have?' Hilda showed no surprise at the question, which she not only expected but had been asking herself numerous times without a completely satisfactory answer.

'You have little idea what it is to be a woman in this man's world, Owerd. He threatened to give me to his men as a plaything before hanging us both. If it had not been for Brother John's intervention, I really have no idea what I would or could have done. It is one of the curses of being attractive to men, who are universally more powerful than women. That is especially so when a woman is alone with her child and the man concerned is more powerful than most and, like many, without conscience when it comes to violating women. All I can say, my love, is that I would not willingly allow any man but you to make use of my body for sex'.

Owerd covered the distance between them in a blur of movement and gripped her in a fierce embrace. He loved this woman and felt for her vulnerability. He also felt guilty that he had not been able to protect her and just as guilty that any female needed male protection. Why was this so, he wondered, casting his mind back to his early church devotions as a novice monk and the oft repeated commentary about it being the fault of the woman Eve that had brought so much evil into the world. He dismissed that thought. His experiences as a warrior almost always revolved around men being the perpetrators of violence and women being the victims. That turned his thoughts toward Sigria. Their maid had previously suffered immensely at the hands of Norman soldiers and had been brought into this nest of male dominance without any consideration for how she was coping.

'We must look to Sigria, my dear', he told Hilda. 'Let us make sure she feels safe and secure'.

Sigria was found sitting on the floor in the adjacent room playing with Breanna. She seemed, to Owerd at least, as a very stoical girl who let the troubles of the world pass her by and who focused her attention on the master's daughter instead. When Hilda lifted her to her feet and expressed concern for how she was feeling amidst all this disruption, a different picture emerged. She pushed herself into Hilda's arms and began weeping uncontrollably. Owerd realized that he could do no good here, so returned to their main chamber and began dressing for Court. Idly, he also examined the weapon that had been dropped by his assailant. It was a vicious long-bladed Hadseax of the type favoured by ordinary Norman soldiers. There was no doubt in his mind about the source and cause of the attack: simple vengeance.

Entering the Great Hall, Owerd could not help noticing the much-reduced number of Norman knights in attendance. That is not to say that there were few people in attendance, for indeed there were many. Most, though, were civilians. Probably, he thought, merchants or men of business who sought the king's favour. King William himself was present and seated upon his throne surrounded by clerks and guards and the occasional noble. Owerd worked his way carefully through the throng until he was on the periphery of the main group seeking attention and paused to watch. Most of the business being discussed was of land transactions and not a few related to complaints of monastery lands being forcibly absorbed into the holdings of Archbishop Odo. Almost all the complaints were dismissed, bar one notable exception which was from a monk pleading on behalf of the Abbot of Evesham. The abbot's representative presented and won a relatively minor case but the rapid decision in his favour spoke much about the abbot's high standing with the king.

The king's wandering eyes spoke of boredom with the business at hand and it was not long before those eyes rested on Owerd. Shortly thereafter the king arose and departed for his private rooms. He had barely left when a court usher approached Owerd to inform him that his majesty wished to speak with him and he obligingly followed the man to a surprisingly small, but lavishly furnished, side room. The room smelled strongly of lavender and rush mats scattered with herbs he could not identify. King William was seated on a chair with arms that extended sideways to form small tables. He had wine to one side and a platter of small eats to the other.

'Welcome our warrior of the sea, be seated'.

That caused Owerd a moment of confusion as there were no other seats in the room and he thought he might be intended to sit on the floor. Fortunately, his problem was solved by a page placing a stool a few paces in front of the king. He sat.

'We are told that you are here, and thus absent from doing your assigned duty, to rescue a lady who, by all accounts, did not require rescuing'. He raised his hand to forestall comment. 'We are informed that she was seen attending the evening meal in Sir William's company wearing a gown some thought provocative and without any sign of duress. No matter, we have more important issues to attend to Sir Owerd. Tell us how your task progresses'.

Owerd could see that arguing his wife's case would be fruitless and possibly risky. He accordingly turned his mind to the ships' strategy he had developed and began to elaborate on the type of ships he was acquiring. As he did so, he realized that he was doing so with a growing sense of enthusiasm which surprised him.

'We accept the sense of basing in the south to protect our trade', the king noted when Owerd had finished, 'but what if our north is attacked?'

'That may well occur, your majesty, in which case we send a squadron of fast ships immediately whilst we activate the bulk of our forces. It is our experience, sire, that the Danes in particular are highly protective of their ships as a way of escape and to return to their homeland. If we threaten those ships then there is every prospect of panic and with the invaders thus being unable or unwilling to leave them to pursue their attacks inland'.

'And how do you expect a handful of our ships to accomplish such a task in the face of hundreds of invading vessels?'

'With fire, my lord'. Owerd paused for effect then permitted himself a brief discourse on his different approach fighting at sea: different to the Viking manner, that is.

The king took a long sip of wine and considered what he had heard for a few moments without expression. 'We are satisfied with what you say, but would like a demonstration of this different manner of fighting. You will arrange one for us immediately after the feast of Epiphany. We think somewhere close to Winchester would suit, for we will be shifting the Court here to Westminster for Christmas and can return there briefly afterwards. We are pleased for now, Sir Owerd. You may go'.

There was a pause as Owerd plucked up the courage to make his request, thinking maybe now or never. The king stared hard at him, which was really only for a few moments, perhaps wondering what more there was to be said.

'Speak!

'Your majesty, I seek a boon. I am about to go about the business of collecting men for your service. They will in all prospect be other than Norman; a mix of Saxon, Waelisc, Cornish and Dane, even some Irish perhaps. They need to be bound together somehow and know exactly who they serve. More so, they need to win the respect of the landsmen, including your majesty's soldiers, and not look like a band of hooligans. I seek your permission to have light over-tunics made for those men bearing your royal badge of the lions'.

The king's eyes remained locked on Owerd who could almost sense the mental cogs whirring. After what seemed an age, he snorted and gave what could have been interpreted as a smile.

'Approved. Make it so. We wish that all of our vassals gave as much thought to their duties and loyalty. Now, no more: go!'

Owerd did not need telling another time. He left with a degree of annoyance at how lightly the treatment of his family had been accepted plus an enormous sense of relief. He went directly to their chamber where he needed to let Hilda know of his new role and ease her mind about possible repercussions about dead Norman soldiers. That nothing had been said indicated to him that Sir William had not had time or opportunity to set in place any legal accusations. That left the miserable ex-tenant Oxenblod who presumably resided with, and had made his accusations to, the sheriff in Gloucester. He would need to handle that cautiously, but for now they could make their way back home in peace. First, though, he needed to attend to some more purchases and convince the horse-master of his need for three more horses complete with tack. He would try to keep his use of his king's authority to a minimum.

As it transpired, it was a further two nights before they were ready to leave and they each left the palace without regret. Their mule was packed high and with Breanna having to be carried, the pace of the journey would be slow. It was fortunate that the early autumn weather was both mild and sunny and the season most simply called "harvest" was living true to its name. This was especially so as they departed the city confines and houses gave way to farmsteads with men and women alike in the fields gathering grains, apples or livestock as their occupations suited. The trees, growing more thickly now as they travelled into the countryside, were slowly shedding their leaves in a fluttering cascade of browns and russet. It was enough to gladden the heart. Less so was the steady crawl of couples, some with young children, and all looking for all the world like scarecrows, plodding miserably towards London.

'Who are all these people?'

Owerd was unsure what to answer but he had a sneaking suspicion. 'One way to find out', he said and vaulted off his horse and accosted the next couple along the road.

'Hail good fellow, what is it that brings you and your family along this road to London?'

'We do naught wrong', replied the man defensively. 'We look for work, food and shelter like all our fellows'.

'But why now and why London, if I may ask?'

'I am of Lincoln, lord, a leather worker, or at least I was. The soldiers burned our house and all those of our neighbours'. He was uncertain as to whether to go on as Owerd's face was growing red with evident anger. After a short pause he decided he may as well continue and his troubles poured forth. 'I did naught wrong, lord, but they killed our chickens and destroyed our goods and all my tools. With no tools to work, no cows about for leather and without food or shelter, what was a body to do? We have been walking now for months, going from village to village seeking work but everywhere between there and here is suffering. There is no food, no work and little of God's charity. I am thinking that London may offer some work, even labouring and I shall take whatever is available'.

'You have some days on the road ahead of you, good man. Take this and my good wishes for your future success'. The man took the handful of silver pennies that Owerd passed him and sank to his knees in gratitude. Meanwhile Hilda had nudged her horse forward and passed the woman a small parcel of food from her saddle. There was little else they could do, so Owerd re-mounted and the group rode on. At their roadside camp that night, the matter was discussed in hushed tones and with much sadness.

'This king and his soldiers have much to answer for', noted Hilda, 'destroying the lives of innocent peasants, including women and children, can hardly be justified. Do you really feel comfortable working for such a king Owerd?'

'I don't my love, but I see little else that is possible. At least this way I can earn coin and gain a measure of power that I can use to help the less fortunate. This

86

situation does not make me happy but doing what I do eases my conscience a little more than simply doing nothing would'.

It was not far along the road the next day when Owerd's reasoning was put to the test. They had passed more bedraggled travelers during the morning when, rounding a bend, they came upon a handcart drawn up on the verge with a soldier rifling through the contents. A man lay unconscious on the grass nearby while a woman looking quite terrified and with her tunic torn down the front knelt before a second soldier holding her at sword point.

'Hold' yelled Owerd as he urged his horse forwards, 'what happens here?'

'Mind your business stranger, we are soldiers of the king returning from suppressing rebels like these up north'. Neither soldier wore mail or helmet but this one spoke in Norman French.

'So, what gives you the right to declare these folk rebels and take their goods, which you clearly are in the business of doing?'

'That be no concern of yours stranger. We have authority to take whatever food or coin we need to fulfil our duties. We have also had a long way to travel on foot, so you had best be away or we may feel it necessary to take those horses in the king's name'.

'I am a knight of the king. You will unhand that woman, leave their cart as you found it and be on your way. I shall offer no further warning'.

In response the soldier drew his weapon and the second soldier turned from the woman to face Owerd. Owerd needed no further provocation. He had offered fair warning and these men would now pay the penalty for ignoring it. He charged and drew his sword in the same instant, running down the soldier without even needing to strike a blow. He turned his mount to face the second soldier but his further involvement was unnecessary. Hilda had passed the reins of her own mount to Sigria, walked up to that soldier and calmly and efficiently disarmed him with a sharp strike on the wrist and a flick of her sword. Both soldiers remained alive, which was a mixed blessing, and Owerd could now give his attention to the victims.

The terrified woman rose and rushed to her stricken husband who was groggily regaining consciousness. She was focused entirely on him, so Owerd was left to deal with the soldiers, and in this he had a dilemma. If he simply let them walk away, they could easily return to finish the job or ambush these victims or others further along the road. He decided to take it one step at a time: first was to collect the two fallen swords and pass them to Sigria, who took them with a look of distaste. She was also holding Breanna so was awkwardly trying to keep the child's wandering hands clear of the sharp steel.

Owerd needed rope. He had no intention of killing these men in cold blood and turned to inspect the handcart. Discarded on the ground was a length of cordage that had been used to tie down the travelers' belongings and he collected that before approaching the unhurt soldier who was still standing frozen still in shock. In fact, he was not unhurt, for he was nursing a wrist dripping blood on to the ground.

'I am going to bind you', Owerd explained, 'but first I shall put some cloth around that wound you have, so stand still while I do so or it will go badly for you'. The man made no comment so Owerd finished his task under the watchful eyes of Hilda and went to investigate their other victim. That man's leg was lying at an unnatural angle and it was probably the associated pain that was causing him to stir. He presented no threat in his present state, so Owerd left him lying where he was.

He turned back to the woman. 'Is you husband capable of walking?'

The woman eased her partner to his feet and he looked around in confusion at what had happened. A closer look revealed a bloody mess to the back of his scalp where he had received some injury but from what Owerd could only guess.

'I am capable', the man declared in guttural Englisc. 'We have come this far and I will not give up now'.

The pair had apparently traveled from near York on much the same mission as the many others who sought to escape exposure and starvation after the widespread destruction in the north. 'I would see these two brigands punished, though, good sir', he added.

'They have suffered enough for now, though you may check their purses if you wish. Otherwise, you need to be on your way as early as you can to put some distance between them and yourselves'.

It was Hilda's suggestion that completed their involvement. The man helped himself to the meagre contents of two purses, packed up his cart and led his wife back on to the road and onwards. Hilda led the bound man further behind the hedgerow, had him sit, and tied him to a young oak of sufficient size to hold him for a while. The other soldier was simply left as he was. He would be chasing down no-one for some time ahead.

-X-

Owerd had relieved Sigria of the soldiers' swords and the party was soon heading homewards once more. A league or so further along, the swords were thrown into some bushes and both Owerd and Hilda felt that at least they had eased a little of Norman oppression from two more folk.

As they travelled further westwards the flow of vagrant travelers reduced markedly, the fields were being tended more often and the easy smiles on those they encountered felt much more welcoming. On the afternoon of the fourth day the sight of Cirencester lifted their weary spirits and they pulled into the stables of Edlif, as much to speak with a friendly soul as to water and rest the horses. He greeted them warmly but with a surprised look on his face.

'My lord, Lady Hilda, I am so glad to see you all, and free of your troubles it seems'.

'Good to be back home, what troubles would those be, Edlif, my friend?'

'Why, rumour had it that you had been arrested, lord, or were about to be. We had been alerted to watch for you by the sheriff's men and report any sighting. Most folk hereabouts simply laughed at the thought'.

'Well, Edlif, we know nothing of all this but I shall make a point of calling on our sheriff as soon as I can to clear up any false rumours. I will probably have some more horses for you to sell soon. Until then, fare thee well'.

As they rode off homewards, Owerd and Hilda discussed Edlif's revelation with concern. 'I suspect the hand of Sir William in this', observed Owerd. 'Sheriff Roger has ever been that man's lackey'.

'Perhaps it is that rogue Oxenblod who has been telling his tale in the hope of reward', offered Hilda.

'Whatever the tale, we need to cautious. I feel a showdown with Sheriff Roger has been long in the making and is now looming. That man needs taking down a peg or two'.

Worried frowns accompanied them during their onwards journey, despite the happy prospect of a homecoming. It was as they passed the home of Dobson, their horse-master, that matters became grimmer.

'Sir Owerd, Sir Owerd!' The cry came from behind them as Dobson came running after them. 'Thank the heavens I saw you passing, my lord', he gushed breathlessly, 'there be sheriff's men at the manor on the lookout for you. They speak of an arrest being planned'.

'Do you know how many of the sheriff's men are there, Dobson, and what about my men-at-arms?'

'I have stayed clear, my lord, I know only what the steward Edward mentioned. There were then at least four of the sheriff's soldiers. I understand there was some sort of fight when they sought to gain entry to the manor-house. Two of our men were arrested and taken to Gloucester.

Another was injured in the fight and remains locked away in one of the out-buildings'.

'Thank you, Dobson', Owerd was pleased that Dobson had used the term "our men" and not simply "your men" but little else gave any comfort. 'Would it be an imposition if I asked you to host Sigria and our daughter for a little while?' He turned to Hilda. 'This could be dangerous, my love, would you stay with Sigria to help look after our daughter or investigate with me?'

'I have a new sword, Owerd, it feels thirsty. We shall go together and see what awaits'.

'Hell's bells Hilda', we don't want them killed unless it becomes necessary. That would bring us even more troubles'. He received only a winsome smile in response.

As they rode, they debated their plan and Owerd was becoming agitated, mostly because Hilda was winning the debate. Eventually he succumbed to her logic and a rough plan was formulated. The horses were tethered in a copse of trees well short of the manor-house and Hilda disappeared toward the nearest tenant's hovel. She emerged sometime later wearing a dark tunic of some rough-looking material and a peasant's cap. She paused watchfully at the roadway, before crossing and disappearing again into the bushes at the side of the manor-house. Owerd made his way cautiously to the edge of the cleared area next to the house and sat nervously to watch and wait.

Owerd found himself biting his fingernails then jumped like a startled hare as a clap of thunder rolled overhead. What followed in its wake was not your usual autumn rain but an absolute deluge. He was soaked within seconds and despite peering intently was unable to even make out the manor-house, let alone watch for any movement. He realized that his nerves were becoming frayed and was sorely tempted to head toward the house to make sure his bride was safe. She had made a convincing argument as to why she should have made the initial approach, not he, but even his absolute faith in her abilities failed to ease his agitation. He rose to ease his body's desire for movement of some sort but thought better of it after walking into a wall of water and retired back to the shelter of the trees.

Regardless of what the monks might assert, time has a habit of slowing markedly when the mind is forced to resist the urge to action. The wait for some development was agonizingly long and Owerd was on the point, for the fifth time, of running toward the house when a sodden apparition loomed over him. His hand had no time even to reach for the hilt of his sword before Hilda flopped beside him.

'It is done,' she exclaimed, dripping even more water over him as she leant in to kiss him forcefully on the mouth. 'Now we wait'.

The rain showed no sign of easing while the pair sat huddled in what little shelter was available to them. Then, as suddenly as it began, it stopped and the sounds of thunder receded into the distance. There was an earthy smell to the air and a distinctive tang that they each seemed to taste. The manor itself was distinctly quiet, the silence broken only by droplets falling from the trees. The grounds were now muddy and pools of water everywhere showed the extent of the downpour. Eventually they could rest no longer and crawled on to an area of soggy grass to seek a better view of the house and barn.

'Cook says it was the Waelisc man Trahern that was injured and has been bound and locked in the old barn. She and Edward are made to join him there at dusk and let out again at Prime to see to their food. There are four of the sheriff's men left here and I have picked up enough rope for all'.

'Did you manage to see to your herbs without being detected?'

'Of course!' Hilda was indignant. 'Do you think I would be lying here in the mire with you if I had been seen? There was plenty of my concoction to send the four of them to the land of dreams and cook promised to share it evenly through their evening pottage. We need to wait another hour or so. Anything you can think of to while away the time?' Her expression as she said that was entirely lustful, but Owerd could only imagine that she was joking. They were both in the open, tired, saturated and becoming colder by the minute. He compromised, as he saw it, by hugging her tightly for mutual warmth.

Their peace was ended soon after by the sound of voices from the house. Cook and Edward the steward were being marched at sword-point toward the old barn, with cook carrying what looked like a platter of food and a flask of some kind of liquid. Edward lifted the holding bar from the doorway and they were then both ordered inside as the door was closed behind them and the locking bar replaced. The soldier returned to the warmth of the house and disappeared inside.

Settling down to wait once more, Owerd found himself constantly fiddling with his sword until Hilda suggested that they release the captive staff.

'Not yet', he replied, 'we might only put them in harm's way and give our presence away before we are ready. How much longer do you think this will take?'

'Patience, husband. That guard was still fully mobile, though he may not have eaten yet. Let us give ourselves another hour, that should be sufficient'.

The hour, as much as they were able to judge it, went by in continued discomfort, not helped by the occasional flurries of rain and a wind that cut through to the bone. Eventually they both rose and tried to loosen up stiff limbs and encourage some blood flow to ease the energy-sapping cold. With a nod and yet another easing of sword in scabbard, Owerd led the way to the back kitchen. Easing the door slowly open he held up a hand, probably unnecessarily, for silence while he listened for any movement within. There was none, so the next target was the common-room. Three soldiers sat at the table, heads slumped forward and patently asleep. They needed to find the fourth soldier and left the slumbering men alone as they cautiously began a search.

Lying spreadeagled on the bed in their chamber, fully dressed but unconscious, the fourth soldier took a little time to be rolled over so as to enable his hands to be bound behind him. He failed to stir so they returned to the common-room where Hilda collected the weapons lying about while Owerd set about binding them one at a time. Other than the occasional grunt or meaningless muttering, none stirred.

'How long before they come around?'

Hilda shrugged her shoulders, which was all the answer Owerd needed or was likely to get.

'These people are not going to trouble us for a while, anyway', he declared, 'perhaps it would be a sensible move to offer our staff a more comfortable abode for the night. We may need their assistance anyway to move this lot and if you feel anything like I do, then some warm product from the cook would not go astray.'

The small barn was dark and gloomy, with the lifting of the locking bar raising no comment from within. Hilda went straight in and called out to those confined. Edward and cook were soon on their feet and eager to leave for freedom but Trahern, whilst awake, made no move to join them.

'My lady, my leg be broke. I cannot walk', he announced with a painful yelp as he tried to move.

'Stay right where you are, I will have to fetch some light and we will then see what needs doing'. With that, Hilda led the others back to the house and directed cook to put together some hot food. 'Without my herbal mix', she added with a smile. She then returned to the small barn with a bronze lamp and examined Trahern's leg. With his left foot splayed at an odd angle to his leg, it was quickly apparent that it was indeed broken and would need re-setting if he was ever to walk normally again.

'How did this happen, Trahern?'

'They caught us unprepared milady, there were eight of them. One tried to barge his way into the manor house and I resisted. His friend tripped me and then he stomped on my leg. Mathew and Lefric were cleaning up the barn and unarmed, but from what cook told me they managed to land a few blows before being taken at sword-point and hauled away'.

'This may hurt', Hilda warned as she removed his boot and then, despite loud protestations, his breeches. From the feel of it the main leg bone, the tibia she had heard it called, was in two parts with the lower section twisted at an angle. Not knowing whether the bones had had time to knit, nor if re-setting was even possible, she left to summon Owerd's assistance.

'Hold his upper leg still Owerd', she directed. 'Sit on him if you need to but don't let him move his leg. This will definitely hurt, Trahern, but is in your best interests; now lie still'.

Using all her strength she twisted the two parts of the leg bone together until they lay in a more normal alignment. Trahern gave out a piercing scream then happily lapsed into unconsciousness. Quickly placing a solid piece of timber along the line of the leg, she bound it tightly with strips of cloth and sat back, perspiring despite the cold.

'He won't be able to stand for a while and not walk for a fortnight is my guess. He now needs to be put to bed; can I leave that to you husband?'

Trahern was ultimately settled in a spare guest room with the aid of Edward and a hand cart, but not without great difficulty. He was a heavy man and the inside corridors relatively narrow. It was thus with great relief that both Owerd and Hilda stripped off their wet clothing, rubbed each other vigorously with dry linen and dressed. Cook then appeared as a ministering angel with platters of hot food and mulled ale. The annoying, but necessary, task was then to relocate the sheriff's men to the old barn where they could be left secured for the night. Owerd took the added precaution of binding their feet but left them in reasonable comfort in the straw.

The mood in the common-room after Edward and the cook had retired was sombre. The oil lamps and occasional candle illuminated worried frowns as the couple shared a jug of light ale and looked to each other for a solution.

'I really have little confidence in a good outcome from all this, my love', said Owerd. 'The sheriff is an arrogant pest, but he has all the authority of the king and can call on the Justiciar and all his troops if necessary to enforce his will. We could take our horses and whatever you think we may need and head for the hills if you would like, but that does seem a touch extreme when we lack information on why he wants us arrested. We could perhaps brazen it out, after all he can hardly lock up a knight and his lady without good cause'.

'Why do we not simply sleep on the matter tonight husband? We are both weary and maybe not thinking straight. We can question our captives on the morrow; perchance they might know of the reason behind this intrusion. I do suspect Sir William as the instigator, whatever the excuse'.

'I agree', said Owerd. 'Mayhap now that Sir William is disgraced and out of the country, we may be able to weaken the sheriff's position on this but he's a stubborn man. We shall have to see'.

-XI-

The sun shone brightly the following morning but without any light whatsoever being shed on Owerd's and Hilda's dilemma about how to react to this prospect of arrest. A good meal of pottage with chicken and cheese did little to ease their spirits before Owerd walked the sixty paces to the small barn and unbarred the door. The four captives looked comfortable enough, but he was greeted with surly outrage and demands for release.

'We are sheriff's men on our lawful duty', one declared, 'you can hang for this'.

'I doubt it', Owerd responded mildly as he seated himself on a bale of straw in front of them. 'I am unused to finding armed soldiers in my house without my leave, so perhaps you can explain to me your purpose'.

The same soldier continued. 'In my tunic there is a writ signed by the sheriff for the arrest of Sir Owerd and Lady Hilda of Birdlip. That be all you or anyone else needs to know, so release us now or the consequences will be that much the harder for you'.

'Do you know the charge which is laid against us?'

'I have no need to know that and nor do you. I simply follow orders, and these orders came directly from the mouth of Sheriff Roger when he gave me the writ'.

'I see', said Owerd, although he really did not. 'I shall have to think upon this for a while. Meanwhile you may rest here and I will have some food brought to you shortly. Did the sheriff perhaps also tell you how long you were to remain here if I did not appear?'

'We stay here until relieved. Be warned, that could be any time so you will have more soldiers to contend with than you might wish, and they will not be happy to see us confined like this'.

Owerd remained silent for a few moments but stared at the angry soldier who was starting to irritate him. 'You call me Lord, soldier. Your lack of respect makes me have fresh thoughts about feeding you just yet. You do your colleagues a disservice'. He walked out, secured the door, and returned to the house having gained no more useful intelligence. He looked at Hilda's enquiring eyes as he entered the house and shook his head with an accompanying shrug of the shoulders.

'Well, I may as well be useful', Hilda announced, 'I shall recover my horse and go fetch Sigria and our daughter; they will be wondering what has happened'.

That reminded Owerd that both their horses had been neglected overnight and he gave a guilty start. 'I will come and collect Satan too. If we end up having to head for the hills, then we will need what horses we take to be ready and in good condition'.

Most of the day was then taken up with domestic issues and those related to aspects of the manor that needed attention. The harvest was now in and the usual selection of animals to be slaughtered for winter sustenance was well underway. A provisional decision had also been made that should matters take a dangerous turn with the sheriff then they would retreat to their manor at Upton. That meant briefing, and to some extent reassuring, Sigria, their daughter and the staff. There was a definite feeling of nervous expectancy in the air as preparations for relocation were actively but discreetly being made. All such activities stopped when horses were heard arriving at the front. Lots of horses!

'You should hide', stated Owerd.

'Like hell I will', retorted Hilda as she fastened her sword and belt around her waist.

Their faces fell as they neared the front door. There must have been at least two score well-armed soldiers dismounting at the front entrance. Owerd decided to brazen it out and walked to meet them with an air of confidence that he didn't feel.

'How may I help you gentlemen,' Owerd began as the evident leader entered the gateway, 'this is ... Oh my good Lord above', he stopped in surprise. 'Sieur Brian of Brittany. Well met sir!'

'And you, Sir Owerd', Brian replied. A second knight, shorter, stocky and heavily bearded, drew up alongside Brian. 'May I also introduce my deputy, Sieur Raymond'.

Introductions completed, the two Breton knights were led inside to the common-room where Hilda had discreetly withdrawn. More introductions followed.

'Sieur Brian leads the Breton knights with whom I was attached by King William', Owerd explained to Hilda. 'Gentlemen, please be seated and accept some refreshment, then you can let us know how this welcome visit has arisen'.

Over cups of ale, they all relaxed and Brian explained. 'We are on our way to disband after the fury of the harrying that King William tasked us with to the north. We are knights, as you know Owerd, and ever willing to fight our lord's battles without demur. What was required of us over recent times was not battle; destruction on a grand scale but not battle. More like savagery, with peasants beaten, even killed, for little reason and even animals and crops destroyed to bring inevitable starvation to women and children. That was not the honourable warfare we were trained and joined the duke for'.

'So, what happens now?' Owerd's query was met by a look between the two Bretons.

'We go our separate ways. I and some others will be going home to Brittany; others to Normandy, and some have been awarded manors here in England. My friend Sieur Raymond here is joining the king's guard as captain. We are on our way to Winchester to finalize matters with the Exchequer but your sheriff denied us accommodation for the night so now, apart from the pleasure of reacquaintance, we seek your indulgence to water the horses and camp somewhere hereabouts'.

'We can do better than that Brian, can we not Hilda?'

'We can'. She summoned Edward and had arrangements made for food and drink to be taken to the new stable building. She then excused herself to go and show the cavalrymen their overnight quarters, explaining as she did the limitations on space for such a number. 'It will be cramped, but at least you shall be warm and dry', she told them, 'I regret the horses will need to remain in fresher air than you will probably have to endure', she finished with a smile.

Owerd also came outside and mingled with the Bretons, renewing acquaintance with many of those he remembered from his time at Launceston. Once all the more junior guests were settled, guest rooms were made available to Brian and Raymond and then they returned to the common room for supper and wine.

Conversation over supper was casual and friendly until the name of the sheriff came up. Brian was annoyed that they had not been given the slightest show of hospitality in Gloucester and was critical of Sir Roger's arrogant manner in which it was denied them.

'We have our own issues with the sheriff', interposed Hilda, 'he apparently seeks to have us arrested'.

'How so Owerd?' Raymond's query seemed pointedly directed to Owerd rather than Hilda.

'Well, we are unsure of the grounds, but we have four of his men locked away here in an old barn'. Owerd looked toward Hilda, uncertain of how much of the tale to tell and received a nod in affirmation. He therefore launched into the story of the attempted rape and then abduction of Hilda by Sir William fitzOsbern and that man's patronage of Sheriff Roger. 'We believe the sheriff has obtained some testimony from an aggrieved tenant who we dismissed from the manor, although we have no details. It takes but a small step from there to believe that the arrest writ originated from a vengeful Sir William before he departed the country in disgrace'.

'But Sir William fitzOsbern has a powerful and honourable reputation, Sir Owerd, I am at a loss to believe such of him', interjected Raymond.

Hilda switched to Latin. 'Be a free thinker, sir, and don't accept everything you hear as truth'.

'And who might have told you that, lady?'

'It is instructive reading, Raymond, which I commend to you. It is one of the sayings of Aristotle'.

There was a surprised look on Raymond's face and a knowing grin forming on Brian's. Not to be silenced, he sat upright in his chair and glared at Hilda. 'Lady, I am your guest and mean no offence, but you open yourself to much criticism as a woman making accusations against powerful men of the king'.

Hilda could not resist an apt response. Reverting again to Latin, she quoted Aristotle once more. 'It is easy to avoid criticism, say nothing, do nothing, be nothing'.

'I suppose that is yet another piece of ancient Greek philosophy', said Raymond who was clearly losing this exchange. 'I could never see the benefit in giving women an education. God made woman to be subordinate and serve the needs of men. Again, I mean no offence, but women are inherently weaker in mind and body than men, so should satisfy themselves by taking guidance from their menfolk'.

'Would you care to prove that assertion with steel, Sieur Raymond?'

Owerd swiveled to stare hard at Hilda, trying to gauge her meaning. Brian's grin vanished in an instant and was replaced with a worried frown as he also sought to see how this might end. Raymond was shocked into silence.

Hilda decided to lighten the mood and produced one of her more beatific smiles. 'Oh, I mean no offence either, Sieur Raymond, but I feel guilty that our poor manor is unable to provide you or your men with any worthy entertainment. I propose a friendly bout of merely a quarter of one hour with blunted or wooden swords for the enjoyment of your men who can then adjudge the winner. It should be fun'.

'Are you serious my lady? What say you to this Sir Owerd?'

'Well, it cannot hurt provided you both show restraint and avoid any injury to body or honour. It may provide a welcome interlude before retiring. How do you see this Sir Brian?'

'If Raymond is willing, why not? It should at least be entertaining'.

The bout was agreed, somewhat reluctantly by Raymond, and the two prospective combatants left to change into more suitable clothing – in Hilda's case – or recover his mail in Raymond's.

Hilda made straight for the large stable where the remaining knights were being housed. 'Mes amies', she began in Norman French, her poor pronunciation alleviated by the lilting tone of her voice. The surprise visit caused many who were resting to rise, and silence quickly descended. She proceeded to explain that some entertainment by way of a practice bout was to occur shortly outside in the training yard. 'But', she emphasized, 'you are guests and guest rules apply to the hosts as well, so if you are asked to judge the bout, I implore you to declare it a draw'.

Not ten minutes later, and surrounded by torches borne by the eager soldiers the combatants entered the ring to scattered applause. That broke into loud cheering and the bashing of drinking cups together when it was realized that Lady Hilda, now dressed in breeches and mail, was to participate. This was quite the unexpected spectacle. Having decided on blunted swords, the combatants squared off with Owerd and Brian acting as joint referees.

'No head-high strikes or thrusts and you both step back immediately if either of us call "hold"', called Owerd. 'Salute and commence!'

Strokes from both contestants began tentatively, neither wishing to be seen to attack in any violent manner. Raymond, for all his masculine dismissal of any woman's mind or ability, had a strong sense of honour and well knew he was fighting, albeit in play, a woman. It was soon apparent, though, that this was no defenceless woman. Her sweeping defensive counters were swift and effective, while her strikes, progressively more forceful, were equally swift and well-aimed. The bout began to heat up and Raymond was hard put to counter a sudden flurry of blows to his shoulders. Inevitably one such strike cut through and he suffered a painful sting to his upper arm. He went on the attack himself but was wary of the watching soldiers considering him to be bullying. He need not have worried on that score as Hilda countered his attempted strikes with apparent ease.

Both contestants were soon perspiring freely and the bout became heated and more exciting. The night air was ringing with the sounds of steel striking steel with a background hum of whispered murmurs, and the occasional shout, of approval. Swords were clashing frequently and with a speed that surprised many of the onlookers, except Owerd who had experienced Hilda's swordsmanship at first hand. A neutral observer would have assessed Raymond competent and the stronger of the two, but Hilda quicker and the more able in using her sword to best effect. Another flurry of attempted blows by both parties suddenly ended with their faces close together and their two swords locked hilt to hilt.

'I would prefer not to arm wrestle you Sieur Raymond', Hilda whispered, 'shall we call this an end?'

Raymond stepped back and lowered his sword, while Hilda did likewise. Sir Brian called for a vote on the winner by acclamation but there was a silence from the assembled troops. 'We declare a draw', called one and he was cheered by his colleagues. Hilda bowed to Sieur Raymond and took his arm to lead him inside.

'You fight well, sir, and undoubtably would prevail in any real fight'.

Raymond was not so sure, but in any event courtesies demanded a similar response. 'You are one of the most accomplished wielders of a sword I have ever met, Lady Hilda and I would not enjoy encountering you in any hostile manner. I take back anything I may have said or implied about any inferiority of the fairer sex'.

'Spoken like a gentlemen sir, let us enjoy some well-earned wine'.

They were not friends, but had at least acquired a degree of mutual respect. After dispensing with their fighting implements and clothing, they joined the others in the common-room. The after-dinner conversation was light and friendly. Their difficulty with the sheriff became a central theme.

'You could always insist on trial by compurgation, Owerd', offered Brian. 'Your oath of innocence would be a powerful statement and certainly acceptable in law'.

'Does that not require a dozen oath-helpers?' Owerd was not familiar with the procedure.

'It does indeed', declared Brian, who continued after a moment's reflection, 'but we have two score such oath-helpers here with us and I dare any to disparage a single one of them'.

'You and your men would do that for us? You owe us nothing Sieur Brian'.

'But you have shown Christian hospitality where the sheriff did not, and you have both entertained us well this day. It could be a good lark too, what say you Sieur Raymond?'

'I say fortune favours the bold', thus quoting Virgil to establish that he himself was not uneducated.

-XII-

A cool but bright sunny morning around Terce the next day saw two score mounted cavalry, in full armour and with lances held erect, canter through the main gateway to Gloucester castle. They were led by the knights Owerd, Brian and Raymond and saw no resistance from the gate guards who simply stepped aside at this unexpected but impressive sight. Forming up two deep in the courtyard facing the main entrance of what was the unfinished castle keep, the cavalrymen quietly grounded their lances and waited in silence. The watchers, and there were soon many, could perhaps just sight four mounted soldiers separate from the rest and with hands bound, looking decidedly uncomfortable.

After a brief pause, Owerd, now wearing his king's surcoat with the golden lions, dismounted to meet up with the captain of the castle guard who was walking toward him with a very uncertain expression on his face. A forced smile of welcome left his face as he recognized Owerd and was replaced with a deadpan mix of respect and nervousness. The two had met previously when the captain was a sergeant assisting Owerd in the defeat of a raiding incursion to the south and had worked well together.

'Welcome my lord, though I am uncertain of your intentions with such a formidable force at your back. It is good to see you again, though I expect that you are aware that the sheriff has placed a writ of arrest upon you'.

'Thank you, captain, and congratulations on your well-earned promotion. Yes, I am aware of this misunderstanding between the sheriff and myself. How be your Latin?'

'Poor my lord, but adequate'.

Owerd handed over his authority from the king. 'As you can read, I have the king's authority to seize men and horses should I choose. I have no desire, and I am hopeful that you are of like mind, for this present misunderstanding to result in a bloodbath here in the castle'. The guard captain, whose name Owerd could not recall, looked momentarily alarmed but nodded his agreement. 'If perchance Sheriff Roger chooses to take unthinking action regarding his warrant, whatever the cause might be, that is a possible outcome. To avoid that, I seek your willingness to stand down the guard, albeit temporarily, so that we may achieve a peaceful outcome. If needs be, afterward, you might properly assert that I had seized control of the guard in the king's name. In any event, I have four of your men who I found disrupting the peace of my manor. I intend handing them over to your custody once I have resolved any issues with the sheriff. I am given to understand that you also hold two of my men and a disgraced ex-tenant here and would have them prepared to be ready to be taken back into my custody'.

The guard captain became very thoughtful and for a moment Owerd thought he might argue the point. He well knew that he was undertaking a monstrous bluff that could easily go very wrong. Eventually the captain accepted the situation.

'The castle guard will be occupied in quarters until you say otherwise my lord', he said with a nervous smile.

Just then another of Owerd's old acquaintances made his appearance scurrying across the courtyard.

'Sir Owerd', the man called. 'Welcome, I think! Sheriff Roger is aware of your arrival and says he is willing to meet with you inside, but unarmed'. He took a nervous look at the impressive array of fighting men in front of him and in low tones whispered 'I trust to the Lord above that you are not intent on taking the castle?'

'Let us see what occurs, Sir Godric. Please lead on'.

As they moved together into the unfinished hallway of the castle, workmen scurried out of their way and Godric added, 'and I have pointed out before my lord, that I am now merely Godric the clerk and lucky to have that position. The sheriff is not known for his generosity or kindliness to the Englisc, previously knights or otherwise'. Godric was a knight whose manor to the east had been forcibly taken over by a band of Norman warriors. Owerd had housed and fed he and is family for some time before Godric could no longer bear living on charity and decided to seek work in Gloucester. At last, they cleared a maze of passageways and entered a sumptuously fitted hall where Sheriff Roger, surrounded by clerks and a few worried-looking guards, sat trying to look lordly whilst his wife Adeliza sat beside him looking much like a frightened kitten. Owerd himself, garbed in helm and full battle array with both sword and seax, looked very much a formidable sight.

'I see that you still bear arms Sir Owerd, despite my instructions to come unarmed. More, I am informed that you entered my castle uninvited with a large body of armed men. Explain to me why I should not have my guard cast you in chains forthwith'.

Owerd decided not to reveal that the guard had been stood down and walked forward with whatever confidence he could summon, and quietly handed the sheriff his authority from King William. Roger read it through twice then looked up perplexed.

'This changes nothing Sir Owerd. I have instructions from Sir William fitzOsbern to pursue your arrest for murder. If you seek to defy me yet again, let alone threaten the castle itself, the king will hear of it immediately and I am cert that his vengeance will be swift and severe'.

'Roger', Owerd spoke for the first time, avoiding any honorifics, 'we both know that these charges, whatever their detail, are just trumped-up acts of vengeance by an ex-Earl who has since been disgraced and left the country. You will, of course, be aware that Sir William has run to Flanders to escape the king's wrath. I am given to understand that his evidence is based on the false testimony of an aggrieved ex-tenant of mine who was dismissed from the manor as a drunken wife-beater. Today, I simply present myself here in case you still wish to pursue the matter, perchance for trial by compurgation, for which I have brought with me two score and two oath-helpers who await outside. Either way, lord sheriff', Owerd sought now to appease the man, 'I urge you in your usual sensible manner, to dismiss these charges as baseless and avoid any unnecessary unpleasantness'.

Throughout Owerd's fairly long speech, the sheriff's face went from a look of obstinacy through uncertainty, even doubt, then finally of interest as a way of out of his difficulty could be perceived. He remained silent for some time and one could have heard a hairpin fall in the leaden atmosphere that prevailed in the hall. The sheriff had no idea, but a great deal of worry, about what Owerd might do should he try to have him arrested anyway. He was not an unthinking man, despite a predilection for personal comfort overriding any desire for good management of his domain, and he eventually struck upon a course that could make this annoying knight, though increasingly powerful it would seem, go away but leave Roger's pride and authority intact.

'The charges against you and Lady Hilda of murder are withdrawn. You are found guilty of threatening the peace of Gloucester and fined one pound'.

A different clerk whispered in the sheriff's ear and he then continued. 'Two men-at-arms of your manor are similarly found guilty of causing unrest and you are fined an additional ten schillings for that. You are to leave the castle this instant and you may take your men with you as soon as the fines are paid'. More whispering ensued from the clerk. 'The serf Oxenblod, who is in my custody, I find guilty of spurious allegations. He is of your manor and I therefore order his transfer to your custody to deal with him as appropriate. You may go. Godric, see to the detail'.

To Owerd, this was the best possible of outcomes and he was tempted to offer some form of obsequious words of appreciation, remembering that as sheriff, Roger held the most powerful position in the shire and held that position directly from the king. He did not want the man as an indefinite enemy. Pride, though, plus personal dislike of the man, decided his actions and he simply gave a peremptory bow and marched out.

Godric accompanied him out and Owerd took the opportunity to find out how he fared in his new role.

'I should really be grateful for any work at all, Owerd, but I have to admit it is trying having to endure Sheriff Roger's whims and disdain for anything Englisc. He is not well lettered so is much demanding in that regard but pays a pittance that barely covers the rent on what is little more than a hovel in the township. As you know, he cleared my previous home and many others for the new castle works and paid no recompense so my wife and children are now forced to mend clothes to make ends meet'.

'That is a sad story, Godric, my friend. I now have to visit the moneylender to pay my fines but rather than return here to finalize the matter, mayhap we could meet at that new alehouse near the abbey. We can share an ale before making our way back to the castle to collect my men'.

'That would suit me fine, Owerd, but here comes our nervous captain of the guard to see what's afoot'.

'Is all well now my lord?' The captain's query was asked in a desperately hopeful tone.

'All is now well captain. I have a small fine to pay for the sheriff's trouble, so you may have your four guardsmen back and I will call to the gate to collect my own men and that rogue Oxenblod within the hour. I claim two of the guardsmen's horses as forfeit for their damages and disturbances caused to my manor-house'.

Turning to Brian and Raymond, he gave them a relaxed smile. 'Your presence ruffled many feathers today, good sirs, but smoothed the waters considerably for my own difficulty. The sheriff and I are by no means friendly toward each other right now but at least we have a truce of sorts. You both have my eternal gratitude and that of Lady Hilda. I look forward to meeting you again for a chuckle over today's adventure, Sieur Raymond, when next I get to Court. May your new life back in Brittany be a satisfying one Sieur Brian, you will be ever welcome wherever I may be'.

With a sharp order, the cavalrymen turned to depart and, much to the relief of the garrison, rode peacefully and majestically through the township and back on the road to Winchester. Owerd's own business with Reuben the moneylender took no time at all and he rode back to the alehouse with a heavy bag containing three hundred and sixty silver pennies. He handed the bag discreetly to Godric who awaited him with two cups of ale to his front. Owerd sat heavily opposite him much relieved at the way the day had been resolved and turned his mind to his important and pressing tasking from the king.

Owerd handed the king's charter to Godric to read after they had toasted each other then sat and watched for the reaction.

'This be an impressive lift in your standing Sir Owerd, my congratulations'.

'How would you care to become my deputy, Godric? I have much need of a man of letters who can manage the business of supplies, accommodation, payments and suchlike. I will pay whatever is fair, but I suspect that is certainly more than any pittance you receive from the sheriff. You would need to move, at least temporarily, to Winchester or Southampton but I would cover the accommodation costs as well as arranging for your family to join you when ready. If all this goes well you have the chance of restoring your rightful standing in society, Godric, but I caution that the work will be challenging and I suspect involve long hours. I am not even sure that I can succeed in the task the king has placed upon me. What say you, my friend?'

The answer was not long coming. A smile, reticent at first to face the light of day, gradually expanded over Godric's usually taciturn face and became warm and expansive.

'I may take that grin as a yes, then'.

'You may, Sir Owerd, and I thank thee with all my heart. I welcome the opportunity and shall not let you down. I suspect the sheriff will not be well pleased, despite my lowly standing in his eyes'.

'Come to Birdlip as soon as you are able and we can make necessary arrangements'.

With Godric's statement to the castle guards of payment having been made of the fines imposed, Owerd collected his two housecarls, who looked especially sorry for themselves, and then also Oxenblod who looked scared.

His men mounted the two horses that the captain had made available, apparently without demur, whilst Oxenblod, still with bound hands, was made to walk alongside tethered to Owerd's mount.

'You mean to kill me do you not?' Oxenblod's fearful question went unanswered until they were well clear of the township.

Owerd called a halt in a relatively remote area of roadway and dismounted as Oxenblod rushed to the end of his tether in terror. That terror exploded into screams of panic as Owerd drew his seax. Pulling the terrified man toward him, Owerd made him kneel then moved behind and made a rapid slice with his seax to cut the man's bonds.

'That is the road north and here are two pennies to keep you alive until you are well clear of this shire', Owerd declared. 'You keep going as far and fast as you can, but be aware that if I hear of you being back in Gloucestershire or I hear of you repeating any of those stories about Normans being killed at Birdlip, I and my men will find you and slice you into tiny pieces. Now go!'

The relieved rogue took off at a run and was almost out of sight by the time Owerd had mounted and begun the trek home. There remained every prospect that the coins would last only until the first alehouse that Oxenblod encountered, but Owerd cared little about that. He needed to get home to Birdlip and share his good tidings with Hilda but a more pressing task was troubling him. He turned to Matthew and Lefric and gave expression to his concern.

'We need more men. I could not help noticing that our sheriff has almost doubled the garrison of his new castle and I trust him not. I have no criticism of your actions that ended in arrest, there was little else you could do, but I would not see a repetition. Matthew, here is a purse for you and Lefric to have a night, or two at most, back in Gloucester. I wish you to recruit up to half a dozen fighting men. Archers or men-at-arms, it matters not, but they must be proficient with their arms and preference should be given to any that can ride. Their background, provided they are not Norman, is of no account but I trust you to select men that seem reliable'.

With a wave of farewell to his men, Owerd dug his heels into Satan's flanks and the horse accelerated effortlessly into a fast canter.

-XIII-

Owerd made a fast and solitary journey back to Birdlip, but if he was envisaging a wife rushing from the manor entrance to welcome him with open arms, he was to be disappointed. The manor-house was quiet and no-one was in evidence as he leapt from his mount. Then he saw Edward, who stood immobile at the entrance door with one hand next to the alarm bell. Recognizing him, the steward let go the bell-rope and rushed towards him.

'All is ready, my lord, Lady Hilda and the others are with the cart and horses at Dobson's farm'.

'Do you mean perchance that they are ready to flee, Edward?'

'For cert my lord, we packed what was essential after you left and put everything in readiness to travel north. I am to sound the alarm bell if any sheriff's men appear'.

Owerd gave a deep chuckle at Hilda's nervous forethought. 'Rest easy, Edward, all is now well. I must go fetch them back'.

Light was fading fast by the time a cavalcade of prospective fugitives made their way back from Dobson's to the manor-house. Once settled inside, Owerd faced a barrage of questions about the day's events and their outcome.

'But where are our men-at-arms, Owerd?'

'Busy recruiting more, my dear. Let us sit quietly with some food and a cup or two of wine and I will tell you all. Sigria needs to be told that there is no immediate need for any relocation, but maybe not to fully unpack just yet'.

Owerd outlined the events of the day, heaping much praise on the behaviour of the Breton knights and the nervous but pompous disposition of the sheriff. 'Which reminds me I need to go back to Gloucester not too far off to repay Reuben the moneylender for the funds he lent me to pay the fines'.

'It is fortunate, husband, that we still have sufficient funds to pay such fines as well as keep the manor going. Having foregone that geld money taken from Sir William, are we at any risk of becoming short of coin?'

A broad smile and a chuckle preceded Owerd's response. 'No risk at all my dear. The only hazard is that the sheriff becomes aware of just how wealthy we really are. You perhaps forget that I still have most of the purse from Earl Tostig's war-chest as well as that awarded by our late King Harold, God rest his soul. We also make good coin from our horse breeding and the other manors my love, so there is no cause for concern about that. What worries me, though not overmuch, is Sheriff Roger's pride and what he might do out of sheer vexation that his authority could be perceived to have been challenged. I am thinking that we might well be more relaxed moving to one of the other manors for a time'.

'I thought Upton somewhat cold and barren as a home, Owerd, what is the other one like?'

'The other is Aust. Still in Gloucestershire unfortunately and one I know almost nothing about, not having visited the manor itself. It may be as good a place as any to avoid the sheriff's ire for a time. In any event I need to be further south, somewhere around Southampton to get together this sea squadron the king seems to want'.

They retired to the bedchamber comfortable that they had the outline of a plan to make themselves less visible around Gloucester. Fired by a heady mix of love, guilt and gratitude, a much-relieved Hilda then made a point of relaxing her husband as well as herself by the simple means of seduction and vigorous love-making that lasted well into the night.

Over a light meal of porridge and some stewed apple, Owerd and Hilda sat breaking their fast the next morning somewhat weary from their night of physical exertion. Hilda was thoughtful.

'Husband dear, if we are now wealthy should we not do something Christian to give thanks to God? I am thinking that the village could use a chapel where the serfs could pray each Sunday should they so choose. We might even attract a priest to say proper Masses one day'.

'I had not thought you so religiously minded, my love. But what you say makes sense and I will investigate what might be done. We have plenty of land near the roadway that is little used and the tenants might welcome access to a place of prayer. I will have none of those money-hungry sellers of false relics and indulgences here though. Let me think upon it'.

The reality was that Owerd's early introduction to religion as a novice monk, albeit for only two years, had bred in him a fierce resistance to the external trappings of Christianity that often cloaked a lack of simple human goodness. He could readily recall the simple life of Brother Radwulf who taught him at Bredon and who was a warrior monk pledged to the aid of the needy. He had lived by his word without preaching or display. Hilda sitting across the table was an example – a slave not only protected but educated in Latin and other skills without demand or thought of reward. Bishop Odo provided an instructive comparison, overtly a cleric of high standing ever willing to preach Christian virtues yet gathering to himself land, wealth and power on the backs of the working poor. Even Owerd living in his rustic backwater could see the hypocrisy and corruption then pervading the Englisc church.

He had cause to further consider the contradictions in the behaviour of his fellow Christians when he deposited a large purse of gold fragments and coins with Reuben the Jewish moneylender. He received a substantial purse of silver pennies in exchange, less the sum loaned for payment of the sheriff's fines. The Church forbad usury, yet almost every Christian lord in the land was quite content to make full use of the services of moneylenders, most of whom happened to be Jewish. His next call was also of a religious character: the Abbey of St Peter on the edge of the township.

Having introduced himself to Brother Thomas, the prior, as one interested in establishing a church or chapel on his manor, Owerd queried the procedure to gain approval and, possibly at some later time, acquire the services of a priest. The process of obtaining the bishop's approval was explained, then the Prior became thoughtful. He was an older monk, clearly suited to a quiet life and comfortable in a fairly cloistered environment.

'When might this all occur, Sir Owerd, if I may ask?'

'I have no set timing Prior; it would depend upon how long such approvals and the necessary construction would require'.

'It is like this', responded Brother Thomas cautiously, 'I have been given notice that I am to be replaced here by a certain reformist Abbot Serlo from Normandy. When exactly, I do not know. However, a small village church would then suit me admirably. I am no young firebrand, but if you would consider me for a position at your new church then I can aid your endeavours with construction drawings and make the necessary applications on your behalf'.

'You have builder's drawings here, Prior?'

'Oh, yes. We are only a small community, just a couple of monks and some boys, but we have made a specialty of collecting construction drawings from anywhere they appear. We have drawings from as far back as Roman times, many acquired from Bath, or Aquae Sulis as it was then known'.

Owerd's mind performed a few inward gyrations as he thought through the possibilities. 'Is there any chance that your collection could include drawings of Roman weaponry, brother?'

'Well, it is possible. I would need to search, but we certainly have some depictions of siege warfare machines, is that the sort of thing you are thinking of?'

It took most of the remainder of the day, but a monk who looked covered in the dust of centuries eventually gave a cry of success and presented them with a bound document headed *"ballista fulminalis"* and Owerd echoed his joy. The Prior delicately pointed out that it would take a day or two and six silver pennies to copy the document, a price Owerd was only too happy to pay. The drawings for a suitably sized church and associated dwelling would be provided without charge on the understanding that Brother Thomas would have oversight of the work and eventually take up a position there.

Owerd could now turn his mind to the small flotilla of warships he was charged with producing, but action needed to await the arrival of his men-at-arms and Sir Godric. That occurred in something of a procession the following day. First to arrive were Matthew and Lefric.

'We identified four worthies my lord. We had a good sufficiency of volunteers but took only the four who showed us they could ride. All are Englisc, mainly from the north. We seek your indulgence to take four extra horses to pick them up as it would be quite a slog here on foot'.

That done, a well-worn nag was ridden up to the entrance and Sir Godric dismounted.

'It was the only beast I could afford, Sir Owerd', he admitted with a blush.

Hilda, unasked, took charge of accommodation arrangements and additional places were made in the new accommodation barn, including one for Trahern who could now safely be moved. His room in the manor-house was now given over, temporarily, to Godric. The four new housecarls arrived toward dusk and Owerd inspected them carefully after he had made them tend to their horses. They all originated from the north around a place named Manchester, of which Owerd had no knowledge, and spoke with a very distinctive but understandable accent. They were a mixed bunch, two of lean and athletic appearance and two broad shouldered and heavily muscled. All were dusty and travel-worn, probably in need of a good feed, but each had a sharp seax at their waist and looked him in the eye when he spoke to them. He decided, at least for now, to trust them.

'The pay is two pennies each day, together with shelter and sustenance', he told them. 'You will each give your fealty to me over all others and swear to protect my family and manor. If this is agreeable, we can all go in and eat and get to know one another'.

All was agreed, but their movement toward the entrance of the house was halted by Hilda.

'You'll not enter my house looking like that. Around the back with you all and use the water cask to clean up. Only then may you come in and enjoy cook's blessings'.

The common-room, despite some extensions instituted by Hilda, was still quite crowded with herself, Owerd, Godric, Edward the steward and the six housecarls.

'My intention is to move the household to the manor at Aust over forthcoming days, but I have pressing business in Winchester and Southampton', he announced. I will decide who accompanies me and who stays with Lady Hilda later. Meanwhile, Matthew, you will escort Sir Godric to Winchester and introduce him to the steward and our other men there. They all need to be briefed. I will write this out for Sir Godric, but I need one hundred and forty warriors urgently. They need to be prepared to serve at sea when called upon to do so; be fit, honest and include as many archers as possible. Further, I need a score of sailors including three competent vessel masters. They will all need accommodation and rations provided around the Southampton area. Tell Osric he is charge of recruiting and that I need it mostly complete by Yuletide. Sir Godric is tasked with arranging the support needed and I will give him a note to the Exchequer for funds'.

There were some wide eyes at this announcement. Some probably wondering at the evident but unexpected level of authority and power their lord wielded. There were no questions, so Owerd finished to call for ale. Edward looked embarrassed.

'Lord, the Norman knights drank us dry. I have only a fresh batch less than a day old'.

'We will needs make do, Edward, perhaps we can provide some honey to smooth the taste. Watered wine will also do nicely if that's no good, but we also need to eat'. He then took Godric and Matthew aside. 'If you can have whatever you may need ready in time, I would have you start out on the morrow.' He received tentative nods of agreement and left them to see to their packing.

The new housecarls especially enjoyed the first hospitality they had received for a long time and imbibed heavily despite the bitter taste of the ale. If they thought that warranted an easy morning next day, they were sadly mistaken. Owerd was up at daybreak and had them all in the training yard with wooden swords and shields as soon as they could be gathered. He paired the new men off initially with each other and then with himself and Lefric. Those not immediately involved were set to work at the pells. It became clear that all of the new men were out of practice with swords, although their basic skill was sound. Once all had developed a healthy sweat, he took them to the weapon store and issued each an Arming Sword and belt. Being one-handed weapons, these would enable them free use of their seaxes with which they were more used to relying on.

'These have had no use for many moons, so I expect a clean blade and sharp edge on them by dusk', he said as he left them.

Back in the manor-house he came across Hilda in the kitchen sorting food with the cook. He swept her up into his arms and told her of his arrangements for a church and priest. She gave a small cry of delight and then pushed him away.

'That is wonderful news my husband and very swift on your part. You stink, though, so perhaps you should best consider that cleanliness is also next to Godliness and go wash'.

-XIV-

The best ironworks in the south of the country were, very conveniently, in Gloucester. Owerd had the specifications for his required iron ballista bolts written out on parchment which he handed to Edward.

'Take this into the ironmongers and pay them for half up-front. I require a dozen as quickly as possible and you can let them know that if they prove satisfactory and the price is right then they may receive an order for many more. They are to be delivered to the manor at Aust where final payment will be made. If you ride in now, you can be back this evening so that I can know all is well before we leave for Aust on the morrow'.

He then had Dobson prepare the cart for a pair of mules and had the housecarls assist Hilda with loading the possessions she considered necessary for the stay at Aust. Not knowing the state of the manor there, much of it was guesswork, but Owerd noticed two crossbows and a quiver of arrows being discreetly added to the baggage. Soon after breaking their fast next morning, the mules were hitched up, with Sigria and Breanna made comfortable in the cart and the convoy set forth. In line with his usual sense of caution, Owerd had one of the housecarls ride half a league ahead to act as scout. If nothing else, he thought, it made for good practice.

With food already prepared and able to be taken on the move, they all made good time, sighting the spire of the little church of St John well before dusk. Owerd decided to call in at the church to thank the priest for his testimony about what had occurred in an attempted incursion that Owerd had prevented a year or so back. The church seemed empty, but that was unsurprising at this time of day. Adjusting his eyes to the gloom inside he was about to leave when he noticed a bent figure on a stool near the altar. He approached.

'Brother Cedric?'

His call startled the monk who looked up.

'My lord above, what happened to you?' The monk's face was badly disfigured and one arm was hanging loose.

'Who are you?'

'I am Sir Owerd of Birdlip, Brother Cedric. You will recall that you testified at Court regarding the attempted raid last year'.

'Ah', the monk muttered, and as he did so Owerd noticed that the man now had no teeth. 'I do recall. Brought vengeance on my head though. The lord of the manor had me badly beaten in revenge'.

Owerd's rage surfaced rapidly. 'That is beyond belief, Brother Cedric. I will seek out the miscreants and seek justice for you. I need to go now but will check on you again very soon'.

'Vengeance is mine, sayeth the Lord', responded the monk. 'Stay your hand Sir Owerd'.

Owerd shook his head in bewilderment at the man's stoic humility in the face of other men's inhumanity and

133

stormed out to his waiting family. Hilda saw the storm clouds forming and wisely chose to stay silent. The group continued on to the manor, some half a league distant. The view as they breasted a hill to sight the manor-house was magnificent: a very large single-storey barn-like structure that must have been nearly one hundred paces wide. The garden and surrounds, though, were neglected and filled with weeds.

Lefric was ahead checking the side of the house when a burly soldier came out of the front door and challenged him before turning to sight Owerd and the others.

'Who the hell are you. This be private property'. He made the mistake of drawing his sword.

Owerd nudged Satan forward and in a single flowing movement drew his own sword and swept it down, edge uppermost, to strike the man's wrist. There was a yelp of pain and the man's weapon fell to the ground. Owerd kept his sword pointed threateningly at the man as two more soldiers, housecarls by their appearance, surged out of the front door yelling and also drawing weapons. Owerd's own housecarls, all still mounted, rode forward to counter this threat, but Hilda beat them to it. Her horse was no battle-trained mount but its sheer size and the flashing sword in her hand were enough. One soldier was bowled over, falling beneath the horse's hooves as he tried to avoid the downward stroke of Hilda's sword. The other turned and ran back for the shelter of the house.

'Hold!' Owerd's order was loud and brooked no argument. He dismounted while still keeping watch on the disarmed housecarl and gave Satan a firm pat on the rump to clear him away. Hilda watched from the saddle but her sword slid back into its scabbard and she urged her mount to the side. The remaining Birdlip housecarls remained watchful a few paces behind their lord and lady with weapons at the ready while Owerd leant to check the fallen man.

'What happens here? Who are you people?' The voice, in Norman French, belonged to a tall, thin man of aristocratic appearance who stood at the manor's entrance, loaded crossbow in hand, pointing directly at Owerd.

'I am Sir Owerd of Birdlip and this is my manor', declared Owerd.

'You are mistaken', responded the aristocrat. 'This is Aust Manor held by my lord Baron FitzRolf who has appointed myself, Sieur de Neufmarche, as its custodian'.

'King William removed these lands from Baron FitzRolf some twelve months past and awarded them to me. I am sure you must have been made aware of that, so I would ask you to lower your weapon and cede custody to myself and my men peacefully'.

The man made no move or comment in response and maintained his aim.

This looked like becoming a messy stand-off until Hilda dismounted and walked toward the Sieur with a smile on her face and her sword still in its scabbard.

'I am sure, Sieur de Neufmarche that you would not wish to see any loss of life over this matter. Why do you not invite my lord the king's Master of Mariners and myself inside and we can resolve the matter peacefully over a cup of wine?'

The sieur was almost frozen with indecision and Hilda continued toward him with an innocent expression that he simply found almost impossible to resist. She was very glad no-one, she hoped, could register her heartbeat just then because it was hammering inside her chest and threatening her composure. A knight wouldn't shoot a woman in cold blood. Would he? All it would take, she realized, was a small amount of nervous pressure on that trigger the man held and her life would be over. Whatever the cause, the man lowered the crossbow. Inevitably the bolt fell to the ground as he did so and it took all Hilda's willpower not to either pick it up or draw her sword and smite the man, to whom she was now very close. Instead, she walked behind him as he turned and re-entered the house.

Owerd went to follow, first ordering his men to watch the injured housecarls and keep an eye out for other danger.

The sieur went straight to what could be regarded as the common-room, though much larger in size than any one might expect to see in a normal manor-house. There he sat and slumped over the table, evidently all thought of opposition or protestation gone.

'Sir Owerd, you say? A king's man by the sound of your title.'

'I am. Sieur de Neufmarche I have no wish to throw you on to the street so to speak, but this manor was awarded to me by the king personally and I have need of it. Do you have alternative accommodation?'

'I do, but those options are distant, London and Rouen in Normandy. Baron FitzRolf did say there had been some disagreement over the manor but was confident the king would restore all his lands once he had calmed down. The baron was the king's standard bearer at Battle you know! He directed me to keep the place ticking as it were, for he was much in need of extra coin'. He looked up and gave a half smile, but a dejected one. 'The hour is late, Sir Owerd. I cede the manor to you, but beg your indulgence for a final night's hospitality in the place. I and my men can be gone on the morrow'.

'Please have your personal possessions moved into a guest room and have the steward attend me, sir. I agree on this night's accommodation, but we need to set in place some satisfactory arrangement for your men so that we have no outbursts of violence in consequence of their injuries'. There was no demur and a few minutes later a sheepish man of middle years entered with his head down and wringing his hands. He was evidently nervous, though whether that was his normal state, in consequence of the recent violence, or fear of a new master could not be known.

Owerd introduced himself as the lord of this manor, explaining that it had been awarded it by the king some twelve months past and apologized to the man for not having made his ownership known personally at an earlier date.

'You are Englisc, my lord!' The steward's surprise was noticeable.

'I am, as is my lady, who you see here also. Is that a problem?'

'Far from it my lord, the manor, staff, serf and tenant alike, will welcome the manor being run in Englisc fashion. I am Arthur, sir. We have had er', and here he paused looking about him, 'what I might call difficulties in living with our Norman masters'.

'That may be so, Arthur, but do not expect any idle life from Lady Hilda here. Meanwhile, I have five housecarls, a maid and my daughter outside who are in urgent need of food, refreshment and accommodation. Please see to them, then return and we will then seek a meal for ourselves and Sieur de Neufmarche. I assume you have a cook here available'.

'We have two cooks, my lord, plus a scullery maid, two housemaids, a stable-boy and myself'.

'Well, please set them to work. I or Lady Hilda will speak with each of them on the morrow. Is there an annex of some kind that could house Sieur de Neufmarche's housecarls tonight?'

'There is, sir, I shall see to it'.

The rest of the night passed without incident. The Sieur proved to be a minor knight who had worked in the household of Baron FitzRolf in Normandy and crossed with Duke William's forces more in the nature of an administrator rather than for any skill at arms. He was amiable company over a meal and reasonably forthcoming over the state of the manor.

'We have some fields of wheat, barley, oats and beans, plus a few head of milking cows the villeins look after but our main income is from wool. I regret to say that the sheep flock is much down in number this year due to murrain'.

'Murrain?'

'A pestilence that the steward asserts is through poor shepherding, although the villeins claim it as punishment from the from the hand of God'.

'Interesting, sir', Owerd acknowledged. 'Do you perchance know what happened to the local priest? I saw him on our way here and he seemed much damaged'.

'Dear me, that is a sad case. I know not the details but when the baron was resident here, he had a sergeant at arms named Ferrant. I only met him for a few days in the course of our handover of the manor but he was an ugly brute with a damaged soul. His anger and brutality were apparently already well known hereabouts when I arrived and rumour had it that he took issue with the priest over some slight to the baron. The results are clear: the poor man now has difficulty with the simplest of tasks and rarely strays from the church'.

'Do you happen to know what happened to this Ferrant? Did he go with the baron?'

'No, the baron dismissed those men that did not wish to stay on. Only two stayed. The sergeant went to seek work elsewhere. I know not where'.

It had been an instructive evening. The following morning, they farewelled the Sieur and his men shortly after daybreak and both Owerd and Hilda rode in the company of the steward on a tour of the manor.

'The main difficulty we have had, my lord, is that the Normans refused to observe the customs of the manor. The farm-folk were much attached to those customs and reacted poorly to their lack of observance. I might add, sir, that the crops did also. For example, instead of rotating the fields and leaving land fallow each three-year period, the baron insisted on growing corn every year on the same land so as to increase his income. The land suffered and little corn now grows'.

That and other signs of poor management were everywhere they looked and the downtrodden looks espied on the faces of freeholders, villeins and serfs alike told a sorry story.

Back in the manor-house, he advised Arthur of his intent to leave two housecarls with him, whose main priority was the protection of Hilda and daughter Breanna but, subject to Lady Hilda's approval, they could be set to work as required.

'Take advice where you need, Hilda my love, but brook no arguments about the running of the manor. That I leave in your very capable hands. I aim to return as soon as I am able, but I have doubts that will be in much less than a month'.

Owerd also briefed Lefric and one of the new housecarls on their priorities and requirements and took the other two new men, Dalston and Cuthred, with him to Winchester. He rode Satan and also took with him one spare horse and a mule well-laden with their food, camp supplies and his "special" consignment of surcoats. He was eager to assess the progress made by Hakon and their Langstone boatbuilder and set a good pace. That lasted until the first pause for food and drink when his two men were so stiff and sore in the thighs from their unaccustomed riding that he was forced to ease to a gentle canter and the occasional walk. As a result, the journey took four days, one of which was entirely taken up in Bristol going hither and thither between carpenters and blacksmiths seeking a pairing that were prepared to manufacture his "contraption" as he termed it. He eventually struck a bargain with two young and eager men who were prepared to work together on the task and he left there lighter in spirit and much lighter in purse.

It was with some relief that his two men were finally directed to rest in their quarters at Owerd's allocated Winchester house. None of Owerd's other men were in evidence and the steward Aelfric was none the wiser. He decided to head down to see Chad the boatbuilder but despite his eagerness the need for food and rest felt very demanding. He slept well. The next morning dawned wet, gloomy and cold but a duck of his head into the provided water barrel cleared head and set him up to break his fast with a hearty meal of hot porridge and fruit. His men were much less inclined to face the day and he had to give some curt directions to get them moving. He avoided lecturing them but hoped the message was getting through: he demanded prompt readiness regardless of their circumstances.

The ride to Langstone was bracing and he began to think his new housecarls were having second thoughts about their employment: they were obviously sore and tired. The mood brightened considerably when he sighted Chad's small boatyard and the hull of a new Snekkar standing on roller logs next to the waterfront. The bare skeleton of a second similar vessel lay a few paces inland.

'All hail, Sir Owerd, here she is as you see'. Chad appeared from a nearby shelter with a beaming smile of pride. 'I did have to change a few elements of the design you requested. She has been in the water but the ram you required weighed down the bow overmuch, so the solid base for the machine you wanted has had to go to the stern. Provided the weight of your machine is not over about four hundred pounds, she should float evenly. I have affixed the tripod you wanted at the bow, though I admit to some measure of intrigue at your intended purpose'.

Owerd walked around the new vessel and was impressed. She was everything he had imagined.

'Three score feet to the nearest half inch', Chad announced proudly. 'All good Danish Spruce I had shipped from Zeeland. I have sufficient for two vessels, the third will need to await your approval. The timber is all first grade, light and durable but costly and I have had it all coated with pitch resin mixed with beeswax for protection. We can ship the mast tomorrow and the sail is nearly ready. Another day to finish the oars and she should be ready for your crew'.

'If she sails as well as she looks, all will be well. You can go ahead with the second vessel and order the remaining timber: my time is short and I will accept the risk. How do we make allowance for my machine? Will she not float unbalanced?'

'We can ballast the stern with rocks until we have the machine itself and can make our adjustments then my lord. Are you not going to tell me what this machine is?'

'I shall keep it to myself until I know it will work, Chad. Until then we keep it as a mystery'.

Owerd left the boatyard in good humour and not a little relief. His concern now was for crew but, on that point, he would remain much in the dark until he could obtain a briefing from Osric.

-XV-

Fortuitously, Sir Godric had summoned a meeting of Hakon and Owerd's housecarls at the Winchester house for just that day to meet the whole team and seek guidance on their requirements. When Owerd rode up to the house in late afternoon, he was thus delighted to see what looked like a whole herd of horses tethered in the courtyard. His entry into the crowded common-room was greeted with a small cheer as they all stood in welcome. He was warmed by their enthusiasm and even more so by the many questions relating to the wellbeing of Lady Hilda.

Getting straight down to business, though, he sought short briefings from Sir Godric, then Hakon and finally Osric. Godric had by far the most challenging task.

'There are no suitable buildings in either Southampton or Portsmouth to house our men, Sir Owerd, but I have found a place nearby that is less crowded, indeed almost barren in parts, called Gosport. There are the ruins of an old Roman fort there that I believe can form the basis of a large building. There is plenty of wood nearby; only a tiny but useable fishing port but good access to the sea.'

Hakon was all smiles. 'I have two good longships purchased for next to nothing and a complete crew for one. They lie near Hastings. My own vessel is ready for sea but I need a cook, and male cooks are hard to find'.

'You also need to find me a derelict vessel please Hakon. Size does not matter, cog or longship, but it must be able to be towed offshore for use as a target for our king's demonstration'.

Osric's brief was the longer. 'Men are easy to come by my lord. We have signed up none yet as they have nowhere to stay but with the ground now too hard for working and winter setting in, we will have no trouble gaining the numbers you seek. There is reluctance to sign on for more than forty days and I hear from Sir Godric that the Exchequer is also balking at paying for men on any permanent basis'.

There was much more detail then discussed. The outcome by day's end was an outline plan with Godric to look after support arrangements with a housecarl to assist, Hakon to see to training with another housecarl assistant and Osric with most of the remaining housecarls to attend to recruiting. By Terce the next day, riders had scattered over the south of England seeking "warrior butsecarls" for their enterprise. Owerd took two housecarls, the more experienced riders Matthew and Rhys, with himself to Aust.

The village of Aust was a blessed relief from the bustle of the larger southern towns and Owerd felt a sense of a weight lifting from his shoulders as he rode into the courtyard of his manor there. Hilda was quickly to his side as he dismounted, as was a young man he had not seen before who took the bridle of his horse, albeit with a look of terror on his face.

'Just keep away from those jaws lad and you should be fine', he said as he pulled Hilda into a warm embrace. For differing reasons, Matthew and Rhys chuckled at all three of them but said nothing and went to tend to their own mounts.

'Come out of this frozen air, husband mine, and tell me how the king's choice of a new vocation for you is suiting his and your own satisfaction and wellbeing'.

'I am content and he leaves me much to my own devices, wife of mine. Now can we not get warm together and you can give me an accounting of the manor'.

They did exactly as Owerd intended, but did not say, which was to bypass the common-room in favour of the bed chamber. Their clothing was soon strewn over the chamber floor and mutual lustful eagerness was slated slowly but vigorously.

'I shall have to work on my fitness, wife of mine', Owerd announced whilst trying to recover his breath, 'you are a demanding wench, for which I am much grateful'.

'I am pleased that you are pleased, husband mine, but I seem to recall that this was your idea, not mine. I do not regret your actions, sir', she added with a smile, 'but mayhap you could in future give more notice and bathe beforehand'.

What followed, fully dressed and enjoying the fruits of the manor at table, was Hilda giving him a full accounting of changes she had instituted at the manor and their results. 'Crop rotation has been one of what I had taken to be a minor element in any overall change but the effect on the tenants has been beyond any expectation. They have begun to smile again, even in this short time, and I am receiving both acknowledgement and suggestions from the steward almost daily. I suspect that our steward Arthur had been browbeaten into a state of effective inactivity under his previous lord. But he did demonstrate remarkable acumen, Owerd, in the finances, for he has shown me the hidden coin for the geld money which he managed to keep hidden from Sieur de Neufmarche'.

A tour of the manor the following morning saw an encouraging amount of industry amongst the tenants and he even saw two serfs weeding the front courtyard area that had previously looked neglected. He stopped to speak with the men concerned and received a courteous welcome to the manor. In doing so, he also saw that the men stood straighter and more confidently. There was still much to do about the place, he thought, but he needed to attend to his other priorities. A step in that direction arrived by cart two days later – a dozen heavy iron ballista bolts.

Another arrival was less anticipated: a messenger from Lord Condor, previously Earl of Cornwall and, as some would have it, the rightful King of the Cornish. Owerd was intrigued.

'My lord Condor offers his felicitations, Sir Owerd, and asks that, if you can make the time, he would welcome a visit. He resides still at Dintagel, or Tintagel as some know it'.

'I am honoured by the invitation; can you advise me of the reason, and perhaps how your lord happens to know that I am here in Aust?'

'My lord, I have no information on the reasons, my mission is simply to pass his message. In the matter of how your presence here was known, I can only say that little occurs in this part of the world without it becoming known to my lord'.

'Please inform Lord Condor that I accept is invitation and will visit within the week'.

Owerd ruminated for some time about the reasons behind this invitation and came to no conclusion. Nor did Hilda whom he consulted and offered the opportunity to accompany him.

'A three or four-day journey, you say. I think not, my love. Our daughter needs my attention more than ever now you are to be absent on the king's business so much'.

Owerd privately agreed that their daughter warranted more of his own attention as well as Hilda's but said naught and decided to go. His curiosity was aroused. Leaving Matthew and Rhys to look after the manor, he took Lefric and one of the new men named Thomas plus a mule well-packed with provisions to keep them in some comfort on the road. A brief stop in Bristol revealed his experimental ballista well on the way to completion. A hard day's ride to Exeter followed and warranted a good night in a commercial accommodation where both he and his two housecarls enjoyed the break from roadside camping. The next evening saw them at Launceston and Owerd begged a room for them at a small village drinking house as the moors at this time of year were becoming frigid. He doubted his likely welcome at the monastery so late in the evening and as it was it took a good supply of coin to convince the owner of the hostelry. It was thus late the following afternoon before the three heavily rugged travelers dismounted at the entrance to Dintagel.

Two young lads took charge of their horses and one received a quick nip on the arm from Satan to let them know he was not to be trifled with. They were then directed down many steps toward what Owerd recalled thinking resembled nothing less than a fortified palace. His housecarls were wide-eyed and open-mouthed at the structure. At a narrow entranceway a steward led Owerd onwards while yet another servant showed the housecarls to their accommodation.

'Greetings, Sir Owerd, welcome to Dintagel. Come thaw next to the fire and tell me of your journey, for which I thank you'. So spoke Lord Condor, a burly man well past his prime but still showing the muscular build of a warrior. 'I have heard much of your exploits Sir Owerd, since last we met. Much the hero of Appledore from what I hear'.

'What you should have heard, my lord, was of a foolish young man getting way out of his depth and paying the price'.

'Well, modestly put but you gained a name for yourself hereabouts that folk still speak of. Now, join me in a cup of wine and whatever small fare that my cook can rustle up. He retired to a bulky armchair that looked much like a throne and had Owerd sit next to him in a similar piece of furniture. Looking around, Owerd could see that the room, large as it was, was quite filled with magnificent ornaments, many of gold, together with luxurious tapestries. Food, equally luxurious, was soon provided and Owerd's palate was pleasantly surprised by the quality of the wine he was served.

'Hello father, am I interrupting?' A well-dressed lad in his early teens wandered into the room brandishing a bone-handled knife in one hand and a crafted leather scabbard in the other. 'Look what Logan helped me make'.

'Manners Cadoc! Sir Owerd, may I introduce my son Cadoc, who has far too much energy. That leatherwork looks to be very skilled, now leave us in peace my boy'.

The lad bowed politely then scampered out and the next half of an hour was spent in convivial conversation, although Owerd felt much as though he was under examination. 'What are your thoughts on our King William? The question was asked in apparent innocence and Owerd responded in careful fashion, admitting that he had been unwillingly tasked by the king to produce a sea force. 'One needs to treat the man with caution, Owerd, he removed my earldom for no other cause than spiteful gossip about my supposed support for the attack of Exeter'.

Their discourse was eventually interrupted by a buxom woman of middle years carrying a well-rugged baby in arms who bowed to them both.

'Why not pass the boy to Sir Owerd, here?' Condor's suggestion surprised Owerd but he took it in good part and reached out for the child.

Comfortably settled in his arms, the boy looked like any other of that age. 'I had not known you had two sons, sir', he commented.

'Oh, not mine, he is your son, or so am told by Wenna'.

Owerd went into instantaneous shock and his whole body went stiff. 'My child?' His question was blurted out without thought, as was the second. 'Wenna's child?'

'You have the sense of it, Sir Owerd. The boy was birthed here not twelve months past by the calendar. Wenna, my headstrong daughter, knew well that you were already married as apparently you informed her of such, but she attests that she was smitten. I know not exactly what passed between you but Wenna claims that you behaved like a perfect gentleman toward her and it was herself that began the relationship. She adores you Sir Owerd'.

'May I speak with her sir?'

'There's the rub, for you cannot. I have no knowledge of her whereabouts and for some time it was suspected that she had gone off to seek you out. We now know that was not the case and anyhow we all doubted very much that she would leave her child. Despite all my enquiries it seems as though she simply vanished. I am hopeful that you might be able to seek her out. That is the reason for your invitation to meet me here but I shall understand if you prefer not to be further involved'.

By now, night was settling in and even the well-banked fire was struggling to provide adequate warmth in the room. It was decided to retire and continue their discussion on the morrow. Owerd's mind was in turmoil. Despite the undoubted comfort of his bed, sleep evaded him for quite some time. Not least of the concerns ricocheting around his troubled mind was how Hilda was going to react to this development. It took a while, but exhaustion eventually won the battle and he slept a sound uninterrupted sleep.

After breaking his fast next morning, Owerd was permitted to hold his son for a little while under the watchful and somewhat amused eye of the wet-nurse. Condor and he then got down to the business at hand. It transpired that Wenna was oft given to riding alone on the moors but one day some three weeks past she did not return. Search parties were dispatched and the moors combed, as much as that is possible in that rather barren terrain, without result.

'Do you ever encounter ruffians wandering the moors, my lord? Is it conceivable that she was abducted by some malcontent?'

'Rarely, Owerd. I might add that any attempt to take a mounted and armed Wenna would have taken more than any wandering ruffian might manage'.

'I will, of course, do my utmost to locate her, sir, but we must each be clear that this is no simple matter and the outcome may well be not to your liking. Is there any particular way of identifying the horse that she would have been riding? I am assuming that has not been found either'.

'She has her own horse, Owerd, a spirited chestnut mare with a white blaze to the bridge of her nose. I seem to recall a white marking to her hind fetlocks too, though I am uncertain of that. And no, the horse has not returned, which gives me hope that she has not been thrown in some remote gully'.

Owerd gathered his things and went to brief his men in the full knowledge that he may be embarking on a fruitless adventure. He did not mention to them the existence of a child but emphasized that the missing young woman was of much importance, both to him and the Cornish lord. He would start his enquiries at the place in Cornwall that he was most familiar with – Launceston, or Lannstevan as the locals called it.

-XVI-

There was no formed roadway to Launceston but there were plenty of meandering tracks which showed where others had passed before them and they were basically reversing their route of two days beforehand. He was not optimistic but nevertheless had his two housecarls ride a hundred paces or so either side of him wherever practical and so as to search a wider area. He tried to avoid the thought that this process would mean they were on the lookout for a body. They saw not a soul on their journey and came across the sight of Launceston before the sun had disappeared below the hills to the west.

The man who introduced himself as steward on their dismounting in front of the monastery looked thin and harassed.

'I seek to pay my respects to Count Robert', said Owerd after introducing himself, 'and mayhap renew my acquaintance with any of the Breton knights present whom I served with here'.

'Well, the count is not here. He be in Somerset. I suppose you seek a bed for the night and to that you are welcome, but your men will need to find berths in the village'.

'Thank you, that will suit very well. Oh, there is one other matter that I was asked to look into which is the disappearance of a Cornish lady named Wenna. Might you know anything of that?'

'I do not', was the terse response, but Owerd noticed the sudden hesitation in the man's movements at mention of Wenna's name. 'I have charge of the administration of near seven hundred of the Earl's manors, Sir Owerd, plus the move that is planned up to the castle. I have no time to concern myself with the whereabouts of one young girl'.

Owerd moved off to brief his men. That man knows something, he thought; I made no mention of Wenna being young. 'Find some accommodation in the village', he told his men, handing over a small purse, 'and keep your ears open. Check the stables also to see if any have that chestnut mare that was described'.

The monastery showed every sign internally of being converted into a very comfortable manor-house. Owerd could easily guess that this was due to the owner now being both the replacement and well-to do Earl of Cornwall and a half-brother to the king. He liked his comforts it seemed. The spacious common-room was almost deserted, just two or three knights sitting at ease and sipping from wine cups. Two of those he recognized, one only by sight but the other he had shared many a ride with.

'Owerd, my friend', one of them called from his seat. 'What a great pleasure to see you back on your feet and looking hearty'. This was Elouan, a Breton given a cheerful disposition and a friendly nature. 'Come join me; we are about to sup I daresay'.

The two shared reminiscences over wine and a meal and Elouan explained his presence being somewhat by accident. He had been badly burned on his right side and hand in the course of clearing a village during their northern harrying activities and had been sent back to convalesce.

'I stayed as I really had nowhere else to go, Owerd. I have no land in Brittany and was rather hopeful that Count Robert might find it in his heart to accord me one of his excessive number of manors here. That now seems unlikely; the count is a rather dull person I find and lacking both heart and any sense of gratitude. I fear I also hear of matters about which I do not approve. His wife Matilda keeps herself, or is kept, closeted for much of the time but some of us have noticed bruising on her and the suspicion is that he beats her. Enough gossip, though, what exactly brings you back here?'

'I have a mission from the king to do with sea defence that brought me this way but mainly I sought to meet up with old friends like yourself. I was also asked if I might enquire about a missing Cornish girl called Wenna whilst on my travels'.

Elouan looked thoughtful. 'I do not think I can help you with that, my friend, the name does not come to mind. Almost all of the Cornish girls have gone now, just those few serving meals here tonight are left'. He called across the room to his two fellow knights, 'either of you good men hear of a Cornish wench called Wenna?' His enquiry was met with silent head-shakes. 'Was that the girl who tended to you after the battle?'

Owerd agreed that it was, then made his excuses so that he could check on his horse.

'You still have that Satan beast?

Owerd laughed, nodded and left. He walked toward the back of the house and had started across the yard toward the stables when a girl came out of the kitchen and they nearly collided. He recognized the girl as the one who had just served them their evening meal.

'You seek the princess?' Her question was hurried and in low tones. He was caught off guard at the reference to a princess, but it came to him that any daughter of what amounted to the Cornish royal family could be regarded as such. He nodded.

'The castle of Trematon', the girl whispered, just as the sound of someone else was heard walking into the yard. The girl scurried off with her head down.

Owerd wanted to question her further but was clearly not going to be given the chance. He mused on that odd encounter as he went into the stables and was welcomed by a whinny from Satan. She seemed in good condition and needed no work by himself, so he walked along the stalls looking for a chestnut mare without success. He gave Satan a carrot and a few strokes on the muzzle then departed for his tiny bed-chamber.

Meeting up with his men outside the gatehouse the next morning, Owerd complemented them on their early rising and asked for any news. There was none from the village, except for mutterings about the Earl and his arrogant ways.

'I need one of you to head back into the village and discreetly find out the location of Trematon castle'.

Lefric rode off and was back in less than half of one hour. 'It lies on the coast south of here about a day's ride', he reported. 'Stay to the west of the river they call Tamar, I was told', he added, 'and you cannot miss it'.

That remained to be seen, thought Owerd, but they headed off in good spirits despite a bitter northerly wind that they were glad to keep behind them. It proved to be a pleasant ride, crossing green fields and being presented with magnificent valley views, but Owerd was nervous about what they would find at their destination. They could see a sizeable township across the other side of the river just as the castle came into view ahead. It was a substantial building and high on a hilltop, exhibiting a look of invulnerability at that distance.

'I have information that Wenna may well be here', he told his men, 'but under what circumstances I cannot tell. From here we must assume danger at every turn. I will use the king's authority to gain entrance and ask that you both stay with your horses in case we need a rapid departure. Take turns to keep a watch on the entrance road. If I ride out, it may well be in a hurry: I have a bad feeling about this place'. He left them then, having noticed them both reaching for the amulets around their necks.

Riding up to the entrance gate, he was stopped by a guard wearing mail and holding a lance. That did not really bode well for a place under no apparent threat.

'King's business', declared Owerd, 'I seek Count Robert or the steward' and handed the guard his writ of authority. He mentioned Robert only to bolster his image of importance, knowing full well that the man was elsewhere. Equally, he doubted that the guard could read, despite his pretence at doing so.

'Wait here', the guard directed and headed off up the hill to the castle proper. He was back after only a few minutes and instead of leaving his post again he directed Owerd along a pathway that led around to the main castle entrance.

'You can tether your horse in the stable a little way along the path on your right', he added helpfully.

Walking Satan along the pathway, Owerd looked about him on the way with great care. The place was evidently built on some ancient Roman fort and the motte and bailey construction had been modified to suit later requirements. The outer walls were high, though he noticed a collapsed section and venturing nearer saw a very steep incline away to what would once have been the motte. Taking the horse inside the stable, he left him saddled, tied him loosely and checked the other animals there. Sure enough, there was a chestnut mare further along that had a clear white blaze to her nose and he could just see the hint of white at her rear fetlocks.

Drawing nearer to the keep, he could not miss the thickness of the walls: they were at least three spear-lengths thick. This place was not intended to be taken easily, he thought.

An elderly man in well-heeled Norman boots and a thick woollen cloak awaited him at the entrance. 'Sir Owerd', he said with a hint of a smile that failed to reach his eyes, 'how can we be of assistance?' He passed back the writ of authority.

'I am tasked by King William to assess the coastal defences', Owerd advised, 'possible landing places, local fortifications, available manpower, that sort of thing'. He made a point of looking skywards at the deepening dusk. 'Perhaps I could also trouble you for a bed for the night sir'.

'I can provide a bed for one night. You had best speak with the sergeant at arms about the rest of that stuff, I am not a military man. Follow me'.

The space inside the keep was not large, though spread over three storeys. He was led into a small common-room that thankfully had a roaring fire in one corner. The steward left him and he took one of the few available chairs so as to give off the air of a man at ease. It was not long before the steward returned, accompanied by a powerfully built soldier who seemed to have a fixed expression of menace.

'Shall we sit and talk of the defences, sergeant, or could we walk the castle while you explain what is necessary?'

The sergeant looked across to the steward who gave a slight nod. 'You may walk the castle, lord, but the third storey comprises the Earl's private apartments and I would ask you to respect his privacy'.

'Certainly', agreed Owerd. He immediately understood that anything or anyone that he might need to find would be on the third storey. 'Lead on sergeant', he said, and followed the man as he led the way through various passageways then outside to examine the vista and defensive arrangements. Owerd kept up a constant patter of questions about possible landing places for pirates, numbers of men in the garrison or locally available and suchlike. The sergeant maintained a dismissive attitude about any possible threat and largely kept his responses short and sharp. Eventually, Owerd tired of the man's company and suggested he had sufficient information and should probably rejoin the steward for a meal.

That night, as was common, most retired early and Owerd did likewise. His allocated chamber was on the second floor and near the stairwell and he peered around his doorway when he heard footsteps ascending further. From what he could see in the dim light of a torch near the stairs the noise was of a soldier carrying a food platter. He was heard coming back down the stairs some minutes later. There was certainly someone up there that needed feeding, thought Owerd, but he was possibly getting way ahead of himself in thinking that could be Wenna. Why by all the Gods above would anyone want to confine a solitary girl and why did he imagine it could be Wenna? His past affection, or perhaps simply lust, for the girl could be colouring his thinking.

He thought hard about his prospects of success in finding and retrieving Wenna and set them as still being low. There was certainly the evidence of the stabled horse probably being hers but this was a fortified and guarded castle. Even if it did prove to be her up the stairway, escape was going to be fraught with danger, even if possible. He kept thinking out options as he tried not to drift into slumber and had lain down fully clothed to aid his wakefulness. He finally decided that he had waited long enough and crept out of his chamber and up one flight of steps. The passageway profited only by a single torch next to the stairs and he could see little. There was a choice of doorways he could investigate but one further along caught his eye. It had a large iron key in the lock.

The lock was well-oiled and the key turned easily and silently. The door, heavy as it was, opened at a mere twist of the handle and Owerd entered as quietly as he could. It was not quiet enough. There was a gasp from the far corner, still shrouded in darkness and a tremulous voice.

'Who is there? Come closer and I shall scream'.

'Wenna?' Owerd was still uncertain. 'It is Owerd'.

From the darkness a figure appeared rushing toward him and only by the starlight from an opening at the far end of the chamber could It be seen to be a woman. She rushed into his arms and clung tightly.

'Owerd, by the Lord and all his saints, I had all but given up hope of ever seeing you again. I am being held here by Count Robert. He means to take me to Normandy as his concubine and has had a ship readied to sail. He said he was looking forward to having a princess as his bedmate'. The words were coming at a rush until she took a deep breath. 'Are we able to escape or are you imprisoned too?'

'We shall try to find a way, Wenna dear, now get dressed and it would please me if you did so quietly'.

'Do not bother yourself, lady, you won't be going anywhere just yet'. The voice from the open doorway was that of the sergeant and a tiny glint of metal showed that he held a bared sword.

With the point of the sergeant's sword inches from his face Owerd's hands went to the buckle of his sword belt and he let it clatter loudly to the floor. He then took a pace backwards into the room's shadow and crouched down. The sergeant was momentarily confused, believing he had Owerd at his mercy, and stood still.

'I wonder whether your memory goes back to Brother Cedric, the priest at Aust, sergeant? He seeks no vengeance you will be pleased to know. I do, however'.

At that moment, and using a move that he had seen Osric perform a few times, Owerd slipped a seax from his boot and launched himself upwards. The seax forced the sergeant's sword upwards and Owerd closed the gap such that the sword could not be used for any useful strike. The sergeant was of very muscular build and Owerd realized that he could not afford to be drawn into any test of strength or wrestling contest. It was a risk to let the sword go free, but necessary in the situation he found himself in, and Owerd pulled the seax back toward him, then upwards in a strike at his opponent's neck. It was a clean strike and the man clutched fruitlessly at his neck to remove the blade and staunch the bleeding. A none-too gentle push had the man on the floor counting out his life's last seconds.

'Dress', Owerd ordered, 'there may be others coming to check the noise'.

Once readied as much as she could be in a rush, Wenna went to check the passageway while Owerd retrieved his sword and, in somewhat grislier fashion, his seax. Much to their relief there was no noise of running feet and the castle sounded still.

'How well can you ride, Wenna; can you negotiate a very steep slope without calamity?'

'On my own horse I can take on the roughest of terrains Owerd, just watch. The front door will be locked but I think we may gain exit to the stable through the kitchen. That still leaves the main gatehouse which is invariably locked overnight'.

Like thieves in the night, the pair made their way silently down the stairway, through the kitchen, which oddly remained unlocked, and down to the stables. Wenna went straight to her horse and began saddling up. That aroused a young lad who was sleeping in the hay bales and he called out to see who it was. Owerd stepped forward.

'Just be quiet lad and nothing will happen to you. The lady and I are just going for a starlight ride'.

What the lad made of that remained a mystery until grilled by the steward later that morning. Meanwhile, the escapees walked their mounts to where Owerd had noticed the breech in the outer wall. He took the reins of Wenna's horse and invited her to go and look at the downhill slope beyond the wall.

'It is very steep, Wenna, do you think you and your mount can make it?'

The steepness of the land there was perilous enough to make any horse rider have second thoughts.

'Is this the only way?' There was a nervous excitement in her voice. To his whispered 'I fear so' she added 'in which case I shall try and I believe with God's help I shall make it'.

They mounted and Owerd let Wenna go first in case of accident on the way. She nudged her reluctant mount forward then hauled back on the reigns as she went over the rise. The horse periodically slid and tried to stop itself as it went down the steep grassy slope and Wenna was almost leaning flat on her back as she sought to keep the horse facing downwards. Owerd could barely see her in the dim starlight but when he assessed that she had gained the flat he nudged Satan forward and they followed a similar path, though with a less reluctant horse.

There were deep sighs of relief as they met up at the foot of the castle mount but no time to waste.

'We go north, cross the river and head for Exeter', he declared.

Wenna was in no mental state to question him further just then, but a few leagues northwards she queried why.

'Why do we not simply head straight across the moors to Dintagel, Owerd? My father can keep us safe there'.

'Because that is exactly what they will expect us to do, my dear. We cannot make much distance across rough country in the dark and need to do the unexpected or risk a conroi of troops riding us down'.

It was well that they had started out before dawn as the sun was sinking fast as they came up to the walls of Exeter. Owerd paused.

'Is there much prospect of you being recognized in the town Wenna? Your father is cert to be well known hereabouts'.

'I think not. I am hardly garbed as an important lady and few will even take notice of me. I have friends here but if we stay clear of places that they are likely to frequent then all should be well'.

Owerd was not so sure but the weather was not conducive to camping: there even seemed the prospect of snow in the air. They walked their tired horses through the town gate with hardly a look from the guards and all looked well. He decided to make for the poorer quarter of the town to find accommodation and picked a likely looking place, a small tavern at random that offered accommodation. The man at the door carried a substantial club so whether that meant the place was used to rowdies or ensured good behaviour was yet to be determined. Owerd realized his error when the man tugged his forelock as Owerd approached. He should have known that his horse alone marked him as a member of the nobility.

Inside was clean and quiet with just a few drinkers at table. His request for ale and food was promptly met, as was an arrangement for a room for the night. The owner winked at him as he agreed that last request, so he took it that this was to be seen as an illicit assignation. All the better, Owerd thought; much less for others to gossip about this way. The pair went to their assigned room early, both tired and relieved to have found a place of temporary safety. There was just the one bed. Owerd said nothing but kept his breeches on as he climbed under the rough woollen blanket. Wenna joined him but showed no such modesty.

'You are the father of my child, Owerd', she said as she wrapped her arms about him. 'You have had me, willingly and joyfully, and may do so again when and wherever you wish'.

'But you know I am married and so committed to another, Wenna. However much I am attracted to you, that fact cannot be avoided'. He was already aroused and had no sooner finished that observation than he found Wenna's hand at is lower belly and groin. He moaned unintentionally. Within just a few more seconds they were making love and neither sought to hide their passion.

-XVII-

Owerd led Wenna down to break their fast the next morning satisfied in body but writhing in anguish mentally. They enjoyed a simple porridge and with only the occasional sly glance from the hostel-keeper they were left alone. The question of the moment was where to go next.

'I need to see my son, our son, Owerd. Can we not head down to Dintagel now?'

'Far too risky my dear. Our son is in good hands and good health last I saw him and the approaches to Dintagel will doubtless be watched for some time. If you think you can face the possible hostility of my wife that I fear may be in prospect, I believe the only safe and sensible place to go is to my manor at Aust. You will at least be safe there and I can send a messenger to assure your father of your wellbeing. There was a nervous look on Wenna's face as he said that, but nothing compared to the trepidation Owerd felt about his forthcoming meeting with, and explanations to, Hilda.

As they walked their horses through the town gate, Owerd looked for any signs of recognition or alarm from the guards but saw none.

'From now on we camp, my dear. I hope you can handle that until I can find a suitable place to sleep where we will not attract attention'.

There was a fairly good road from Exeter all the way to Bristol and they maintained a steady pace from dawn to dusk, making a roadside camp each night. They made love twice more on the way despite the cold, or possibly because of it in a need for warmth, and were both in good spirits. As Bristol loomed, Owerd explained his need to check on the progress of certain equipment he was having constructed and speculated that those in charge of the work could perhaps provide Wenna with more comfortable lodgings for a night. That is exactly what occurred and they spent a chaste night in a workman's cottage of one of the carpenter's men. Owerd was delighted with the ballista they had produced and gave approval for a second to be made. All would depend upon a successful test firing, they all agreed.

'We will be in Aust before Sext, my dear', Owerd advised as they said farewell to the carpenter's workman.

'I am nervous Owerd', said Wenna. 'What if Lady Hilda attacks me or insists that I be thrown on to the street?'

'Hilda is not like that, my dear, I am sure all will be well'. He exuded a confidence that he did not feel.

As it was, Hilda appeared in a rush of billowing skirts as they rode up to the manor-house. 'Owerd, where in heaven's name have you been? We expected you more than a week past. And where are your men?'

'We encountered some trouble, my love', he said as he dismounted. 'I will explain all over some ale. Meanwhile, may I introduce Wenna, daughter of Lord Condor of Cornwall? Wenna, meet my lady wife, Hilda of Birdlip. Wenna seeks refuge for a while'.

Hilda looked at Wenna, then back at Owerd. She knows, Owerd realized, she absolutely knows. Regardless of anything he might have expected, Hilda broke into a charming smile of welcome and went to give her a hug as she dismounted. Wenna responded timidly. Looking at the two women together, Owerd was struck by the difference in their appearances. Hilda was clearly the elder by about six years and had the solid physique of a woman who was supremely fit. Wenna, by contrast, was especially slender, looked vulnerable, and her deeply black hair emphasized the pallor of her skin. He liked them both enormously but reminded himself of his ultimate loyalty to Hilda.

Seated around the table in the common-room, Owerd explained the events of the past weeks and that he considered Wenna still at risk from Count Robert's lustful intentions. Equally, vengeance against Owerd for his dispatch of the Count's sergeant-at-arms could not be discounted. The absence of his two housecarls he could not explain but he had confidence in their ability to look after themselves. He would somehow get a message to Lord Condor to assure him of Wenna's wellbeing but did not wish to denude the manor further of manpower just yet.

With a subtle shift of her eyes, Hilda indicated that she wished to speak with Owerd privately. In their bed-chamber she sat on the bed while he took a seat in an armchair.

'She is the woman you shared a bed with in Launceston, is she not?'

'She is, Hilda. But there is more. Apparently, she had a child in consequence and now has a son, as therefore now do I'.

Hilda almost physically reacted. 'So, do you now think that you might keep her as a bed-mate "on the side" so to speak?'

'Absolutely not, my love. I vow to you that I shall be true only to you for as long as we both shall live'.

'You once vowed that same thing to me at the manor in Birdlip, and then again in the church at Evesham. I suppose that in this man's world you live in it is acceptable to have sex with whomever at whim provided only that you are a man. It is typical of male ego. But, let me tell you now that it is not acceptable to me. Be under no illusions, husband dear, that I cherish you more than life itself, but if I so much as get a hint hereafter that you have taken up a lustful relationship with another woman then I shall strike off your male member and feed it to the pigs. Now if we are clear, I need to go arrange a bed-chamber for our guest'.

The lord and lady of the manor together with their house guest all awoke in a happy state of mind the next morning. Owerd that he still had his member; Wenna that she had not been murdered overnight, and Hilda? Well, Hilda was feeling merciful, and she had made her point. They broke their fast together and discussed options for getting a message to Lord Condor.

'I am reluctant to send Matthew or Rhys when I still feel at risk from the Earl or his men', he said. 'I will wait until the morrow in the hope that Lefric and Thomas will return'.

In the event, that became unnecessary. In the early afternoon, Trahern rode in albeit with his previously broken leg still heavily bandaged.

'Welcome Trahern, is that leg good enough to hold up if it comes to a fight?'

'It is my lord, thanks to Lady Hilda's ministrations (he actually said "mistrations"). Are we expecting trouble?'

'We may; but maybe not. We have two of your colleagues missing at present so I am on edge is all. Go eat and refresh yourself then I would like you to find Matthew and get you and he a workout in swordplay to see how far behind you may have fallen'.

He then called for Rhys and briefed him to depart at first light the next day to take a missive to Lord Condor at Dintagel. 'If you are stopped for any reason, just say you are seeking employment with the lord'.

Matters here were becoming settled, he thought, but the king's demand for a sea-fighting demonstration was steadily approaching and he still had much work to do. His concerns were much reduced when another dusty and weary pair of housecarls rode in.

'Lefric, Thomas, your lord and lady are much relieved to see you safe. What happened?'

Lefric dismounted and explained. 'My lord, we waited as you instructed but saw naught all night. Then just after dawn, it was like someone had kicked an ants' nest in the castle grounds; there were men running in every direction. We stayed hidden, then shortly afterward a group

172

of near a dozen mounted soldiers galloped out and headed toward the moors. We thought to follow them for a while and did so, but the country was barren and we stood a strong chance of being sighted so we returned to the castle. When you had still not come out by the end of the day, we were at a loss my lord. We retired to the local alehouse and sat to warm ourselves and take refreshment. Word around the drinkers was that some robber had broken into the castle and slain their sergeant. They seemed much pleased at that and all believed the robber had somehow escaped. We spent a little of your coin, my lord, in a meal and a good night's sleep then decided to make for here'.

'You did well, both of you. Take some rest and then I have more tasks for you.'

He next summoned Matthew. 'How did your bout with Trahern go?'

'He has become a touch out of shape, milord, but his skills are sound'.

'I will have him work out some more over the next few days perhaps. But I have another task for you which involves a ride to Winchester. Are you up to it?'

After Matthew confirmed he was ready for such a ride, he briefed him on what was required and retired to set his instructions on to parchment. That gave him another idea and he recalled Rhys.

'While there, find out whether a longship can beach at Dintagel too please Rhys'.

The manor was bereft of good horseflesh, in all probability taken by Baron FitzRolf and his men when forced to vacate the place. What remained was one mule and an old and tired Rouncey that was suited only as a packhorse. Owerd had the mule added to his own to make a pair for the cart which was still loaded with the ballista bolts. Taking Lefric and Thomas with him, he left Trahern to offer what he might in protection for the manor. This was a risk, he conceded to himself, but he needed fit men with him. They were heading for Bristol, a reasonable day's ride away at a steady pace.

An overnight at a comfortable hostelry put them all into a good frame of mind the next morning and Owerd's first call was on the sheriff at a rather grand manor-house. When he was introduced, Sir Harding leapt to his feet and welcomed him warmly.

'Welcome Sir Owerd, I recall you well from the day I was awarded this office here. To what do I owe the pleasure?'

'Simply a courtesy visit, lord sheriff. I am here to meet some of the new ships our king has tasked me to organize and loading some armaments made by your good citizens'.

'Interesting. As it happens, I was asked to watch out for you and report your movements to our earl. A garbled message I am sure: something about an attack on one of his castles and making off with a young female ward of his'.

Owerd gave a loud guffaw. 'The so-called attack was a brief overnight visit and the so-called ward was the daughter of Lord Condor of Cornwall who the earl had abducted and planned to take to Normandy as his unwilling concubine'.

'That makes sense Owerd. The earl was ever the self-indulgent dullard who cannot even read Latin. Anyhow, I am the king's authority here in Bristol and he can go look for you himself, although I suspect he might rue the day that he did find you'.

They parted on good terms and Owerd proceeded down to the port to call on the port reeve. Here he received a polite though less effusive welcome and explained his needs.

'The berthing is no problem, Sir Owerd and if they be king's ships then I shall not attempt any collection of dues. Loading is something else: you will need to negotiate with one of the larger fishing vessels that may assist with a boom'.

Next was the carpenter's workplace where his new ballista looked fresh and gleaming. His men had already backed the cart up to the machine and the carpenter had sensibly fitted two rails beneath it so that it could be loaded by dragging it. That was no easy task and it took all the manpower they could readily lay their hands on to accomplish it. Owerd sought the carpenter's agreement to leaving the weapon, cart and mules there until his ships arrived and that was agreed. Owerd considered staying in Bristol but it could be a week, even all being well, that the ships made Bristol. He and his housecarls retired to wait at Aust.

It was Matthew who brought the news that the two vessels Owerd had requested would, weather permitting, be in Bristol in another three days. He also had a scroll with him that had been delivered to the Winchester house which Owerd set aside and promptly forgot about. Rhys had also returned from relieving the worry of Lord Condor who also advised that a small beach below the castle was useable by a shallow draught longship but only for transfer of people. The next few days saw Owerd in a mood of frenzied impatience and he managed to annoy most of his family and housecarls at one stage of another. Hilda had been remarkably tolerant and spent much time with Wenna and thus keeping well away from him, although her tolerance was sorely tested by Wenna constantly making eyes at her husband. It was to her great satisfaction that Owerd was able to tell them he would be sending Wenna back to Dintagel by boat.

There was a tangible air of relief in the air when Owerd, Wenna and three housecarls rode out to Bristol three days later.

-XVIII-

Happiness, relief and pride were all present when Owerd saw the "Merry Widow" secured alongside a short timber jetty in the Avon River with his, or rather the king's, new longship next to her. The meeting with Hakon took place on the vessel's after deck and Owerd was surprised to see so many men either working or lounging around the vessel.

'The longship crew', Hakon explained as he waved his arm around. 'I decided to berth them onboard rather than seek accommodation ashore for fifty men. I would not delay here too long though, unemployed men become restless quickly'. He then realized that he had not welcomed his lord, and did so with a beaming smile. 'All is going to plan, Owerd, we have crews for two longships as well as for mine own ship, and the first crew, the one that brought the ship here, has proven quite capable. Let me introduce you to her skipper'.

'Dierk, meet Sir Owerd, the king's Master of Mariners', he said loudly, patently with the intent of capturing the attention of all the crew within earshot.

'Well met Dierk, I suspect you are Danish by your looks'.

'I am, my lord, and perhaps I could say the same for you'.

'Looks are ever deceiving Dierk, for I am a Briton. Now, tell me what you think of your new vessel'.

'She's fast, my lord, faster than anything I have come across before now. The high sides allow for good protection in heavy weather and the crew seem pleased with her also. But she does need a name, my lord, if we are to keep the Gods and the superstitious appeased'.

Owerd looked at Hakon for confirmation as he responded that he planned to have her names "Adeliza" after the king's eldest daughter.

'That will do nicely, my lord, I shall have that painted about her stern. I do look forward to seeing this contraption I hear you plan for her and how we are to manage it'.

All three then disembarked and went to the cart where the ballista and all twelve bolts rested. There was then a little awe at the sight and much debate about the best way to have it fitted. Ultimately it was decided to beach the longship at a suitable spot further along the river and manhandle the weapon aboard. That took some time, but eventually worked and Thomas was dispatched to bring the carpenter for him to complete the fitment.

'I have additional cargo for you too, please Hakon, meet Wenna, daughter of Lord Condor who needs to be landed at Dintagel. I am told the beach there is adequate and a landward trip would place her in some peril. If we can all wait yet another day, I believe the second ballista may be ready which "Merry Widow" could transport to Langstone'.

'I could use an ale', laughed Hakon, 'but perhaps we should test this machine beforehand. What do you say sir Owerd?'

Owerd could only agree as he was himself becoming thirsty despite the chill in the air. First things first, he thought to himself and looked around for a suitable target. On the opposite side of the river and a little downstream was a large oak which stood out from its surrounds. He decided on that, but first the ship had to be floated off its muddy beachhead and stone ballast thrown overboard to level the keel. With all in readiness, and Owerd and Hakon watching from shore, together with a small crowd of onlookers, the Bristol carpenter supervised the loading of one bolt plus the winding of the torsion spring and moved out of the way.

With a wave to Owerd, Dierk aimed and pulled the release. There was an almighty bang as the bolt flew across the river. It struck the tree at about the height of two men, completely shattered it and kept going into the scrub, flattening bushes and small trees on its way. There was a stunned silence amongst the watchers, until Dierk called across the water.

'I think that will do it, my lord'.

That was met with raucous cheers from the crew and much muttering and shaking of heads among the uninvolved townsfolk watching. As the longship was left to make its way back to the "Merry Widow", Owerd, Hakon and Wenna returned to the ship where two more carts awaited. One was food and ale for the crews, the other contained a pile of Indian calico bags whose contents remained hidden, together with two lidded iron cauldrons. These were loaded on to Hakon's ship just as a third cart arrived with the second ballista.

'You may leave for Dintagel and Langstone whenever you are ready, Hakon my friend, I think that we are done here. Please ensure that Wenna is safely returned to her father with my thanks'. He was then embarrassed by Wenna saying farewell with a hug and a fiery kiss on the mouth. Saying nothing, he gathered his housecarls and mounted for a return to Aust despite knowing that they would be unable to make it back before dark. He was keen to judge Hilda's mood and that he considered important before telling her that he would need to be away on the king's business for an indefinite time.

As it happened, Hilda was not interested. She was in a dreamless sleep when Owerd quietly joined her in their bed and, apart from a gentle murmur of annoyance at the interruption, continued to slumber. The morning gave no hint of any sense of upset or otherwise in Hilda's manner until she had finished her porridge and fruit.

'Are we good husband dear?' The question seemed innocent enough but Owerd was uncertain and used the excuse of having half a pear in his mouth to simply nod.

'I am pleased that is so, husband, as I believe I am now with child again'.

It took a moment for that to sink in. Owerd then stood, smiling broadly, and walked around the table to give his wife a kiss on the crown of her head.

'If you are pleased, my love, then I am doubly so. That is very happy news indeed'. There followed an awkward minute or so while Owerd contemplated whether now was the right time for his own news. He decided that he could not sensibly put it off.

'Hilda, you know that I am tasked by the king for this sea squadron he has a mind to form and methinks I must now move speedily to see it done. I have much to do in preparation and must be in Winchester or Southampton to put things in order. I may be absent from the manor here for some considerable time. I will, of course, leave two housecarls to see to your protection, but in other ways, will you have all that you may need with another youngster on the way?'

'I will be well looked after, Owerd. In other circumstances I might prefer to have the child at Birdlip but with matters as they stand, I am content to remain here. Before you plan on riding off, though, you should read this', and passed across a scroll with the king's seal. 'This came while you were off in Bristol', she added.

Owerd opened to scroll and gave an audible sigh of frustration. The scroll read:

"His majesty King William summons you as a member of his council to attend him at the Palace of Saint Oswald's Priory at Kingsholm on mid-winter's day. There you shall give what advice may be sought and stand witness to the formal wearing of the crown which is King William's by right".

'I am summoned to Gloucester', he said as he passed the scroll across to Hilda. 'That is barely a week away, so I need alter my plans. I will go from there direct to Winchester, my love, provided I survive this meeting of the king's which will put me amidst the enemies I seem to keep making'.

'Owerd, for you enemies are merely evil men you haven't killed yet!'

'That be a wondrous way of putting it, Hilda dear. We shall see'.

The word "wondrous" came again to Owerd's mind a few days later when he and his three housecarls came upon the sight of Saint Oswald's Priory and the nearby palace of Kingsholm. They were marvelous buildings, mainly of stone, many storeys high and set in a vista of rolling green pasture edged with a lofty mix of Oak, Elm and Beech, now devoid of their leaves. Just as surprising was the large number of soldiers about the place, mainly lounging around the palace next to various forms of tentage. If these were mainly housecarls or servants, he thought, there must be close to a hundred members of this king's council that he was apparently now a member of.

'I shall see what is available, but by the look of this lot I suspect you men will be camping', he told his men. 'Go now and find a spot. Keep your eyes and ears open and see what news or gossip you can pick up'.

His horse having been whisked away by eager grooms, Owerd entered the palace to be met by the chamberlain who checked his name from a parchment and had a servant relieve him of his sword and seax. Moving into the main hall, Owerd saw that his earlier estimate of numbers was about right, all of whom were milling around in groups or taking morsels of food from tables laid along both sides of the large hall. His appearance caused a brief lull in conversations. Most, though not all, were dressed in flamboyant court clothing while Owerd still wore his mail, together with a smart leather surcoat that Hilda had made for him. He stood out as being every inch the warrior, even without his weapons. He saw few there that he recognized but his feeling of isolation was eased by a nod and warm smile from Sir Harding of Bristol, followed by a meeting with Alwyne, Sheriff of Warwick and brother to Owerd's first wife.

A throne sat majestically, as was to be expected, at the far end of the hall on a raised dais and surrounded by monks and guards, though there was no sight of the king. There was then a call from an usher of some sort that Owerd could not quite catch and William marched in accompanied by Lanfranc, the new Norman Archbishop of Canterbury and a host of other prelates and monks. He was wearing a simple open crown decorated with crosses and fleur-de-lis. The Usher waited until William was seated and then loudly exclaimed in Latin "Hail the King". The assembled lords were clearly expected to repeat this and Owerd joined in, though without the enthusiasm of some.

'We are not expected to say anything else', whispered Alwyne, 'now we go do penance at church'.

Alwyne's statement was proved wrong within seconds when Count Robert burst forth.

'Your Grace, I object to the presence in this august company of that man Owerd of Birdlip. He has blood on his hands'.

'Do not we all, brother. Explain!'

'He just lately gained access to my castle at Trematon under some pretext of examining coastal defences, killed my sergeant-at-arms and made off with a treasure'.

'What say you Sir Owerd of Birdlip?'

Owerd was right at the back of the assembly and could not help noticing that many made a clear space around him, not wanting any guilt by association. He thought he might best avoid any public criticism of the king's brother.

'The outline of events the Count describes are correct, your Grace. I would beg your indulgence, sire, in not offering the details in this place to avoid embarrassing my lord the earl'.

There was many a gasp around the hall at that and looks of open curiosity of what this might be about. The lords loved intrigue.

'We will attend to this at another time', declared the king, 'we will now attend to our duties to God and seek his blessing on my reign and for the good of this land'.

With that the procession moved off and meandered its way to the church of the Priory some few hundred paces away. Owerd had suffered many a boring sermon in his days as a novice monk but that from Archbishop Lanfranc exceeded the worst of them. It was with relief that the service finally concluded and the assembled lords made their way back to the hall. William removed his crown and took his seat on the throne where he was served a platter of meats and fruits. As he ate, he spoke with various of his lords and Owerd watched from afar until a clerk informed him that the king wished to speak with him. He approached, noticing that Count Robert was also summoned. The crowd around the king made way for them but many hung back, eager to hear of this potentially juicy gossip.

'So, Sir Owerd, explain yourself', said King William.

'My liege, I was on a tour of the Cornish coast examining places where pirates might land and what defence on land could be brought to bear. One such place was the count's castle at Trematon where, during the night I heard moans from one of the sleeping chambers. Investigating I came across the daughter of Lord Condor, the previous Earl of Cornwall, who claimed to have been abducted and was being held against her will for use as a concubine. She sought my assistance to escape which I provided but was accosted by the Count's sergeant on the way out who attacked me. In the course of a fight, he was severely wounded so I took the maid away fearing more bloodshed. I assume the maid was the treasure my lord Count spoke of'.

Owerd had no guilty conscience over his stretching of the truth of the matter as all essential elements of what he said were accurate and he had been careful not to accuse the count personally of any wrongdoing.

'That all seems reasonable, brother. Sir Owerd is now our Sea Lord and appears to have been going about his duties admirably. Does that account rest more easily with you?'

The Count stared hard at Owerd for a few moments before speaking. 'It may be that one or other of my men had acted improperly, your Grace, but Sir Owerd should have first approached me about the matter. I should be recompensed for my loss'.

'We think not, brother, if you had any more land or coin then you would possess more than the Crown. That does depend, Sir Owerd, on what you have done with this maid you claim to have rescued. If there were to be any motive of personal gain in this then we should think differently'.

'She has been taken back to the care of her father, your Grace'.

'So be it', said the king. 'You may both go with our thanks for attending'.

Owerd could not leave the palace quickly enough and gathering his men from their meagre camp-site he realized that they were of the same mind.

'We will spend the night at Birdlip then direct to Winchester', he announced as they all mounted and rode away.

-XIX-

The arrival at the manor-house in Winchester was disappointing: there were none of his men there. The steward informed him that they had all relocated to a place named Gosport but was fortunately able to provide directions. After having had a few days in the saddle, Owerd decided to stay the night anyway and ride further south on the morrow. He was glad he did for early the next morning a monk arrived from the Winchester palace to make arrangements for the king's "demonstration of sea-fighting" as he put it.

'You will call on His Majesty at Prime on the day after the Feast of Epiphany and escort him and his entourage to a suitable vessel which you shall provide. He will spend the daylight hours with you but no more. An adequate meal is to be provided at about Sext'.

Detailed discussion resolved various matters to do with numbers in the entourage, dress and the like and the pair separated reasonably satisfied with requirements. Owerd collected his men and rode to Gosport, content but nervous about the state of preparations he was likely to encounter. The sight that met his eyes was astonishing. A new building at least two-score paces long stood proudly on the rise and, from where he sat on Satan, he could see not one, but two, of his new longships rowing furiously down the adjacent waterway. It was evidently a race.

Hakon saw him from a nearby vantage point and left off his own viewing to greet him.

'Welcome to our new home lord. Come and look through the place while it is still empty'.

As they did so they were joined by Sir Godric who looked slightly harassed. 'These men take much looking after, Sir Owerd. The clerk of the exchequer is becoming increasingly nervous about the coin I have been forced to spend. Locals cannot supply that which we need so I have had to hire a small vessel to fetch goods from across the water. If I may be excused, I need to go down to the jetty now to collect the latest delivery'.

Hakon led Owerd inside the building which was set up in similar fashion to the hall of a Norse Jarl. Sleeping spaces along both sides were separated by hanging curtains. A series of rough-hewn tables ran down the centre and large firepits blazed at each end. There were two doors, one the entranceway and the other leading to an open cook-house. Owerd could only be impressed.

'We used the crews to fell the local trees and build the place. It proved good exercise for their muscles and kept them out of mischief when not rowing. We have room to house four-score should we have need', he finished.

'This is all good, Hakon, my friend, but it is the ships and crews that demand more of our attention just now. Are the crews competent in their maneuvering? We have but a week to have things in readiness for the king's perusal'.

Much discussion ensued over the next few days on devising a plan for the demonstration and arrangements that they needed to make. The day of the Epiphany dawned with a thin layer of cloud but no evidence of imminent rain or snow. Hakon had all the men mustered in front of their building and Owerd climbed on to a makeshift platform to their front.

'Men', he began loudly so as to capture their attention. 'Today your training is finished. Today you become king's men'. He nodded to Osric who had his men behind the butsecarls begin to hand out their bundles of red surcoats with the king's lions stitched to their front. 'Wear these surcoats with pride. With these on you men can hold your heads high in any company. You are the point of the spear that the king will use to rid our waters of pirates and invaders who prey on the weak and defenceless. I cannot promise an easy life but what you do will be God's work and may save many of your fellow countrymen from death, bondage or sale into slavery. We will show those engaged in evil no mercy. I might also add that should an enemy or pirate vessel perchance be captured then you will share in the booty'. That brought a loud cheer.

'There is a small difficulty that you need to overcome before beginning this task. On the morrow King William and his nobles will be examining the performance of our vessels and crews. You will need to impress or all this work until today will go to waste. I have faith that you will do well. Today is a rest day. Enjoy. God speed'.

Owerd had decided to spend the night at Winchester so as to be ready at first light the next day and shared a warrior's grip with Hakon, Godric and each of the longship skippers and rode off by himself. His housecarls had duties to perform locally on the morrow so were left to enjoy a free day.

The day of reckoning, as Owerd regarded it, began with promising weather: a light north-easterly and no sign of rain. He pulled into the palace courtyard and was delighted to meet up with Sieur Raymond, the Breton knight who had evidently taken up his position as captain of the king's guard. Pleasant greetings were exchanged and they awaited the king and his nobles who appeared shortly afterwards. Owerd dismounted and approached the king, going down on one knee as he came near.

'Rise! Is all in readiness for our day's entertainment, Sir Owerd?' Owerd managed no more than a nod before the king turned 'you have met my brother Odo, I believe, and this is Earl Robert de Beaumont, a doughty warrior in whom I have much faith. So, let us be off'.

The troop of guards formed up at front and rear and it was an impressive procession that rode out of Winchester on the road to Gosport. It would be a long ride so, with Sieur Raymond alongside him at their head, Owerd encouraged a fast pace. As it was, they barely made their destination in time for a midday meal. On arrival Owerd's men rushed forward to act as grooms while the group dismounted and made their way into the new hall.

'This looks like it has cost our purse a sizeable sum, Sir Owerd', said the king as he looked around.

'No cost to the exchequer, sire, all built by your butsecarls from local timber felled and cut by themselves'. He then introduced Hakon and Godric who both looked justifiably proud of their efforts.

Archbishop Odo joined in the conversation as they eyed a table laid with fruit and trenchers of cut meats. 'These servants all have the look of warriors to me, Sir Owerd, are we safe?'

He was referring to Owerd's men, thankfully unarmed, who stood waiting to serve wine. 'Well noted my lord archbishop, they are all men-at-arms, my own trusted housecarls. Right now, my lord, added to his Grace's own guards outside, we are possibly in the safest room in all of Christendom'.

The meal, short and simple as it was, went smoothly and, on completion, Owerd led the nobles down to the waiting ships. The whole contingent of nine nobles followed the king over to the port side of "The Merry Widow" to stare at the longships secured alongside. All two-score and two oars were being held vertically by the butsecarls sitting brightly in their red surcoats. Owerd briefly explained the build of the vessels before nodding to Hakon to proceed.

'That is a nasty looking weapon at the stern, Sir Owerd, I can see its logic. But why all that netting at the bow?'

'These ships are built for ramming sire, so the only point of contact will be at the bow. The netting is an added safeguard to avoid being boarded'.

Within a few more minutes all vessels were heading into open waters, with the longships making ground a little upwind. The cog passed the stationary target vessel, a dilapidated cog riddled with woodworm, which had a longboat alongside and a few watching seamen aboard.

Hakon manoeuvered his own cog to seaward then had the sail lowered. Owerd began his commentary upon what they were about to see, then a large yellow flag was waved from the stern. The longships immediately approached at a fast pace then reversed oars smartly to take station just astern and picked up tow ropes trailing aft from the cog.

Once the longships were settled Hakon waved a striped red and white flag. 'That means enemy in sight my lords. May I ask what you see?'

The crews of the longships had put their heads down, such that the vessels looked much like unmanned vessels loaded with red cloth.

'I see much red', muttered a jocular Bishop Odo, 'what is the point?'

'At a distance, my lords, this will look like a merchant cog towing two loaded longships. That is a prize no pirate could possibly resist. We would plan to await them closing to an easy distance and then order the attack'.

As he said that, Hakon waved yet another flag, this time red. The longship crews sat up, released the tow-lines and the vessels made their way rapidly upwind under oars. The onlookers' attention was then drawn to the target vessel which now had her sail raised and with the crew scrambling into their longboat and rowing away as fast as they could. Next seen were the two longships under full sail sweeping toward them at the pace of a galloping charger. They split to pass either side of the target and two pairs of fire arrows streaked outward, striking the target's sail and setting it alight. The longships lowered their sails in unison and turned upwind to pass the target once more under oars. As they came abreast the target a storm of arrows flew into her from both sides, including a few fire arrows. Causing the onlookers to give a gasp of surprise, there were then two loud cracks and steel bolts few across the water. The after castle of the target disintegrated, spreading splintered timber in all directions.

'Should that not finish the enemy vessel, we would administer the coup de grace', Owerd advised. The two longships were then seen turning directly toward the target and ramming her. Oars working heavily, they then pulled back and, with Hakon waving the yellow flag, returned to their tow positions astern of "The Merry Widow".

'I am impressed', said the king as the target vessel was seen slowly sinking beneath the water, 'what say you gentlemen?'

There was a momentary silence amongst the nobles before Earl Robert, probably the youngest of the group, remarked 'I am glad we did not meet you off Hastings Sir Owerd'.

The sail home was smooth, as was the chatter amongst the nobles, and without incident, but it was getting late and the sun was well on its way down.

'You need not accompany us back to Winchester, Sir Owerd', said the king, 'but we would know your intentions now'.

'We have received reports of pirates interfering with trade and fishing vessels off the South-West coast sire. With your consent I would go to investigate and see if we might make those waters safer'.

'We approve, though do not linger too long. We expect to call on your team for some possible tasks which I see looming in the east. You have pleased us greatly Sir Owerd, fare the well'.

Owerd congratulated both Hakon and, once ashore, Godric and had them muster the men in the hall. Once gathered, he stood on a bench to address them.

'Men, you have performed above expectations. I shall not give you any long speech, but be prepared to leave soon for real action. For now, enjoy the ale which is from my purse in thanks'. The men were elated and cheered, especially when the housecarls brought out jugs of ale. Owerd himself was equally elated and decided that if there were any evening when he could let his guard down and enjoy a surfeit of wine then it was this one. He became happily drunk and was led to his sleeping berth by Osric just as the fires were being banked for the night.

-XX-

While preparing to sail a few days later, the two longship skippers put a damper on the mood by reporting the start of cracking in the base-plate of one of the ballistae. Owerd and Hakon both went to inspect the matter and, tiny as it was, the crack would inevitably spread and probably also arise in the other vessel.

'These boats are built with their strength fore and aft sire', explained one of the skippers. 'When we fired abeam the force was absorbed cross-ways, where the boat is weakest'.

Owerd pondered for a full minute or two then smiled. 'The Parthian Shot', he exclaimed and received very curious looks from the three seafarers.

'It is written of in the old Latin texts of the Roman wars', Owerd explained. 'Some time before Christ our Lord was born, the Romans attacked a land called Parthia. They had a powerful force but it was almost exterminated by the Parthians. The barbarians had a clever trick which was to feign retreat on horseback and then fire volleys of arrows over the rumps of their horses. It became known as the Parthian Shot. We can do the same. From now on we fire the ballistae only aft. That should enable to force to be borne by the hull, though I accept that this will take practice'.

The experienced skippers looked at each other, then nodded. 'We do not like the idea of being seen to run away from a fight, Sir Owerd', said one, 'but I can see how that might work'.

Back on the water two days later the three vessels sailed westwards in relatively light winds, remaining just in sight of the coast. There were a few fishing boats about, which raced inshore at the sight of the warships, but little else.

'Trade seems to have dried up hereabouts', remarked Hakon toward the end of their first day. There were certainly no trading vessels to be seen then, nor had there been earlier in the day. 'Ahead is a dangerous point off Portland that locals call "The Beel", infested with shallows and hidden reefs', he added 'we could pass well clear but there is a village at the mouth of the river this side of it which could make a good place to stay overnight and gather intelligence from the fisherfolk'.

Owerd agreed and the ships headed inshore. Just as they did so a small vessel, little larger than a skiff, came hurtling around the point. Her helmsman saw them and began to turn away but perhaps thought better of it and sailed toward them. Onboard could be seen a man, a woman and two small children.

'Ware, raiders inshore' the helmsman yelled as he came within hailing distance.

'We are king's ships', Owerd called back. 'Approach and tell us more'.

The boat's skipper did so and they managed a brief conversation though with sparse detail. The gist of the tale was that raiders had landed in the night and plundered the village, taking many villagers as prisoners. This man had managed to take his wife and children to his boat and thus escape, but the raiders were still ashore.

Owerd swung into action, calling both of his longships alongside their cog. He briefed Hakon on what to do, which was to block any escape then buckled on his sword. He clambered over the side and into one of the longships, trading places with the after oarsmen.

'Inshore, we attack', he called so that all of the crew could hear him. Turning to the skipper he asked how many archers were in the crew to be told about half, which gave him a score of archers and a score of men-at-arms. Plenty, he thought. In front of him, men were rowing and awkwardly feeling for bows, arrows and seaxes at the same time. As the men progressively found their weapons, the oar stroke settled and became faster such that they rounded the point heading toward the river mouth at good speed. Ahead, much became clear. There was a longship of the Norse variety beached near the river entrance with a large group of people clustered nearby. More concerning was a large open-topped cog with shields arrayed along her sides riding at anchor off the beach.

'We leave the cog for now, make for the longship and be prepared to disable her by ramming', he told the skipper. Standing, he called out to the crew. 'Men, today we fight for king and our people. I want no reckless acts of bravery. Once we beach, we will form up and only attack when we are ready. We will use the archers to defend the ship and men-at-arms as they land, then have them join us ashore. We give no quarter to pirates'.

As they closed on the beached longship, Owerd could see that there was but a single guard left aboard.

'Change of plan, beach us right next to that longship. We will try to take her intact'. He then called toward the bow. 'Bow archers, take out that guard on the longship'.

Moments before they grounded on the beach, two arrows flew across the water and appeared in the enemy guard's chest. There were then a few moments of near chaos as men lurched forward as their own vessel ground rapidly to a halt on the sand. Leaping over the side, Owerd was disadvantaged in being at the rear and went into water above his waist and he struggled to keep his sword clear. He was also trying hard to control his breathing as he realized that the excitement of battle was upon him and his heart was racing. Wading through the shallows he took stock of their position and formed the men-at-arms in front of him and the archers to the rear facing landward. The only potential opposition looked to be from about six warriors guarding a miserable huddle of villagers and a pile of goods of some sort about two score paces along the beach.

Owerd looked back at the raiding longship, thinking that it should probably have a sizeable crew. He contemplated his priorities. The six men further along the beach presented no threat right now, but the village would be in the other direction. He did not want to leave six soldiers at his back.

'Six archers, step out', he called. 'Take a walk along the beach and take out those ruffians down there. Try not to kill any of the villagers'.

Just as the archers went in one direction, a man appeared from the other end carrying a bundle of what could only be plunder. He dropped whatever he was carrying in surprise at seeing a large body of men between him and his vessel. He gave a loud cry of alarm and disappeared the way he came. Owerd's mind was racing and his first thought was of probable shield walls forming. But if they were lugging booty from the village, he thought, then they would not be burdening themselves with shields. He was also conscious that none of his men, himself included, wore mail. Turning his attention back to the beached longship he could not help but notice that her sides were lined with shields.

Turning to the nearest man-at-arms he pointed to the longship. 'Take ten men and gather those shields off the longship, share them out as much as you can'.

His men struggled back with a pair of shields each just in time. As Owerd took one, he looked to the end of the beach to see a roaring mass of irate warriors stream on to the sand. A leader of some sort managed to put them into some sort of order, this being as close as possible to a shield wall but without the shields. This was apparently the way in which these men were used to fighting and though at a disadvantage in numbers they still presented a fearsome threat. Knives, axes and the occasional sword were being waved in the air and the whole group was issuing loud cries of anger and menace.

Owerd felt the need to steady his untried men in the face of the coming onslaught and tried to keep his voice calm and steady. 'Hold fast men, let them come to us. Archers move to our flanks and thin them out when they charge'.

As if they had heard him the raiders swarmed forward but lost cohesion as a group as the more motivated or braver ones outpaced their companions. Arrows flew across the sand with a whirring sound as the king's archers let fly and those in the front rank of the raiders began falling, whether injured or dying. As they did, those behind stumbled and lost momentum so that it was a loose rabble of fighters that struck Owerd's front rank. Owerd found himself facing their leader, a rough-looking individual who was all brawn and anger. He also smelled, both in body and breath, and the stench was enough to qualify as a weapon in its own right. He swung an axe in a wild swing that connected with the shield Owerd was carrying, sending ripples of pain up his arm. Splinters flew in all directions but the shield, thicker and thus heavier than he was used to, held together.

Owerd dared not check how his men were faring as his opponent had now drawn a vicious looking knife and was seeking to slash his sword arm while simultaneously driving him into the ground with blows of his axe. Men were now falling to left and right and one of the raiders suddenly lurched in front of Owerd, screaming in agony. Owerd managed to take a half pace backwards as the falling man came between himself and his own attacker but his opponent was less fortunate and stumbled. That was

Owerd's chance and he took it within an instant, driving his sword in a straight thrust to the man's chest and twisting it free ready for a second strike. No second strike was necessary: the man gave an incomplete snarl as his eyes glazed over and he collapsed with blood dripping down his chest.

Owerd took the opportunity to survey the battle's progress and was relieved to see very few of his men lying on the sand. That could not be said about the raiders, who lay about either moaning in pain or having taken their last breaths. There was one fierce contest still going on toward the end of the line where one of his men was being harried by a thin wiry raider who was wielding a long seax in each hand and looked to be winning his battle. Owerd did not delay: honourable combat be damned. He took a few paces to his right and swung his sword across the shoulder-blades of the raider with as much strength as he could muster. It was enough, indeed had it been an inch or two higher his stroke would have severed the man's head.

A tired and weary but exultant cheer rang out. His men had won a resounding victory over the raiders but Owerd was worried that he had lost touch with events at the other end of the beach. He had no cause for concern. His six archers stood proudly in front of the collected villagers, seemingly unhurt. That could not be said for all his men. Two of the men-at-arms lay prostrate with blood oozing from wounds to their neck or head and a couple more were nursing blood-soaked arms.

'Nearest men see to our wounded', he called. 'Well done all of you'. He looked about but could see no raiders still standing, although one or two on the sand a little further away seemed to have life in them yet. He let them lie. Calling to his longship's skipper, a Frank named Piers, he had him look over the raider's longship with a view to checking that she was seaworthy while he went to the villagers to check their wellbeing.

'Also, Piers', he said quietly, 'I see men cutting the purses from the bodies of the dead raiders. I am not averse to that, but the coin needs to be shared amongst the men. Will you see to that'.

'Aye, sir, I will'.

An older but fit-looking man in sturdy boots, breeches and a woolen cloak was then seen walking toward him out of the group of people that had been captured.

'I am Chad, sir, village headman of this here village of Wyke. I thank thee, and thank God above for your arrival, for without your timely aid we faced lives of penury and hardship as slaves or worse. Might I ask your name sir?'

'I am Lord Owerd, the king's Sea Lord', came the response. Owerd was thinking that having been given that title by King William he may as well make full use of it. 'This matter needs reporting to you sheriff, how far away would he be?'

'About three leagues, my lord. We have a donkey in the village if it still lives: mayhap I can have someone ride to inform him, though I doubt that he would be of much help'.

'Do you have injuries amongst your folk Chad?'

'Not in this group, sir, but I fear for those that were left in the village. They brought only the fittest of the menfolk and prettiest of the young women to the beach. We here are all sorely hurt in the mind but just bruised and bothered'.

'Well, you may tell your folk they have nothing more to fear and may collect from that pile there what belongs to them. Then perhaps you could take me with you to the village to see what state it is in'.

Chad led the way to the village which was only a few hundred paces from the beach. Owerd took two of the men-at-arms with him in case there were any raiders taking refuge there. The village was a mess. The contents of the village huts lay scattered about and there were at least half a dozen dead bodies visible. There were few signs of life: mangy dogs sniffing through the detritus; an old lady weeping over a body outside a hut; and a dazed and naked child of about two years wandering aimlessly.

Owerd was appalled but realized that there was nothing they could do for the place that the surviving villagers could not handle themselves. Further, he needed to check on Osric's progress with the raiders' cog.

'We go men', is all he said, and began his return to the longship in deep thought. If this is what they could come across almost by accident, what other places around the coast must be suffering a similar fate. He needed now to consult with Piers about what to do with the raiders' beached longboat. That took only moments. Piers was dubious about towing from their own longship and much more positive about putting a dozen of their crew aboard the raiders' vessel. Owerd agreed and as he was rowed out toward the anchored enemy cog was pleasantly surprised to see her intact with "The Merry Widow" lashed alongside and the second longship tied up on the other side.

'You seem to have matters well under control here, Hakon', he muttered as he scrambled aboard the cog. 'How did it go?'

'The pirates had left but very few men aboard her, Owerd, so taking her was not difficult. Two of the more foolish fellows threatened to fight it out but some well-placed arrows resolved that. The few others left saw the number of men we came with and threw down their weapons. So, we now have three prisoners and the interesting part of that is that one of them seems to be Norman. Even more interesting is a sight that will gladden your heart, come with me'.

The vessel's hold did not look particularly inspiring at first sight, but peering through the dimness below, Owerd could make out a large quantity of bulging sacks.

'I have not examined them all but there are quite a number that contain silver crucifixes, holy books and the like. It would seem that these people have been at their trade for quite some time. You may be especially interested in a separate storage'. Hakon led him aft and then lifted a flap below the steering platform. Tucked inside were three iron-bound chests.

'Mainly silver, my lord, but enough gold in addition to purchase a small fleet of longships if that were your wish'.

'Best keep this find between us, Hakon. Let me think upon it, but I have no wish to have us accused of piracy ourselves. Meanwhile, can you tow this thing?'

There were thus two cogs and three longships that returned to Gosport late the next day.

-XXI-

The rough-hewn oak table in their Gosport hall looked magnificent. At least one end did, with it being laden with ornaments and books more suited to a grand manor-house or a cathedral. The hall had been cleared of all except the officers who sat wondering what this haul of plunder could be worth.

'We need to be of one mind about this', declared Owerd. 'I promised our men a share of any booty. The question to be decided is what share. I will offer you each a chance to speak, but first we should be prepared for the king to demand all of it. I do not propose to offer him that chance. It is the coin boxes that are most significant and I believe Sir Godric has now made an estimate of their worth. Please share that information my friend'.

'My initial count is of forty pounds value in silver and something like half that amount in the gold pieces and coinage, much of which is Byzantine'.

'From my experience gold can be a difficulty to exchange for useable silver so I propose most of that goes to the exchequer. I suggest three quarters. The silver must be seen as a reasonable balance so I suggest half of that. If agreed, that would leave us with five pounds in gold and twenty of silver to share about. My expectation is that the king will be more than content with a windfall of some forty-four pounds in ready coin. The goods we can seek the crown's decision upon. Godric, you have control of the accounts. Can we afford to give each of the men say five shillings?'

'That would amount to a little over ten pounds, sir, but may I suggest four shillings each and one gold coin?'

'What about the officers, my lord, do we take similar shares?' Piers seemed disturbed.

'How would one pound each for the officers plus two gold coins suit? I would reward my men-at-arms out of my share. What remains I will keep as a separate reserve to fund any requirements of the squadron that the exchequer will not'.

A mix of vague shrugs, smiles and nods followed so Owerd took that as an agreed plan. 'Right, the officers can take their shares now. Godric, if you would muster the men who went on our last voyage and see them paid. That includes the injured of course, all of whom I hear are likely to recover'.

Owerd then turned his attention to the prisoners who were herded into the far end of the hall. One was Frankish, one claimed to be Norman and one spoke a language none could understand which Hakon thought to be Irish.

'You are charged with the heinous crime of piracy', spoke Owerd, 'how say you?'

The Frank just shrugged; the man from Ireland, if that is where he was from, also said nothing, while the Norman declared his innocence as he had been captured and forced into sailing with the others.

'He lies', spat the Frank, 'he joined the crew in Dublin'.

'The sentence for piracy is death', intoned Owerd with no outward emotion. 'Take them out'.

Calling Osric to him, he first apologized for giving him an unsavoury task. Take them down to the village and hang the Frank and the Irishman. Let the bodies swing afterwards as a warning to others. For now, the Norman is to be kept safe for the king's justice'.

The ride to Winchester was not the triumphant progress that Owerd would have liked. The cartload of plundered goods and the coin chests was well covered from idle examination and he had his four available housecarls as escort supplemented by two of the more experienced archers manning the cart. The element that drew unwanted attention was the sight of a bound man tethered to the back of the cart and occasionally forced to jog. Owerd had no sympathy for him. It was also beginning to depress him that he was brought to this, so far from his visions of the glorious warrior. As he had come to realize, no-one was exempt from committing one or more of the seven deadly sins, himself included.

The cart was paused only briefly to drop off one of the coin chests for safekeeping by the steward of his Winchester house, finally stopping inside the palace grounds. Owerd had two of the housecarls take a coin chest each and follow him in to see a clerk of the exchequer where he asked to see Sieur Charles, head of the exchequer, personally. That man came out of a side office with curiosity written all over his face and an even more intrigued look at the sight of two heavy coin chests.

'Welcome Sir Owerd, or should I call you Sea Lord, as that is what I now hear you referred to as?'

'Owerd would be fine thank you Sieur Charles. I come with the proceeds from the capture of some pirate vessels. I wish to see that they are accounted for in proper fashion without the inevitable fees and deductions that would occur should they handled elsewhere. In short, Charles, I believe you to be an honest man and I do not trust some others. I have not personally checked every penny but believe there is something like thirty-five pounds in gold and silver in these chests. The coin is for the king's exchequer. I also have a cart of stolen valuables retrieved from the vessels outside and would welcome your advice on what should be done with those and the two vessels themselves'.

'You honour me Sir Owerd, though in reality I am but a simple keeper of accounts. The coin will be much welcomed by his majesty as I can advise you that he was beginning to express concern at the size of the costs your endeavours are incurring. This will help balance the books admirably. As for the other goods I will have my people take a look. The vessels are more in your own demesne Owerd. If you are able to put them to good use, in whatever manner, then I suggest you do so and I will inform the king likewise'.

'Is he here, for I should report to him of events and of a matter needing justice?'

'He is back at Westminster, but Archbishop Odo is here. Perhaps he would suit your needs, although he could be one of those "others" you mentioned', he added with a smile.

With a handshake and good cheer, the two parted and Owerd headed for the main hall after telling his men to make sure those checking the captured goods knew that their cart and horse were not part of the plunder.

The palace chamberlain was inside the hall resting on a stool looking for all the world like a man with the weight of the world on his shoulders. He rose with a weary sigh on sighting Owerd.

'Welcome Sir Owerd', he greeted. 'The Court has moved to Westminster, so I am left without enough servants and the high cost of food to meet in a time of famine. The demands of those nobles remaining do not diminish, however'.

'Famine?' Owerd's query was genuine for there were few signs of it locally.

'It is mainly the north but those who usually sell their product at local market are well appraised of the situation elsewhere and choose to make their profit where it is highest. Less product here means higher prices as you might imagine.'

'I see your difficulties, Lord Chamberlain', said Owerd, knowing full well that he neither saw them nor sympathized. 'It is the Archbishop I would now wish to see in lieu, I gather that he is here'.

'He has a guest with him at present my lord but I will see'.

A servant was summoned to announce Sir Owerd to the archbishop and he returned with an affirmative answer more quickly that Owerd expected. He was becoming used to the practice of many nobles to attest to their authority and importance by keeping visitors waiting. Following the servant he recognized the king's private dining room, where Archbishop Odo was now acting lordly, reclining on a couch and sipping from a silver goblet of wine. Nearby was a tall, athletic man who was both well attired and bore the air of one used to authority.

'Welcome to our new lord of the sea', called Odo from his couch without standing. 'Come, meet Sieur Hugh de Port, a friend and colleague of mine of many years standing'.

A handshake with Sir Hugh told Owerd much about the man. He had the air and firm handshake of a warrior and looked him directly in the eye as they met. This is a man to beware of or befriend thought Owerd.

'My lord archbishop, I come to seek your guidance, though on a matter more temporal than spiritual'. He explained the events of the past few days and had obviously gained the close attention of both men.

'The matter at hand is that one of the captives from the pirate ship claims both to be of Norman origin and aboard under duress. That is despite a fellow crew member denouncing him as a liar on the latter count. Being barred from hanging him myself, I have brought him here to face the king's justice'.

'Well', said Odo after a thoughtful pause, 'you are in the right company here. Sir Hugh is about to take up his new position as Sheriff of Hampshire this very week. What say you to this Hugh?'

Sir Hugh spoke eloquently with a clear confident voice. 'This man must be of the lower sort even if he is Norman as he claims. But why barred Sir Owerd, I understood that it was common practice to hang pirates as a matter of course?'

'There is a king's edict against anyone causing the death of a Norman and with rather severe consequences Sieur Hugh'. Owerd knew that he was on thin ice here, as he had personally disposed of many Normans.

'My chartered term as sheriff has not yet begun and I have nowhere to keep him anyway. I am unsure that I can be of any assistance just now'.

Odo stood, belched rudely and eyed both men. 'I am bored. This man may warrant a trial, so let us have one. Sir Owerd, bring the rascal into the main hall. Sieur Hugh and I will act in judgement'.

Owerd gave a slight bow and left the pair to find his men helping unload their cart. Unhitching the pirate from the cart he had two of his men-at-arms escort the man, now a thoroughly despondent individual, into the main hall. The archbishop now sat upon the king's throne with Sieur Hugh sat next to him on a slightly lower stool and both accompanied by a few of the palace guard.

After a few preliminaries, the accusation of piracy was levelled at the man. He gave his name as Brenno, declared that he was a Norman from Caen and had been abducted by the pirates. A few more polite questions from the archbishop saw the accused grow in confidence until the matter of where he had first stepped aboard the ship came up. He was clearly about to lie but thought better of it and admitted that it was in Dublin.

'So, how long were you aboard until captured?'

'Er, I forget my lord, I lost track of time, perhaps a few weeks'.

'Your vessel pulled into a number of ports in the meantime I expect', said Odo with an innocent expression.

'Yes my lord, many small ports'.

'So, why did you not manage to escape'.

The man became confused. He hung his head and declared that he had been mortally afraid. 'Those were vicious men my lord, I was affeared'.

'Show me his hands', Odo directed the men-at-arms who turned the man about and held up the palms of his bound hands to be seen. Having looked closely he stared at the man once more and noted callouses on his right hand that were absent from the left. 'You were a soldier', he announced. 'I believe you also to be a coward and a pirate'.

The archbishop stood. 'Brenno of Caen I find you guilty of the heinous crime of piracy, for which the sentence is death. Guards, take the prisoner out and have him hanged as soon as that can be arranged.'

So, justice was seen to be done, thought Owerd, although it was a tedious process and he was left blameless for the death of yet another Norman. Bowing to leave, he was stopped by a call from the archbishop to come closer.

'Was there booty upon these pirate vessels Sir Owerd?'

Odo was obviously allowing his more avaricious side to see the light of day. 'There was my lord archbishop. Some gold and silver coin, many bags of domestic goods and some church ornaments and religious books'.

'Where lies this booty now, sir?'

'I have placed it into the custody of the head of the king's exchequer, my lord. I believe he is unloading it outside as we speak. The exception is the two captured vessels themselves, which are probably of little value. Sieur Charles suggested I try to find some use for them in pursuit of his majesty's wishes'.

Odo was on his feet. 'Items of a religious nature belong to the church. I as Archbishop of Canterbury have responsibility for such and I shall see to their distribution personally'. He marched out, leaving Owerd ever thankful that he had placed the funds and goods with the exchequer before Odo could manage to redirect them to his own use.

He had to await the complete unloading of the cart before riding off and it was becoming marginal as to whether they would make Gosport before nightfall. He decided to stay the night at the Winchester house and was just briefing his men accordingly when the chamberlain rushed outside toward him. It was unusual to see the chamberlain rushing anywhere, so Owerd was nervous about what this might portend. As it happened, it was merely a message scroll from Westminster that had arrived the previous day. Owerd opened it.

"You are directed by his majesty to assemble his majesty's fighting ships assigned to you at the port of London with all expedition. The port reeve of Dover, assisted as required by the Earl of Sussex, has been directed to assemble ten ships of war and crews to attend in the king's service for twenty days from two weeks hence. The port reeve of Sandwich likewise. You are to take command also of those vessels and muster together in London Port. When this sea force is assembled you are to report directly to his majesty at Westminster."

A strong expletive was forming in Owerd's throat and probably about to burst from his lips when he thought more on it. The expletive, whatever it may have been, did not reach the evening air. The opportunity this gave him to alleviate any boredom building amongst his butsecarls and mayhap see some more action himself, was too good to be churlish about.

-XXII-

At midday next, Owerd's senior men were again gathered around their hall table addressing the forthcoming deployment. The atmosphere was businesslike and rather than any dismay, Owerd detected an air of anticipation verging on excitement.

'I will ride so that we can maintain some form of communication overland and take Osric and three of my men with me. I also need an experienced man to check on my lady wife and the manors at Birdlip and Aust – Cuthbert can do that and then join us in Winchester afterwards. Godric, I leave you with the task of setting the third of our new longships to work. Hakon, mayhap you could advise him on a suitable man to be appointed as skipper'.

Owerd was approached by Cuthbert later in the morning.

'My lord, I wondered whether you might consider taking me with you to the east and having Osric check on Lady Hilda and the manors'.

This was a most unusual request, especially coming from the normally very reticent Cuthbert.

'You will need tell me why that should be, Cuthbert'.

There was a very evident sense of embarrassment about Cuthbert's approach. 'Er, well, it be like this sir. Osric has developed a liking for the maid Sigria and it is apparently returned. I believe Osric has it in mind to come to an arrangement with the girl'.

The image of Osric, the burly no-nonsense warrior and Sigrid the timid and much younger maid as a couple sat curiously in Owerd's mind. It was certainly unexpected, but he supposed that pairings such as this were inevitable. He agreed to the change.

The rest of that day was occupied with restocking the ships which then sailed promptly on the following morning's tide. There was still no word on the reason for this sudden requirement and Owerd wasted no time in idle speculation. They would doubtless be told when they arrived in London. Getting there by land in any direct fashion would be difficult, but word had it that an old Roman road led from the other side of the river past Winchester and on to Silchester. It was thus on that road, now muddy from the Spring thaw, that a party of five armed and mailed warriors made their way toward London.

The group was an impressive sight. The horses, including their two spares, were curried to perfection and their riders were uniformly dressed in new hose, long boots and leather jerkins similar to the one Hilda had made for Owerd. They met few on their route and those that they did gave them a polite wave or simply stepped aside. The travelers were less shiny as they ultimately arrived at the gates of Westminster but were waved through readily and Owerd went to find the Chamberlain to beg a night's accommodation.

Walking into the Great Hall, he saw a few resident courtiers standing around sipping wine or grazing from the supply of food at the near end of the long central table. At the far end, though, he could see a group of nobles huddled over some documents or maps and conversing eagerly. He went forward for a closer look, hoping to see the Chamberlain, but instead saw King William. What initially seemed worse, the king saw him.

'Ah, my Sea Lord', exclaimed William, 'come join us'.

Owerd still wore his sword and seax so hastily removed them before bowing and joining the group.

'Gentlemen, if you have not already guessed, this is Sir Owerd, our Master of Mariners who seems to be generally known as the Sea Lord. Sir Owerd, meet Ivo Taillebois, Lord of Holland and Kesteven and Sieur William Warrenne, a doughty knight and another of our other counsellors here with us'. There were polite nods all around but nothing more. 'We discuss our plans for ridding ourselves of that nest of vipers inhabiting Ely'.

This was the first hint Owerd had received of his likely task so listened intently. It transpired that the Danes had landed again near Ely where the rebel Hereward held sway. He looked around the rest of the group and noticed Brother John the Intelligencer at the back looking very relaxed next to a priest who looked the opposite. John had an easy smile on his face and nodded as he caught Owerd's eye, whilst the priest had a grim expression and was staring intently at Owerd. His own attention was brought back to King William.

'Sweyn Ulfsson is with them and commands more than two score ships. I am loathe to attack while he stays. Can you remove him Sir Owerd?'

'I can certainly make his stay very uncomfortable Your Grace. Mayhap he will leave, but the outcome of any fight is in the hands of the Almighty, sir, so I do not forecast it'.

'Do it! Go now, take what ships you need and rid me of this Danish presence'.

'With a bow of acknowledgement, Owerd left and, after retrieving his weapons, tried again to locate the Chamberlain. He had almost immediate success and was just thanking him for his courtesy when Brother John came up and took him by the arm.

'Well met, Owerd', began John. 'The king's anger has been aroused by the rebel Englisc under Hereward joining with the Danes to sack and burn Peterborough. The clergy are outraged and that Ivo Taillebois you met is stoking the anger. He has lands around Ely from which he gains no income because the rebels control the area. You will need to beware the fens there Owerd; they lead into all sorts of dead-end marshes and traps which the locals know well. You might also beware that priest you may have seen me standing next to. He certainly saw you, and I could almost feel the antipathy emanating from his soul. He is Osbern fitzOsbern, younger brother of your old enemy William. He is supportive of his elder brother and good friends with the king, so not to be trifled with'.

'You are full of the sort of useful information that a man should know, friend John. I thank thee and shall tread warily.'

Housed comfortably, Owerd and his men had a good night's sleep and rode out the next morning in good spirits. The road to Dover was well-worn and in reasonably good condition so, without pushing the horses, they were making good time. It was but a few leagues into their journey when Matthew, the Englisc archer, rode up alongside Owerd.

'We are being followed, lord. Just the one that I can occasionally glimpse, but there could be more'.

Owerd had complete trust in his archer. 'Could simply be another traveler for the same destination, Matthew, but best to be safe. Put yourself in the bushes up ahead where you can avoid detection and let whomever it is go past. If safe to do so, come back and let us all know what you see. If I see you not within a few leagues further then we shall make early camp for the night in a suitable spot and await who follows'.

A touch less than half an hour later, and with no sign of Matthew, Owerd directed his men off to the side of the road into a likely looking grove of small trees. Tethering the horses further away, they took up a suitable vantage point sheltered by clumps of Dogwood and Privet. The whole area was very quiet such that they could almost hear each other breathing and even the wildlife seemed to be having a rest in the early afternoon sun. The stillness of the Spring air did not last long, giving way shortly afterward to the clip-clop of horse's hooves. A lone rider came into view. Definitely a soldier of some kind, staring intently ahead. He had a good mount, though poorly equipped, and looked to Owerd to be of the mercenary type.

Not long afterwards, the sound of horses again broke the stillness. This time five riders, again soldiers, and equipped in a miscellany of outfits and weapons. Owerd had little doubt that these were mercenaries and of ill intent. They exuded confidence as they rode past, chatting amongst themselves and paying little attention to their surroundings. Owerd had a dilemma. The group including the apparent scout outnumbered his own men. Letting them go onward unmolested as he had intended left themselves open to an ambush further along the road. Equally there was just the slightest uncertainty about their intentions, though not much, he thought. He needed an advantage and decided to assume the worst of them and rely on surprise.

Once Matthew returned, which was not long after, the men were mounted and prepared for a fight.

'There is a good prospect of them realizing that they have missed us somewhere along the road and doubling back to check', he told his men. 'That being the case we try to take them unprepared, so be ready to charge without warning and have your shields ready. That may provide us with an advantage against the odds. Mathew, you take the rear with the spare horses. Let them run if we meet our enemy and use your bow as you see fit'.

Owerd led them out at a trot, increasing to a light canter half a league further on, the better to ease into a gallop should the need arise. A disadvantage, he thought, was probably that they would be unable to hear horses ahead of them and would need to rely on a sighting. The relaxed mood of the morning's ride was gone. He was tense with anticipation and sensed the same in his men. Satan, also sensing the demeanour of his rider in that mysterious way that horses have, pricked up his ears and Owerd could feel an increased tension in his muscles. Horse and rider were both ready for battle.

Their opportunity was not long coming. Rounding a slight bend in the roadway, the six mercenaries came into view. They were in disarray, scattered either side of the road searching for some encampment or resting area of their quarry.

'Charge!' The order was probably unnecessary as the whole group broke into a gallop at first sight and rapidly closed on the enemy. Owerd's sword flashed before any of the opponents had managed to draw a weapon and with a forward slice he struck the leading man across the chest, severing his arm in the process. Continuing, he rode down a second horseman, whose mount was no match for Satan. The enemy horse went down in a flurry of tangled legs with a scream of agony that matched that of its rider. Pulling hard on the reins, he managed to slow Satan and turn him to face the way he had come. Two others of the mercenaries were on the ground trying to staunch the blood pouring from wounds which left two still mounted to be attended to. Digging his heels into Satan once more he aimed for the nearest, only to see him fall from the saddle with an arrow sprouting from his chest.

The remaining mercenary had had enough. He dropped his sword to the ground and raised his arms in surrender. One of Owerd's men rode up alongside him and pulled him from the saddle. He landed with a gasp of surprise but was out of the fight, completely winded.

Owerd spent a minute attempting to calm Satan, no easy feat as the animal had absorbed Owerd's own battle rage and was ready for more. He eventually managed to hand the reins to Matthew and dismounted to investigate the human detritus on the roadway. Much to his relief his own men looked to be intact. Three of the enemy were dead: two lay injured, one still trapped beneath his horse; and one sat at sword-point facing two of Owerd's men.

Owerd took another moment to catch his breath, then approached the man beneath the horse. He kicked a fallen sword further away from the man's outstretched arm then knelt beside him.

'I will free you as soon as you tell me who you are working for. If not, I shall leave you to rot. What is it to be?'

'I was not informed who the paymaster is', claimed the man in a guttural mainland accent that Owerd could not work out.

'So be it', said Owerd who rose and examined the horse that was shivering with pain and had a clearly broken foreleg. He gave a short sharp upward thrust with his seax and put the animal out of its misery. He walked across to the seated prisoner and gave the man a similar ultimatum.

'Tell me who you work for, or end your life here on this roadway'.

The man was scared, that much was obvious. 'A priest', he blurted. 'I know not his name but he is one of the nobles at the palace'.

That was quite sufficient for Owerd to put two and two together.

'Osbern fitzOsbern', he called to his men, 'a man of God, or perchance the Devil. Take what you wish from the fallen men, they were probably well paid for their dirty work. The bodies can go into the bushes to feed the ravens and the horses come with us: take one or two in tow each. As soon as the mess is cleared, the sooner we can be on our way again'. The two mercenaries still alive were left to fend for themselves.

Owerd and his men continued along the old Roman road most knew as Watling Street and set up camp just past the turn-off to Hastings on the outskirts of a town named Maidstone. They settled comfortably, knowing that it should be an easy ride to Dover the next day. That it turned out to be. The exception was the weather as they rode down to the sheltered river which provided the basis for the bustling port. Storm clouds loomed and the first drops of freezing rain fell upon them as they sighted the warships. His own longships looked empty, with just a guard crew of two aboard but the Cog was seething with men. They rode toward the cog and were quickly soaked to the skin.

'Take yourselves off to find some accommodation', he told Cuthbert. 'There must be a good market for horse flesh here from arrivals from the continent. See if you can fetch a fair price for our five newly obtained beasts and come visit me on the morrow here at the ship'.

A cold and dripping Owerd climbed the boarding ladder to be sighted by an amused Hakon who gestured him to the aft accommodation cabin.

'Greetings Lord Owerd', said Hakon with a broad grin, 'it is only fitting that the Sea Lord already has his feet wet as he joins his motley crew'.

'Not just my feet, Hakon, but if you wish to remain my friend you will conjure up some ale and food at the speed of a lightning bolt. Let us talk business once I am returned to a fit state'.

Settled some little while later on a couch originally fitted for Queen Edith, Owerd queried the ships' journey thus far and was mightily pleased with the response.

'We fed and housed the men from our longships overnight aboard the Cog', Hakon reported. 'They all seem in good spirits and I have had no issues of discipline. The longship masters know their trade and apart from demonstrating that they can outrun me at every turn, have behaved themselves well. The crews of the other vessels brought together under the old Scypfryd mustering arrangement are a different matter. They are a belligerent lot, mainly fishermen who dislike being told what to do. And the ships themselves are not the best. Most are Karvi, the smallest that one could consider as longships, and as the king failed to specify the type of ship to be provided the Reeve has made up numbers with some fishing boats. There is one Irish-made Skeid longship here, of near one hundred feet, but it has the appearance of neglect and the Reeve claims he would be unable to man it'.

'Mayhap Sandwich may be more productive', offered Owerd. 'Anyhow, the good tidings are that we now need not put into London town. We sail direct for the Isle of Ely'.

That brought an unexpected reaction. A look of mild horror came over Hakon.

'Lord help us', he exclaimed, 'that place is an island of mud, fens, marshes and demons. It is approached through an area known as the Wasche where one can sail in during the morn and be high and dry by midday. We shall never get near the isle itself without a local who knows the river and streams'.

'We are tasked with ridding the place of Danes, my friend. Let us speak with the longship skippers and see if they may find a man who knows the place. If not them then mayhap one of the fisherfolk may have some intelligence of it. Either way, we need our ships to be at sea with the first tide on the morrow. I will talk to the Port Reeve about the arrangements for the Scypfryd vessels'.

-XXIII-

Owerd felt a tinge of sympathy for the few hundred seamen standing before him on a green sward at the water's edge. They were a motley lot: most in poor clothing unsuited to the chill morning air, while he himself wore his full war gear less the helmet. He was standing on a fallen log with Hakon beside him and was fortunate in having an offshore wind so that his voice carried.

'Men, I am Lord Owerd, the king's Sea Lord, and will command this attack. We go to rid the coast of Danes and pirates, in that order. My deputy here, Master Hakon, will be skippering the "Merry Widow" from which all orders for our array and deployment will come. He will explain the signals to be used shortly. Our destination is Boston on the shores of the Wasche. There is intelligence of a large force of Danes at Ely and our priority is to have them leave or be destroyed. On our return voyage we will seek any pirates who harass our trade and fisherfolk. The value of any plunder taken will be shared with you all'.

As he finished his speech, during which an annoying man in the front kept up a constant chatter with those around, he could see that not all were happy about this venture. Then that same annoying individual called out loudly.

'So, what foolish folk do you think we all are that we would trust a pair of Danes such as yourselves?'

If there was ever a time to exert his authority, Owerd thought, now was it. He stepped forward a pace,

227

glowering at the man. 'I am no Dane'. That made no difference to the man's demeanour and he then made matters worse by spitting. The phlegm landed half a pace in front of Owerd's boots. That was it! Owerd took two paces forward and felled the man with a punch to the stomach followed with an uppercut that had him out cold.

He turned to Cuthbert who stood a few paces behind him with the rest of his available housecarls. 'That man smells of ale, fear and cowardice', he shouted for all to hear, 'take him and cool him off with a good dunking in the river. He will not be sailing with us'.

That garnered a few smiles and enough respect to allow Hakon to finish his own briefing in good order. 'We sail with the tide', Hakon finished.

'I ride for Sandwich now and will see to what arrangements may have been made there. I intend joining you aboard from then on'.

The ride to Sandwich was an easy one and Owerd and his men were there in good time to partake of some ale and rare fresh pigeon pies before attending the Port Reeve. That official's success in mustering men and ships, or lack of it, was much on a par with that of Dover but at least the man was more cooperative. He was a jolly, rotund man of middling years who ran a very busy trading port with evident efficiency. The place was clean and well-ordered and he had set berthing space aside for at least a few of Owerd's ships-of-war.

'I have gathered six longships and crews which is as many as I have found possible. The seamen know they will lose coin and be put at risk in these musters so they either vanish to sea in their fishing boats or take positions on trade vessels leaving for foreign ports. I can provide two crewed cogs should you have a use for them. One has archers' castles fore and aft so could prove useful'.

'I will count those in your numbers Sir Reeve', said Owerd, 'it would add to the count if you could load a half dozen casks of water and a few kegs of ale on to one of them'.

The reeve gave a wan smile but nodded his agreement.

'My ships should be here before nightfall and I will take accommodation in one of those, but it would be a kindness if you would recommend a place to stay for my four men and our horses'

All was done as Owerd requested and he walked aboard "The Merry Widow" with relief when she arrived as the sun was disappearing behind the low hills to the west. As the lead vessel she gained a berth at the port jetty but most of the longships were forced to beach nearby. It was noticeable that the Dover vessels beached well clear of those from Sandwich.

'I gather that there is no love lost between the crews of these two ports, friend Hakon, so best to keep them separate as far as we are able. They compete for the fishing grounds and I am told often come to blows over the matter. For now, though, let us eat and sup a little ale for I have both thirst and hunger'.

The morning briefing of the Sandwich seamen followed a similar script to that at Dover, but without the unpleasantness. It would be a three-day sail to Boston depending upon wind and sea and how the amateur fleet managed to keep up and organize themselves for night beaching. Owerd was not confident and mentally allowed for at least a four-day journey. It was much like herding wild mice, Owerd thought. As it was, the fleet, now numbering some twenty-one vessels, kept a reasonably tight formation on the way north and there were no obvious breakdowns of men or machines.

Now being aware of the animosity between Dover and Sandwich, Owerd had directed the Dover ships to beach on the eastern shore of the Wasche rather than in Boston. He would detach one of the cogs there later with supplies to keep the men in rations. The sea was in benign mood throughout the journey and a light westerly wind prevailed. It was as the fleet turned west into the Wasche that a man in the bow called the alarm.

'Sails ahead, a league and a half, Vikings by their look'.

Owerd rushed to the bow for a better look, with Hakon at his heels. There were at least a score or more longships with their distinctive carved prows heading seaward along the far coastline. There was a sizeable gap then another three longships trailing behind.

'Signal "enemy sighted" please Hakon', said Owerd softly. 'We will not catch the main body of that lot, and I suspect should not try. The three trailing vessels look to be within striking distance however. We will give it an attempt. Call "Adeliza" alongside, I will transfer and lead the attack in her. Two other longships should suffice if they can keep up'.

Owerd climbed down into "Adeliza", which necessitated two of the aft rowers giving up their bench and retiring aboard the Cog. Within a matter of minutes, the two new longships and two of the Sandwich vessels had their sails taut and at full stretch with all of the ships building up impressive bow-waves. Inevitably "Adeliza" and her sister ship "Cecilia", named after the king's second daughter, drew ahead of the others. Their opponents looked to be maintaining their seaward heading, and Owerd wondered if they could be laden with booty and reluctant to engage in a fight.

'Ready fire arrows forward', called Owerd as they closed on the nearest target. He then looked toward "Cecilia" and gestured for her to attack the next ship in line. He received a wave of acknowledgement and focused on the enemy ahead.

'We will go for the sail first', he called out so all could hear, then spoke quietly to the skipper. 'Keep us well off but within bowshot, just as practised. If we get ahead of her, I would use the ballista. I have no intention of risking our vessel for the sake of any booty she may be carrying. Beware they do not turn towards'. A solemn 'Aye Lord', was all he then needed to hear.

Three fire arrows struck the Danish longship's sail. One lower down fizzled and achieved little: the other two flared brightly and within seconds the sail was ablaze. Sailors could be seen rushing forward to lower their sail and dowse it with buckets of water, but Owerd's objective had been achieved. The ship slowed to a halt as she lost any benefit from the wind and oars were being rapidly put out. "Adeliza" was now well ahead of the Danish vessel which was trying to regather way.

'Give me a stern shot please skipper', said Owerd, fumbling with the torsion gear with which he was not as familiar as he would like. Fortunately, the ballista was already loaded so, once tensioned and the vessel heading directly away from the target, he was ready. The enemy longship was still coming on and now picking up pace as her oarsmen began their work. Owerd fired. The crash of the bolt's release shattered the air. What followed was absolute mayhem as the bolt traversed the Danish longship from end to end, taking arms, heads and anything else in its path. The vessel was now no threat to anyone and slowly lost steerage way amidst great howls of pain, rage and misery aboard her.

There was a second clap like thunder as Cecilia's ballista also released. That one took out their opponent's mast before sending splinters and body parts down the length of the vessel. Another complete success without having to burn their ships, Owerd thought.

'Down sail, out oars please skipper'. Owerd had seen that the third Danish vessel had realized that their doom was imminent and turned toward shore. 'She is trying to beach for them to escape over land', he said, 'follow her in'.

He had them back water as they came close to the beached longship. 'Archers, thin them out and let none escape off the beach. Fire at will'.

The reason for the ship lagging behind the other Danes was clear as they drifted closer. There were less crew than one might expect because the centre of the ship was mounded with plunder almost as high as a man. The archers were having a good effect, so Owerd nodded to the skipper to beach the ship.

'Archers keep firing at will; the rest on me', he called as he leapt overboard into waist-deep water. An angry Dane decided to take revenge for being denied his booty and charged at him in the shallows with a double-headed axe held high. Owerd felt decidedly vulnerable, having no mail and no helmet and raised his sword in preparation though knowing that he would be fortunate to avoid being hit or worse. An arrow appeared in the charging man's shoulder and slowed his movements, just sufficiently for Owerd to make a thrust to the chest beneath the swinging axe. It was a lethal blow for the Dane, but still a damaging one for Owerd as the axe went over his head and swung down into his back. He fell sprawling on top of his dead attacker and grunted in pain.

Owerd felt himself being dragged by the arms through wet sand and only vaguely heard the surrounding clash of metal on metal and yells of threat, anguish and hurt. He needed to have a short sleep, he thought. That is all he recalled until he felt his tunic being roughly ripped over his head and a voice that he did not recognize calling for more cloth. He was being held face down and becoming very uncomfortable and sore. He struggled to rise.

'My lord, you need keep still until I get this bleeding staunched', came the voice.

It took some time, but eventually Owerd was able to sit up and survey the scene. There were bodies strewn around him and the shadow of someone standing over him. He looked up with difficulty. It was the skipper of "Adeliza" and he struggled to recall his name. Dierk, that was it, he remembered.

'Dierk, is it over? Could you help me up?'

Dierk gave him an arm and hauled him to his feet, which caused a ripple of sharp pain across his back.

'Lord forgive me, for I am a sorry mess, Dierk. My back feels like the gates of hell opened and spat fire on it'.

'An axe head embedded in one's back will probably do that, my lord. The men surrounded you when you fell and took a heavy toll on any who approached. We have won the field and yours is the only significant injury. Mayhap charging ahead by yourself was the cause of that, if I may be so bold my lord'.

'Let us examine our catch, skipper', he said as he took a few tentative steps towards the Danish longship. The vessel itself looked to be intact, with what could only be captured booty scattered about her and in small piles leading up the beach.

'That is quite a haul', he noted with admiration for the pile of well-stowed valuables behind the mast in the longship. 'Have the men take what they wish from the bodies, then leave them lie. Dropped treasures need to be returned to the longship, then float her off and have her rowed to Boston. We shall go check out the other longships, though it seems from here that our other vessels have them in hand'.

'Whatever it is that you plan my lord, I suggest we do so without delay', said Dierk. 'There be a storm coming and my bones tell me it will be a real bastard'.

Owerd looked to the sky without seeing anything unusual, but did note that the wind had dropped. 'Very well, let's move'.

Bodies were still being thrown into the sea from the two remaining Danish longships as "Adeliza" approached. The two Sandwich vessels had each attached a towline to their respective captive longships but as yet had not recovered all their crew or begun their return journey. Owerd hailed each skipper in turn, calling for them to make best speed to Boston. "Adeliza then joined "Cecilia" and still in calm wind, but with a now-threatening sky, began rowing toward Boston. Hakon had been thoughtful and secured a good berth for their Cog, so it was a simple task to tie up alongside her. The first heavy drops of rain fell just as they were doing so.

The three captured vessels and their escorts were less fortunate. By the time they made their way into harbour the rain was pelting down, although "down" was relative as the wind had risen to a near gale and was driving the rain sideways. The sodden crews managed to beach their vessels nearby but even that was challenging in the conditions. A mad rush toward the shelter of the cog then had to be halted as the overcrowded vessel was becoming top-heavy. Owerd saw nothing for it but to brave the elements and go ashore to seek accommodation for some two hundred men. For the first time he gained a measure of satisfaction from the fact that the fleet was smaller in number and size of vessel than planned. Two barns, one of which doubled as a warehouse for wool exports, were made available for an excessive amount of silver and the men progressively transferred there for shelter. Food and drink would need to wait.

-XXIV-

The storm lasted for two nights and all through the intervening day with a constant howling gale and drenching rain. Hakon had to detail off a steady stream of his crew to bail out their two longships. They did so naked and for some it would have been their first good wash in many weeks. Owerd and Hakon remained closeted in the Cog's cabin chatting and exchanging views of the progress being made with the king's tasking and how long it might take for him to be satisfied. Owerd was concerned about Hilda, now pregnant, and more immediately about his housecarls who had still not appeared. He would need to find a horse or horseman shortly, he thought, so as to inform the king that the Danes were gone.

The first rainless day was welcomed by all but frantic in pace to put things back in order. The three captured vessels were each brought alongside "The Merry Widow" to transfer their load of valuables and then towed back to the beach. One was in good shape and would probably be taken on as part of the king's squadron, Owerd believed, whilst the other two would provide the locals with firewood for some time. Hakon dispatched a second Cog across to eastern coast of the Wasche with provisions for the Dover contingent and to discover how they had fared in the storm. Being more exposed to the strong northerly gale, some damage could be expected. Owerd was beset with requests for everything from replacement bowstrings for the many ruined in the rain to the need to find men who could cook a decent meal. He was beginning to feel the absence of

Godric who was far more accustomed to this level of administrative labour than he himself.

Owerd's frustration at the demands upon his time was not helped by the constant pain in his back. He had taken many wounds in his life but this one seemed to be causing more soreness than most and taking longer to heal. The need to have someone repeatedly bind his upper body with fresh linen to staunch the oozing mess that he could feel but not actually see was also testing his patience. That patience was about to be further tested.

A knock on the cabin door was followed by a head peeking around. 'You are wanted on shore, my lord'.

'Who by?'

'Some Norman lord, sir, I know not who'.

Owerd let Hakon finish securing the linen bandage around his chest and went on deck. A Norman knight sat impatiently on a large well-equipped Courser, surrounded by half a dozen armed guards. Owerd was shirtless and without his sword. The man looked doubtful.

'I seek the man who call himself Lord Owerd', the knight called brusquely.

'I am oft called Lord Owerd, and especially by the king, so I suppose that is I. Who asks?'

'I am Sieur Turfold Lincoln, Sheriff of Lincoln. I am informed that you have something for me Lord Owerd'.

'I do indeed sheriff, would you care to come aboard to see?'

The sheriff dismounted without a word and launched himself up the gangway, pausing at the top to simply ask 'where?'

Owerd signaled for two of the sailors to join him and led the sheriff forward to the hold. 'Bring them up', he directed.

The sheriff looked nonplussed as the sailors brought nine bound men on to the deck.

'Danish prisoners, sheriff, hereby handed to your custody'.

'I have no transport for prisoners', argued the sheriff angrily, 'it is their plunder I come to secure'.

'I cannot give you that, lord sheriff, for it is destined for the king's coffers at Westminster'.

'But that is plunder taken from the sack of Peterborough and the Fens, entirely within my jurisdiction. I hold the king's authority to seize it'.

'And I hold the king's authority not to let you have it', said Owerd. 'What do you wish done with the prisoners?'

'Hang them!' The sheriff realized that he was getting nowhere and stormed off the ship, called to his men, and rode off, or at least he tried to. Just then a group of five armed men rode through the sheriff's men, scattering them. In the lead was Osric waving a closely rolled parchment in front of him and shouting 'King's business, move aside'. The sheriff and his men were thoroughly discomforted but moved aside and tried to quiet their alarmed horses. Osric dismounted before his horse had come to a complete halt and raced up the gangway. He made a solemn bow to Owerd and handed over the parchment.

'So, what is all this theatre about Osric? I am very glad to see you and the others all safe and well, but I fail to see the rush'.

'We stopped off at the stables where you have been feeding the men so as to take a drink and watched as that Norman noble rode past full of his own importance and pushing people aside with unnecessary force. I thought he might use a little of his own physik'.

'Well, they have gone now, so what is this urgent message you carry?'

'Oh, my lord, I forgot. Simply a note from Lady Hilda'.

Owerd had a good laugh and felt it was not before time. 'Get yourselves fed and watered and be prepared to leave again first thing in the morn. We will be going fully armed and in mail. I trust neither the sheriff's men nor the local rebels'.

A council of the leadership was summoned that evening and some pleasant wine was consumed in the cramped cabin.

'Firstly, I want this cog well-guarded day and night. Hakon, could you make sure the hold is battened down? I accept that means we cannot shelter the crews onboard but needs must. In fact, I think it may be best if you anchored off. As soon as I let the king know that the Danes are gone, I expect he will attack. Our task is to make sure none fleeing over water escape the Wasche. The two Sandwich cogs can anchor in the centre as support vessels, one for each of the Sandwich and Dover contingents. At least one longship from each contingent is to be underway and patrolling day and night.

With as much as he was able to plan being well in hand, Owerd retired and slept like the proverbial log. He was an early riser and immediately set to work in an attempt to rescue his sword from its exposure to salt water. He was rubbing the metal vigorously as Hakon walked in.

'This is unseemly, my lord Owerd, you need a servant for tasks such as that'.

'All very well, my friend, but I would need a man also able to ride and fight if he were to be worth his salt. Such men are rarely prepared to undertake menial domestic tasks'.

Nothing more was said about the matter as they broke their fast, which was interrupted by Osric announcing them ready for departure. Owerd struggled into his mail, with his painful back and chest binding making things more difficult, then joined the others ashore.

'The king indicated that he would muster his army at Peterborough, but would himself encamp some way to the east of there at a village called Brandon. We shall aim for there'.

241

'We came through Peterborough on our way to meet you sire', said Osric. 'That is where I met the others. Always the safe course when looking for Cuthbert; head for the nearest large town and seek out the busiest place that serves food and ale'.

'I heard that, you churl', called Cuthbert from the rear.

'I mention it sire, because the place was full of mercenaries and cut-throats, all bent upon taking a share of the riches supposedly resting at Ely. It is a good place to avoid at present'.

'We shall do that if the bogs and marshes of the fens will allow of it', responded Owerd lightly. 'But tell me now, how is the Lady Hilda'.

'All is fairly well there, sire. She claims to be eating like a horse and getting fat but I observed no sign of that. Your daughter is becoming mischievous and is into anything and everything: she has much energy. There has been some sort of pox going around both there and at Birdlip with a few tenants succumbing but it is more the case in Gloucester and Bristol where whole families have been lost. Lady Hilda and Mistress Wenna both decided that they would stay away from the towns for a while'.

'Mistress Wenna? What has she to do with this?'

'I believe Lady Hilda was planning to tell you of it my lord. She has asked Mistress Wenna to accompany her during her preparations for childbirth'.

With a guilty start, Owerd realized that he had not yet read her note. He went to reach for it but recalled leaving it onboard the cog. Later, he thought. The rest of the ride to Brandon was tortuous and required many diversions to avoid deep streams or boggy patches but became easier once they crossed the River Ouse. The king's "camp" once they reached it was surprisingly opulent for a monarch more known as one used to the rough and tumble of battle. Perhaps he was becoming used to an indulgent lifestyle, Owerd thought. They approached a string of guards and were required to dismount and leave their horses before approaching an enormous marquee surrounded by smaller ones set on what would have been the village green. Owerd left his sword and seax with a guard at the marquee entrance and walked into a scene that was as close to debauchery as he could imagine. A scattering of nobles lazed around on cushions, together with a bevy of ladies who from appearances were more used to frequenting the streets at night. Some were naked to the waist and being casually fondled by their nearest companion.

The king sat slightly separately, hunched forward from his stool and focused on a game of some sort involving dice that he shared with Ivo Taillebois. He looked up at the intrusion and waved Owerd forward.

'Sea Lord', he exclaimed, 'welcome to our little rustic camp. What have you for us?'

'The Danes are gone, your Grace, probably to hell and damnation'. He had the king's full attention now, as with other nobles who sat up to listen. 'We captured three of their ships of war laden with plunder. The others

243

vanished into a storm that even the hardiest of seafarers believed would prove to be their ruin'.

The king took another sip of the wine he was nursing, then stood.

'We attack!' The king's announcement was evidently welcomed by all except the ladies in the tent. There was a great cheer, followed by the men busily setting their clothing into order before cursory bows to the king and a mass departure, presumably for weapons and in readiness to ride.

'You have done us proud yet again, Lord Owerd, go now and see that none escape the net to sea. I shall expect you at Westminster once the rats' nest has been cleared'.

Dismissed once more, Owerd left to find his men. He did so with them being gathered around and chatting courteously to a tubby, businesslike woman. He should have realized the cause: she was the chief cook and was plying the men with pastries in direct proportion to their compliments. Not foolish enough to stand on ceremony if a meal was in the offing, he joined them and was rewarded with both a cup of ale and a handful of some of the tastiest pastries he had ever encountered.

Owerd looked up as he heard Taillebois marching past gesticulating and urging his men to prepare to ride. He turned to Osric.

'Osric, it seems to me that the men are deploying but leaving the camp intact. Have a word with some of the servants and see if there will be spare tents for the six of us tonight. It seems shameful to waste the opportunity for a restful sleep before our journey back and mayhap enjoy some nourishing food into the bargain'.

That evening was spent in good company and in equally good humour. Owerd and his men shared a campfire with the servants and were well fed and supplied with ample good quality wine. They slept in comfort and rose ready for the ride back to Boston well contented. Owerd even thought, though he could have been mistaken, that he saw a few of the ladies from the previous night leaving his men's tents in the pale light of dawn.

The ride back to Boston was taken at an easy pace and it became clear as they skirted Peterborough that the king was mustering his army there. Dusk was upon them before they had traveled much further and Owerd decided on an overnight camp next to a river the locals called "Welland". It was far from being in the salubrious nature of the previous night but comfortable enough for men used to camping rough. Much to the amusement and surprise of his men, Owerd even took the opportunity to shed his clothes and bathe in the river. None other even contemplated such an activity, fraught with the hazards to health and wellbeing that it was widely known to be.

The scene at Boston looked peaceful. They had received a second visit from the Lincoln sheriff, this time with a larger contingent of guards. Once he had seen that the cog lay offshore out of easy reach, he and his men had given up their quest and departed. Work was in hand on hewing new masts and spars for two of the Dover longships that had been dismasted in the storm. Otherwise there had been no seaborne encounters and Owerd considered it likely that the men would become bored, and thus disaffected, if this situation persisted for much longer.

After consulting with Hakon, Owerd decided to release half of the vessels provided under the Scypfryd arrangements, including the cog with the archers' nest fore and aft. She was an unwieldy vessel, easily outmaneuvered, and he could see little worth in her without the availability of a surfeit of archers. Another day or two of tedious administration saw him pacing the deck aimlessly and beginning to think the Lord above was either testing him or preparing him for purgatory. The crews had developed their own routines, which were working well, and the life of the Sea Lord was becoming monotonous. He desperately needed some action.

-XXV-

Calling for the skipper of one of the Sandwich longships, a Kentish man named Fuller, he had him brief his crew to be ready to sail at first light the next day. 'I am going to see what is afoot inland, Hakon', he told his friend when next he saw him. 'I will take one of the Sandwich boats as they are smaller, flat-bottomed and draw less than our own longships. Do you think you can locate that man who supposedly knows the inland waters hereabouts?

By early the following morning all was in readiness and Owerd embarked in the longship together with a fisherman who claimed to have frequented the area in the past. He was a craggy older man named Watt with a scruffy grey beard, sallow skin and an attitude that endeared him to no-one. None of that mattered to Owerd provided the man knew his way about the local waterways. The ship was a Karvi, a variety of longship of similar construction to a Snekkar but with only a dozen oar-benches. Owerd had made sure to ensure there was a good sprinkling of archers in the crew.

They entered the river just south of Boston and Owerd was surprised to see how wide it was. 'That width be misleading', announced Watt, 'most of it is mudflat covered at all but the lowest tide and set to capture any vessel that strays from the midpoint'.

The land about was almost uniformly flat and the river wended its way towards the Wasche in a lazy flow of muddy brown. It was also very quiet. The gentle splash of

247

the oars was just noticeable, despite the seemingly languid stroke of the oarsmen. There was little sign of life, mainly the squawking of Gulls and Kittiwakes or the occasional honk of a late-departing flock of geese. There was certainly no sign of habitation. A break in the monotonous landscape loomed ahead in the form of a hillock, not much of one but sufficient to stand proud of its surroundings.

'Nose her in to the bank next to that hill, please Fuller. I would have the men in the bow take a look from the top'.

The longship duly touched the muddy bank and the two bowmen jumped for the shore. They came to an embarrassing halt as they sank into almost a foot of slimy mud while their momentum carried their upper bodies forward to land in yet more mud. There was a great cheer from the rest of the crew and much ribald banter then followed the two as they extricated themselves and fled up the hill away from their tormentors. They were not there long. There was plenty of peering in different directions and the occasional pointing arm but no signs or sounds of alarm as they returned to the ship.

'The land looks to be empty, my lord', called one as he retook his oar-bench, 'the only movement about as far as we could see was a small boat well up the river. Too far to tell what sort but probably just a local fisherman'.

'We will go on for another league of so, then return to Boston', Owerd told Fuller.

The boat which had been seen from the hilltop eventually came into view and it was certainly no fishing boat. She was an open and grossly overloaded sixteen-foot row-boat full to the gunwales with armed men and perhaps three heavily cowled women.

'Archers ready', called Owerd as they closed on the boat. 'Skipper, stay clear of her but back oars when we are abreast until we discover the nature of this discovery'.

'Wrong way Dane, the others have all gone home to their women', called a stout man standing in the boat's stern.

'I am no Dane', called back Owerd. 'I am the king's Sea lord and on the king's business, so identify yourself'.

'Which king?' The retort was sharp and heavy with cynicism.

'You know well that William is king hereabouts. I warn you now, identify yourself'. He then turned forward and called the archers to readiness.

Faced with over a dozen archers with drawn bows at near point-blank range, there was a sudden and dramatic change in the demeanour of those on the boat. Most showed fear, some anger, and the women in particular looked terrified. The man in the stern simply looked resigned.

'I have heard of you Sea Lord. Owerd is it not? I am Hereward of Bourne, late of Ely and we here are all good Englisc so why do you threaten us when we mean only to pass on our peaceable business to our own northern pastures?'

Owerd had an immediate attack of conscience and doubt about how to proceed. This man was the leader of the Ely rebellion and so should be taken into custody to face the king's justice. But Owerd knew well the kind of justice usually meted out to Englisc rebels. He had himself suffered under the Norman yoke but had taken the opposite course to Hereward and submitted to what he saw as a lawful ruler. Here was a man who could have been himself had he chosen a different route. Regarding himself as being entirely Englisc he had profound sympathy for this man and his people, but he had a duty. He needed to interpret where that duty lay.

'I take it then that you are bound for the north without any rebellious intent'.

Hereward saw a spark of hope. 'That be our intention, north without rebellious intent'.

'In that case Hereward, you had best be on your way because I am busy hunting for rebels. Make sure you go north; other directions are unsafe'. He then turned to the archers and directed them to stand down. They were all facing him at the stern as they sat and Owerd was certain that he saw a mix of relief and approval in their faces. His crew were all Englisc after all, and probably held a degree of at least moral support for Hereward at one time or another. The boatload of Hereward's people wasted no time and their single pair of oars began working feverishly to distance themselves further down river from the longship. With a wave in salute from Hereward they were gone.

Owerd was surprised at the degree of satisfaction he felt about his decision. He considered that perhaps he had made some measure of restitution for the actions he had previously taken during the landing by King Harold's sons in the south-west. He waited another half a league upriver then had Fuller turn the ship about for return to Boston.

Tying up alongside "The Merry Widow", still at anchor, Owerd was surprised and delighted to see Brother John, the king's Intelligencer, awaiting him with another man he did not immediately recognize. Clambering over the ship's side he rushed to shake Brother John by the hand and gave him a broad smile and a warm welcome. The smile was not immediately returned and the monk looked unusually sombre.

'Methinks you should speak with your man Osbald here first, Sir Owerd', he said.

Osbald, his Cornish housecarl who now appeared beside John, looked many years older than when Owerd had last left him at Aust.

'I failed to recognize you at first Osbald, what brings you here to Boston?'

'My lord', Osbald began then faltered. With his head bowed and looking absolutely miserable, he finished. 'My lord, it grieves me beyond belief to be the bearer of ill news. The Lady Hilda has gone to God'. He passed across a rolled parchment 'this from Mistress Wenna', and stepped back trying to look invisible.

Owerd could not readily believe what he had just heard. 'This cannot be, Osbald, she was reported to be in robust health only recently. Perhaps you mean something else has occurred?'

'No, my lord. She passed very quickly, but it is cert that she did'.

Owerd felt himself go numb in mind and body. John wrapped an arm around his shoulders and shepherded him to the ship's cabin and, without asking but nodding to a silent Hakon, poured Owerd a cup full of wine. He took a full mouthful of the wine which tasted like ash in his throat and stared at nothing in particular. Then he became angry. 'If any Norman had a hand in this then I will slay all of them that come my way', he declared, beating his fist against his knee with one hand and fondling the hilt of his sword with the other.

'No Norman involved, Owerd. Maybe best if you read the letter and learn the truth of it'. John handed over the letter that Owerd had earlier let slip to the deck in his confusion.

'This may unman me', declared Owerd firmly, 'pray give me a few moments alone to absorb this news'.

The others left and Owerd ripped open the letter. Written in a clear feminine hand, presumably Wenna's, it began 'my beloved friend, it is a sad day that befell us all yesterday....' Continuing, Wenna wrote that there had been a few cases of pox in the area for some time but Hilda and the manor people had seemed untouched. Then one morning Hilda announced a tiredness upon her and retired to her chamber but with little concern arising amongst them. When Wenna had gone to check on her before the evening meal she found her in a sweat and with tiny red spots upon her skin. A physik from Gloucester had been sent for and arrived late in the evening to announce that Hilda had some form of Pox and should be allowed to rest and be kept warm. By next morning she was gone.

Owerd felt torn asunder. Hilda had been part of him for most of his adult life and they were a partnership that he had thought would last forever. He had seen himself growing old with her, though had never managed to picture his Hilda looking aged. He bowed his head and let tears fall to the deck.

By evening Owerd's grief was well entrenched. John tried to distract him with news of the fighting around Ely. The king's forces had eventually won the day but only after a series of failures and much loss of life. Despite all the rumours there was virtually no treasure to be had in the rebel fort and many mercenaries had fallen out between themselves in frustration. The king was on his way back to Westminster satisfied that no internal rebellions remained. 'Earl Morcar has been imprisoned and his brother Earl Edwin has been killed by some of his own disaffected men, which leaves only Edgar the Atheling as any threat and he has fled to the land of the Scots'. How much of this was sinking in, John knew not, so would leave him in peace. 'I shall pray for her soul, Owerd, and mayhap you might do the same'.

Owerd awoke the next morning feeling no better. He had roundly cursed God and all the injustices of life and had little venom left in him. He took a turn around the deck, stripped off and dived into the water to the alarm of the guards on deck. Hakon and Brother John, who had both slept on the deck overnight, rushed to the ship's side fearing the worst but relaxed when they saw Owerd swimming strongly around the vessels. Dripping and almost exhausted, he was seen clambering on to the longship alongside and then making his way back on board the cog.

'I shall ride to Aust today if the king will allow it', he announced. 'Hakon my friend will you see to the ships' dispersal and perhaps more importantly the delivery of the plunder to the exchequer?'

'There is no difficulty with you leaving', said John. 'The king has released your ships from further service for the present and is well pleased with what you have done. I shall inform him of your loss'.

Hakon left to organize a skiff to take Owerd and Brother John to shore, while Owerd asked John to make sure that proper arrangements were made for the captured treasure in London. 'For there is a large amount of it, John, and it will doubtless attract the sticky fingers of any intermediaries. I will probably take the old Roman road they call Fosse from Lincoln, why do you not join me on the way there? There are still plenty of bandits about and your company would be welcome'.

'That is kind, Owerd. I need in any event to visit the sheriff there to discuss a few matters and will beg a bed from him. He has a rather nice new castle there: would you wish to join us for the night?'

'I think not John. The sheriff was not too happy with me when I refused to transfer the captured booty to his custody. He tried a second time with what I suspect was intended force but I had shifted the cog out of harm's way so he was denied'.

'Another move in your favour, Owerd. With no treasure gained from Ely I suspect his majesty will be more than usually joyous at receiving an undiluted windfall through your hand. I will make mention to the king of the sheriff's interest and your protective instincts in case of any foolish complaint'.

Owerd spent a little time rounding up his men and horses but they still managed a relatively early start for Lincoln. They were all in varying degrees of depression over the loss of Hilda and the ride lacked the usual happy chatter. Owerd and his men parted ways with Brother John that evening and looked for lodgings that were not excessively rowdy. Osric took the men aside at one stage and briefed them to have two or more always with their lord. He was in a fragile state of mind and it would not end well for any locals, especially any of Norman origin, that managed to offend him in some way. In the event none did and Owerd, though not outwardly morose, was quiet and kept his thoughts to himself until they all retired.

Spring may have been in the air next morning but none would have known it from the atmosphere surrounding the silent riders as they left Lincoln town. Owerd slowly became aware of the effect his own mourning was having on his men and tried to restore some normality.

'Six days to home, men. We will camp overnight until Birdlip if you bunch of tired old grey-beards can handle that. I believe it to be about three score leagues to Aust so we shall try to manage ten leagues each day. I expect no trouble on this road but we will have a scout out if you please, just in case'.

It was not until nearly nightfall that Owerd's expectations were proven wrong and his decision to have a scout out front proven correct. Cuthbert was out in front at the time and, as they rounded a gentle bend, he was seen to have halted with his arms out to the sides. They all knew their signal for a threat of some kind and automatically halted and felt for their weapons. Signaling for the others to wait he rode forward to join Cuthbert. He had no need to ask the problem for as he came up alongside Cuthbert he could see that a large elm had been felled to block the roadway.

'No roots showing, so definitely felled', said Cuthbert. 'We could go around but that just leaves some other poor souls to suffer'.

'I agree', answered Owerd. 'What do you suggest?'

Cuthbert looked at Owerd in surprise. He had never before been asked to offer advice on the way to fight. Was he being tested?

'We know not how many there are, my lord, nor do they know that of us. They have probably already seen you and I but that leaves the others unseen. Also, we know not exactly where they lie in respect to the fallen tree. Might I suggest that we split: three to ride in at the gallop and jump the tree with the others following after a short delay at a slower pace. That way we can attack from either side of the obstruction'.

'A sound plan Cuthbert. Go back and brief the others. Make sure whomever you choose to join us is capable of jumping that sort of obstacle whilst mounted'.

Cuthbert rode back to the others delighted that his plan had been accepted, though already he had nervous doubts as to its suitability. He set those doubts aside and briefed the others, taking Osric back with him as the best of the riders. Owerd drew his sword and kicked his mount into a gallop as soon as the pair reached him. The distance to the fallen tree reduced at an alarming rate and they each had to ease their horses' speed before launching into a jump. None baulked at the obstacle and Owerd was much relieved to see the three of them on the other side in one piece.

Four men in ragged but usable soldier's kit charged at them from the brush wielding seaxes. That flushed them out, Owerd thought, but it was not ideal as they were now outnumbered on this side of the tree. The other three could be seen from the corner of Owerd's eye as they rode to join the fray but did not do as expected or briefed. One went into the brush; one went the other side of the road to find a way around, and the last jumped the tree. Owerd was too busy to watch his own men further as he was in a furious fight with the leading attacker. The man was either a trained mercenary or a soldier with no master, for he kept expertly striking at Owerd's vulnerable legs and it was taking some effort to ward off those blows. Satan intervened. He rose on his hind legs and turned to attempt a vicious bite at the man's head. The bite was unsuccessful but forced the man backwards on to the defensive sufficiently for Owerd to sweep his sword across the man's neck. A spray of blood covered the ground as the attacker dropped his weapon and grabbed fruitlessly at his neck before collapsing.

A tight turn saw Owerd behind the second attacker who was focused on killing Cuthbert's horse. A blade in the back was rarely an honourable thing to do, but Owerd was in no mood for niceties. He urged Satan forward and thrust his sword directly between the man's shoulder blades until it would have appeared out the other side. The man fell forward and took Owerd's sword with him. He drew his seax and looked for another opponent but none were left. One lay on the roadway shrieking and grasping at the stump of his arm from which blood flooded the ground. His arm, grotesquely still holding a seax, lay a pace away. A fourth attacker lay sprawled on the ground, not moving. That was hardly surprising as his head lay a good distance away. That must have been some strike, thought Owerd, as also apparently did Osric who sat looking intently at his blade.

'Let us get this mess cleaned up', called Owerd, 'we have a ways to go yet'.

'Lord, there is cart back a score of paces into the brush and I thought I saw two women tied to the wheels'.

Owerd rode off the roadway to investigate. The cart was where Trahern had said it was. Two women, one of middle years and the other much younger, perhaps twelve or thirteen were both sat next to one of the wheels, evidently bound to it. He pulled out his seax and gently cut their bonds, helping them slowly to their feet.

'You are safe. My name is Owerd and I will help you on your way from here. How long have you been captive?'

'I am Bronwen and this is my daughter Alice. Those men took us on our way to Snotingham for my husband to take up an offer of work. They killed him without mercy and had none for us either. They badly used the both of us these past three nights'.

'Is the cart yours?'

'It is lord. It has our own belongings loaded plus some goods those men took from others that attempted to pass'.

Further investigation revealed four human bodies lying in the undergrowth a little way from the robbers' camp and a mule tethered even further off the road. There was not a lot to be done about the bodies, so Owerd had the men concentrate on getting the mule hitched up to the cart. There was little of any real value in the goods in the cart, so Owerd let that aspect rest: rather small compensation for what the women had endured, he thought. The tree was problematic but one of the spare horses and a rough harness of reigns attached to one end managed to see it shifted such that it no longer fully blocked the road.

Nottingham, as Owerd knew the name to be although the woman had called it Snotingham, was a thriving town with a significantly Norman proportion of residents and a new castle dominating the skyline. The sheriff greeted Owerd courteously when he called on him to report the attack further along the Fosse Way and agreed to have men recover or bury the bodies. An invitation for an evening meal and overnight stay was declined as Owerd thought he would be poor company and wished to stay with his men. That was welcomed by his men as any night in a hostelry beat a roadside camp, especially as their lord was paying. A small purse taken from the robbers was given to the rescued woman and she and her daughter went on their way independently.

Owerd felt purged of his anger. He would miss Hilda with an intensity he could not yet imagine, but his anger was gone. What was left was a hollow feeling, but he also knew that he had a daughter to care for, and perhaps a son he should also consider making arrangements for. His own sense of loss, extreme though it be, needed to be set aside. How all that was to occur occupied his mind as he drifted off into a troubled sleep.

-XXVI-

Apart from the crackling of burning twigs and the occasional hoot of an owl there was no sound as Owerd and his men sat around the campfire two days' ride from Birdlip. All were content with their own thoughts and it was an easy camaraderie that prevailed. Owerd was trying to come to terms with life after Hilda and having some difficulty in imagining it. He rose to his feet and gestured for Osric to walk with him. Ambling casually back along the roadway for a little way he looked closely at Osric in the moonlight.

'How do you see yourself in the future, Osric?'

The look in response to the question was startled. 'Is this about Sigria, lord?'

'Not entirely. I would know how you would wish your future to look'.

'I am content in your service lord, but I do know that a warrior cannot be such all his life. Mayhap I could one day have some land of mine own. I fear you may have become aware too soon that I have developed an understanding with Sigria. I have been meaning to seek your approval of the match and I have saved enough coin for maybe a virgate or so of land upon which we could perhaps then settle. I had not thought to leave your service and I hope this matter does not sit ill with you'.

'This matter, as you put it, does not sit ill with me Osric. What are your thoughts on Birdlip?'

This sudden change in the subject completely threw Osric, who struggled for an answer. 'I like the place well, lord. Yourself and Lady Hilda made it a welcoming home'.

'That thought has occurred to me powerfully over the last few days, sergeant, and I fear I cannot now live there with such strong memories about. It is also occurs to me that it is well past time that you were rewarded for your loyal service over the years. In other circumstances I would like to gift you the manor of Birdlip. I cannot do that, as it is held directly from the king, but I can rent it to you. I would set a rent at half of whatever one year's past annual income would show. That would allow you to take any extra profits for yourself and Sigria, assuming you will go ahead and wed. What dost thee think?'

Even in the dimness of moonlight it was obvious that Osric was in a degree of shock. He said nothing for a full minute. Even then he made a few false starts. 'My lord, I do not deserve this generosity but I take it that you approve my wedding Sigria'.

'You need no approval from me, Osric, you are a freeman as is she a free woman. I am happy for you both. As for generosity, it is only as much as you deserve and I will look to receiving rents promptly when due. We will need to come to a separate agreement regarding the horse breeding which has become a separate business under Dobson's guidance. We can discuss details later and have papers drawn up. For now, let us share a cup of watered wine around the fire and enjoy God's blessings'.

A similar conversation took place with Cuthbert on their ride the next day. This time it involved the gift of a Burgage in Gloucester town, one of a number that Reuben the Jewish moneylender had advised him to acquire. Rent would be in the form of continued service with Owerd, with the added status and payment as sergeant. Cuthbert would take some convincing that he warranted this generosity but Owerd would later speak with Osric to have him convince Cuthbert of his worth.

The mood became sombre as the warriors pulled into the forecourt of Birdlip. That mood continued into their overnight stay. Every wall hanging, piece of furniture and ornament spoke of Hilda. Owerd felt her presence everywhere; perhaps about to walk in and scold him for being late at table or making a randomly wanton offer of joining him in the bed chamber. Owerd even noticed that all of the housecarls had religiously dipped their hands and head in the outside water cask before entering the common-room for the evening meal.

A similar mood prevailed at Aust, though less evident among the staff who had so much less exposure to Hilda's charm. Owerd's first act after dismounting was to hug his daughter Breanna and lead her by the hand down to the village church to say goodbye to his beloved wife. There was a lovely inscription on the headstone which read of a beautiful, strong and generous lady, for which he thought Wenna had perhaps had a hand. He knelt in the dirt to say a prayer over the grave and Breanna joined him so had evidently been schooled in the process. Afterwards his thoughts returned back to his house guest, who invariably churned his mind in a mixture of lust and confusion at every encounter'.

Back at the manor-house, Wenna was busy seeing to her own child — our child, Owerd corrected himself. At the first opportunity he invited her into the private solar away from the bustle of the servants for a quiet word.

'So, tell me Wenna, how is it that you are staying here?'

Wenna was the epitome of correct behaviour and sat with her hands demurely folded in her lap. 'Did you not receive Lady Hilda's letter my lord?'

Owerd was plunged into embarrassed guilt. He had not opened it and recalled that it now lay somewhere in his saddlebags. 'Tell me in your words, Wenna dear'.

'I received a note after you had reportedly gone off to sea. Hilda explained that she was away from her usual home and lacked friends with whom she could be comfortable conversing and sharing the worries and emotions of looming childbirth. She asked if I would consider staying with her until she had birthed her child or you had returned. I agreed without hesitation and we developed a very warm relationship. Did I do wrong, my lord?'

'You did no wrong, Wenna, and for goodness' sake please stop calling me "my lord". To you I am simply Owerd. I am most pleased that her last days were spent in good company. What vexes me now, and bearing in mind all that has passed between us, is what happens about us. I am, of course, in mourning and as a widower it may not be considered seemly to be hosting a single lady in the house so soon'.

'I am yours Owerd. Deal with me as you please'.

That was such a stark statement of what should have been obvious to him that Owerd was shocked. He did not consider himself the sort of man who would or could take advantage of a woman's possibly fragile infatuation. Equally, infatuation is what he appreciated he had himself felt for Wenna, despite his marriage to Hilda. He decided that he must honour both women.

'Wenna, I have much regard, indeed great fondness, for you; but now is not the time to indulge in sentiments that may lead us down the wrong path. I need to attend to my duties in Winchester very shortly and may be absent for a month or more. If you would accept the continued hospitality of the manor I would be honoured if you would stay. After a little more time has passed, then our paths may become clearer. Is that acceptable to you?'

'That is as I would wish it Owerd. There is one more matter that has not been addressed. My brother Cadoc has expressed a wish to become a warrior like our father. My lord father is conscious of his own advancing years and would wish him placed elsewhere with someone he trusted. He trusts you Owerd and asks that you consider taking Cadoc into your service as his mentor. He would come with a tutor if that assists'.

Owerd was honoured and suspicious. Was this a trap to tie him permanently to Condor and his daughter?

'I am no great lord, Wenna', he began, noting that Wenna raised her eyebrows in what could be either questioning or disagreement. 'I am not averse to the idea, but please allow me to think upon it a while. Cadoc is young yet and there is no rush'.

The business of the manor occupied the next few days, after which Owerd took six of the housecarls as escort to Winchester. The house he had been allocated there was both cavernous and empty. Nevertheless, it provided for a good night's sleep for all before continuing on to his new hall at Gosport. There he found his king's seamen, those who had not deployed east, on the water with one older longship and their new-build which still awaited a name. In the hall was the solitary figure of Godric, hunched over what looked like accounts.

'Good day to you Sir Godric, how goes the wrestle with men and money?'

'God give you also a good day, Sir Owerd. The wrestle seems never-ending but at least our small navy is solvent and manpower is abundant. I just hope the king's exchequer is prepared to meet some of these extra expenses we seem to have accrued'.

The pair addressed matters financial and organisational for some hours and Owerd finally called for ale well satisfied with the manner in which all was being managed. They were embarking on their second cup of ale when a messenger arrived from the palace.

'My lord Chamberlain sends his good wishes, Lord Owerd and was optimistic that I could find you here. He has a message for you from the king'. He handed over a sealed parchment.

'The king is here?' Owerd was surprised that this could be so but needed to check.

'His majesty is at Westminster to the best of my belief my lord. Is there any response?'

'Allow me a few moments to check. Over there', he pointed to a side table, 'you will find some ale going spare'.

'Curses and the Devil's damnation!' Owerd's displeasure was clear. 'I am summoned to Westminster and no reason is given. At this rate they shall have to start calling me the Saddle Lord, the amount of riding I seem to be doing'.

Horses, equipment and supplies arranged and housecarls briefed, Owerd and his team left for London the next day. Another four days in the saddle and they entered the mire and malodorous streets of London. Owerd went straight to the Palace Chamberlain who allocated rooms and allowed him time to change before announcing him to the king. Joining the throng of nobles, monks, clerks and servants hovering around the throne, Owerd noticed Ivo Taillebois looking very pleased with himself and Archbishop Odo looking like he had just been deprived of a choice morsel. King William scanned the crowd and seemed to notice Owerd but gave no acknowledgement and continued his discussion on what sounded like plans for a hunting expedition.

With no apparent change in the king's demeanour, Owerd saw him nod and a cleric called out 'Sir Owerd of Birdlip come forward'. Owerd did so and took a knee in front of the king who stood and, without any ceremony declared 'We appoint you Sir Owerd as Vicomites – sheriff – of Wiltshire' and stepped forward to hand him a rolled parchment. 'This is your letter patent. Now, walk with me'.

Without further ado, the king walked off and Owerd followed clutching his parchment. They ended up after a series of short passageways in a private courtyard at the rear of the palace.

'We are sorry for your loss'.

Owerd bowed. 'Thank you, your Grace. It was a grievous hurt'.

'You have pleased us Sir Owerd. We will not take on all that you have suggested regarding our sea defences. That is a matter of financial prudence. We do, though, like the idea of the three squadrons of more permanently employed sea warriors and you may make arrangements for that to be set in place. We counsel you to also set in place deputies that can manage all that entails, while you stand ready as necessary to temporarily set aside your Shrieval duties to command at sea. We will maintain the system of Scypfryd as an adjunct'.

'Your recent successes have also come at some gain to the exchequer, for which we commend you. We have been informed that you protected but took no part of that treasure recovered from the Danes for yourself. Is that true?'

'Yes, your Grace. The treasure was not mine to keep'.

'Rightly said. We would reward you and as it happens, we have a manor going spare. Wilton is a large one but there is a catch. The catch is in the form of a widow: Aubreye de Beaumont by name. Her husband has passed to God but this lady is of noble heritage and has relations here both wealthy and powerful. We would not see her put out. Should she prove suitable to you then we will give her to you as wife. Otherwise, you may simply keep her as bed-mate. Either way she is to be kept content. Do we make ourselves clear?'

'As ever you Grace'.

'You may go. See the Clerk of Chancery before you leave and he will provide you the necessary documents regarding Wilton'.

Owerd bowed and walked back to the Great Hall in something of a trance. He had arrived at Westminster still in a mental fog as to his own way forward in life and here he was finding yet again that others were deciding much of it for him. The Chancery clerk when he found him was full of advice and direction regarding the duties of sheriff and gave him two names, both Norman by the sound of them, as suggested candidates for Under-Sheriff. In an aside he also mentioned that rumour first had it that he was to be made earl, but had been discouraged from that course as it would place too much power in the hands of the de Beaumont family.

'Both of Lady Aubreye's brothers are already earls, you see', he added. 'One is Earl of Warwick and the other Earl of Leicester'.

More information and a couple more rolled manuscripts followed before Owerd was able to make his way from the palace to find his housecarls.

'You men now serve the Sheriff of Wiltshire', he said when they were gathered.

This caused many looks of consternation which turned to congratulatory glee when he explained. The men were also buoyed by the obvious improvement in Owerd's spirit. He was slowly managing to put his grief behind him, or at least bury it a little deeper.

'We additionally have a new manor to investigate. We remain this night and ride on the morrow at first light'.

The four days in the saddle that followed were accompanied by far more light-hearted chatter than on the journey to London. Owerd was peppered with questions about his new station but was mostly devoid of any useful answers. He would, he thought, make a point of calling on the sheriff of a neighbouring shire at an early date to gain more insight into the role.

They arrived at the allocated house in Winchester unmolested on their way and in good spirits. The steward, rather gloomier than they, then announced that he had received notice from the palace that the house was to be vacated to permit the housing of royal guests from the following week. Owerd's plans for a change in domicile would need to be advanced more quickly than he had expected.

-XXVII-

Osric was directed to visit Wilton Manor and give notice that Lord Owerd would arrive on the following day. He was to seek accommodation for the night and make discreet enquiries amongst the staff there as to their likely reaction to Owerd becoming lord of the manor.

Dressed in his better clothes, Owerd rode into the forecourt of Wilton and could not help being impressed. It was a grand house built in stone and set within equally magnificent grounds which were adjacent to, and once part of, the grounds of Wilton Abbey. His arrival, though not specifically timed, was expected and the entire staff seemed to be in evidence as he rode up and dismounted. A lady stepped forward to greet him in the French style and he was astonished to realise that she was young – probably a few years younger than he. She was also good-looking and of aristocratic appearance. This might work, he thought.

'God give you good welcome, Lord Owerd'. She spoke in Norman French.

Owerd responded in like fashion and they moved inside to what he took to be the solar.

'I apologize if it appears, as it doubtless does my lady, that I have been imposed upon you. I am hopeful that we can make an arrangement that suits us both for the years ahead. Perhaps we could begin by having the steward show me around the manor-house and introduce the key staff'.

'I shall do that myself, my lord if you would care to follow me'.

'Please call me Owerd', he responded as they left the room, 'I am not one to stand on formalities, especially as we may spend much time together'.

'As God and my lord will it, so let it be', she said. Owerd thought that a very odd response and followed up by asking of her ability with Englisc. That was apparently nearly non-existent.

'I shall call you Aubreye if you will permit it', he added.

Conversation became stilted thereafter, and downright awkward when she showed him the master sleeping chamber. 'I have my own chamber adjacent', she mumbled, 'but would join you should you request it'.

It was not until the evening meal, taken apart from any housecarls or servants, that an easier conversation flowed.

'Regarding our sleeping arrangements, Owerd, I ask you to understand that my husband was quite elderly. He was', here she stumbled in search of the right words, 'er, unable to meet what some call marital obligations. It was a simpler matter to sleep apart. I know not your own intentions but I recognise that I am yours to do with as you wish and I shall not object'.

'I would never take a woman to bed without her willing consent, Aubreye. We have only just met. Let us see how this works out for both of us'.

That night Owerd slept alone and awoke early thinking of Wenna.

Breaking their fast, Owerd noted that Aubreye crossed herself and said a short prayer both before and after her meal as she had done the previous evening. This was evidently a religious woman, he thought. She then surprised him.

'You did not wish me to come to you last night Owerd?'

'Aubreye, I would have been delighted had you come to share my bed last evening. It must be your own will that brings you. If you have a mind to do so, the invitation stands for this evening'.

He could have sworn that she blushed scarlet but he left her to her own devices whilst he went to check on the men and gather their thoughts on the manor.

'This be a Norman stronghold, my lord', offered Osric. 'I spoke to the staff and few except the lowliest even speak Englisc. It be a grand manor, but! The stables could house most of the herd from Birdlip by looks and the accommodation building is also stone and could sleep a hundred. I suspect this was once a royal palace sometime before the Normans came'.

'You may well be right Osric. I shall do something about the servants in the fullness of time. I would value your help for a little while yet before you head over to Birdlip. I need to find my feet as sheriff to begin with. Mayhap you could visit the Reeve in Salisbury town and have him call on me. I would know what could be expected if I called upon the posse comitatus and how well armed or trained they might be. There are also the matters of when the County Court and Hundred Courts were last met and I would know whether the Tithings are properly recorded. You may add to that the status of Geld collection. There is much to learn. Take Ralph and Osbald with you. Meanwhile, Cuthbert, bring the rest and we shall ride to view the extent and state of the manor'.

Looking and feeling dusty after his day-long tour of the property, Owerd was intent on bathing but could see no cask of water available, whilst the lake looked anything but healthy. He wandered into the common-room and asked the nearest maid. She became quite flustered and beckoned for him to follow her to the main bed chamber where she mimed removing his clothes. Owerd took the hint and stripped to his undershirt while she disappeared. She reappeared carrying a large tub which was placed near the window and was followed by others bearing buckets of water. This will do nicely he thought and, stripping off his undershirt, climbed into the very cold water.

Movement behind him had him turn to find Aubreye with a few squares of cloth with which she knelt and began rubbing him down. She blushed as she came to his more private area and he took the cloth from her to finish the task. Nothing was said. Dried and fed, Owerd retired for the night feeling comfortable, though expecting to dream of Hilda or Wenna.

That was not to be. A timid knock on his door saw Aubreye enter wearing a loose garment over her undergarments. She said nothing but shed her overgarment and climbed beneath the sheets with him. Owerd thought she may expect to make love like that.

'Undress, my lady', he directed.

She seemed quite shocked. 'You mean to see me naked, Owerd?'

To a muttered 'I do', she complied and re-joined him, clearly as tense as an over-stretched hawser. He caressed her body and breasts gently while muttering of her beauty and, once satisfied that she was sufficiently relaxed, entered her. She gave a sharp cry of pain as he did so, but then settled into a rhythm that gave them each pleasure. He made love to her once more during the night. In the morning she was gone, leaving a bright red blood-stain on the sheet. 'Lord and all the angels above, that was her first time', Owerd exclaimed to himself.

She came to him again next night and seemed to have a more pleasurable experience but left immediately afterwards. At the morning meal she let him know that she would be visiting the abbey.

On her return from the abbey, Aubreye asked to speak privately and they went to the solar. Over a cup of wine, she thanked him for introducing her to the pleasures of the flesh but admitted that these were not for her.

'My confessor has counselled me about having sinful relations outside marriage and advised me that taking pleasure in the act is much against the will of God. Marriage is an option that is not in mine own gift, Owerd, and I have an enormous fear of becoming with child, wed or not. I have spoken with the abbess about my situation and she believes she can find a good position for me at a sister abbey in Normandy.

'You would be a nun, Aubreye?'

'I would sir. I have taken pleasure with you when I am affeared I should not have and have thus placed my immortal soul in danger. That is no fault of yours Owerd, but my mind is fixed'.

Two weeks later Aubreye de Beaumont, having written to her brothers to record the kind and honourable treatment she had received from Lord Owerd, took passage to the nunnery of St Leger de Preux in Normandy. Owerd dispatched a rider the next day to invite Wenna to bring his son and daughter to Wilton.

Most of the Norman staff were given notice. The exception was the steward who expressed a fervent desire to stay and had demonstrated his capability with the well-run nature of the manor. He was given the task of recruiting replacements which would be vetted by Owerd himself or Wenna as appropriate. One matter Owerd needed to attend to personally was the organisation of the sea squadron and he rode to Gosport for that purpose. He found Sir Godric at his usual endeavours, this time arranging more supplies from across the water.

It consumed a whole day to ensure that all was in place for the basing of the three sets of longships and their crews. The third new construction, now named "Matilda" after the king's third daughter, would stay at Gosport. Sandwich and Harwich were selected as the other bases.

'Do you see yourself being able to remain in this role of deputy to manage the sea squadrons Godric?'

'Thank you for asking Owerd. The work is satisfying, but I do not need to spend all my days here in this rather remote place and I would much value the opportunity one day to settle my family'.

'I have a possible solution, Godric. Osric will be taking over the manor at Birdlip under a rental arrangement. I would welcome you doing the same at Aust. How would you feel about that?'

Godric was delighted with the offer and they decided to work out details at a later date when Godric could speak with his wife. The prospect of his own manor once more clearly made him a happy man.

Back at Wilton, the manor was buzzing with activity, not least because of the arrival of Wenna and two young children. Owerd gave her a hug as she busied herself unpacking and making staff, meal and other arrangements with the steward. Owerd made an early point of accepting the role of mentor for her brother Cadoc.

Owerd retired early after a full day. Wenna was not shy about physical relations and joined him as he was drifting off to sleep. A night of tender and mutually enjoyable lovemaking ensued.

'This all feels like it was meant to be', declared Wenna over a lazy meal the next morning. 'Wyrd!'

Owerd had one last call to make. He took his housecarls and rode in full dress and mail to the abbey. This was the site of one of his first humiliations when directed to the servants' entrance as a novice monk. This time he would go through the front door to meet the abbess as the most senior noble in the shire. He greeted the abbess whilst still contemplating how far he had progressed in life. No more would he need be concerned about having people demand that he "know his station".

AUTHOR'S NOTE

Many of the characters herein were real people who lived at the time and I have attempted to meld the tale with actual historical events, at least as insofar as the "Anglo-Saxon Chronicle" records them.

The character of William I of England (William the Conqueror), then known dismissively as William the Bastard, is shrouded in mixed opinion. He was certainly a healthy and robust warrior monarch but variously given to acts of piety, cruelty and mercy depending upon the chronicler. He never succeeded in learning Englisc (Old English). He had four sons and at least five daughters.

Sir William fitzOsbern did leave England to seek the hand of, and fight for, Countess Richilde in Flanders. He was killed in battle there in 1071.

Ivo Taillebois was a powerful Norman who led King William's army at the siege of Hereward the Wake's rebel fortress at the Isle of Ely. He was regarded by many as an evil man.

Condor (or Cadoc, sometimes Candorus) of Cornwall was probably the last noble of the royal line of Britons. Though initially submitting to William, he was stripped of the earldom after the siege of Exeter. His son Cadoc may have regained the earldom (but that is another story).

Aubreye de Beaumont did become a nun, becoming Abbess of St Leger de Preaux in Normandy and then returning to England as Abbess of Eton.

Despite regular incursions by the Irish, Welsh and Scots, by far the greatest threat to England at the time were the Danes, or Norsemen. They were also intrepid mariners, sailing their open "longships" often over great distances. The more common ship types were the Knarr and Cog, both types more suited to cargo, and, in increasing order of size, the Karvi, Snekkja, Skeid and Drakkar all powered by both oars and large square sails of woollen cloth.

Britain did not have a permanent navy until the mid-16th Century when Henry VIII assembled a standing maritime force known as the "Navy Royal". Fleets of warships were much earlier assembled under a system known as Scipfryd requiring the provision of one warship per a given size of landholding. William I allowed the Scipfryd system to lapse but did occasionally assemble warships for specific purposes. Embarked sailors were mostly also warriors and known as butsecarls.